PARTY OF
THE YEAR

PARTY OF THE YEAR

WITH EXCERPTS FROM
The Legend of the di Castigliones, Annotated

John Crosby

STEIN AND DAY/*Publishers*/New York

First published in 1979
Copyright © 1979 by John Crosby
All rights reserved
Designed by David Miller
Printed in the United States of America
Stein and Day/*Publishers*/Scarborough House
Briarcliff Manor, N.Y. 10510

Library of Congress Cataloging in Publication Data

Crosby, John, 1912–
    Party of the year.

    I. Title.
PZ4.C9485Par   [PS3553.R55]   813'.5'4   78-24694
ISBN 0-8128-2606-X

To Anne and Arnold

BOOK ONE
Windletop

Among the shards of rumor and hysteria, there were a thousand disagreements. The Earl of Canossa, a beautiful young man of twenty-six, caught the first bullet. Some said His Lordship, dressed in black velvet, was dancing the gallop with feline self-absorption when the .375 caliber (Russian make of inferior quality) tore into his throat sending a thin stream of hot scarlet all over the white lace of his shirtfront. Splashes of scarlet encarnadined the Princess Paola de Bruxelles, a lovely and passionate girl of twenty-two, the Earl's companion in the dance, herself shot a few moments later through her lovely breasts (her most stunning feature) which had been perhaps too conspicuously displayed in black chiffon. The burst of machine pistol fire almost cut her in two. This was only one version of the beginning.

Each survivor had a different encapsulation of the opening moments in this terrible ballet, each adding his little extra touch to the larger picture, illuminating the tragedy like a flashing strobe light with little bits of personally observed detail. "Jessica de Angelis plunged headlong into the pâté de fois gras which had been carved into the shape of a swan," said Jeremy Wild, the distinguished author and playwright, as quoted the next day on the front page of The New York Times. *He was speaking of the Duchess de Angelis, known as the Flying Duchess; she was pulled from the pâté by the police, who found—after they'd wiped her off—an expression of duchessy disdain imprinted on her dead features. So said* The Daily News *who got it from a police sergeant.*

Twenty-six dead. Everyone agreed on that, but there was considerable initial disagreement about how many of these were the terrorists. These days, snapped Joie de Printempts, the gossip columnist, it was difficult to tell the duchesses from the terrorists, the way people dressed. The columnist was especially bitchy because she had NOT been invited to the party and she was furious. Joie de Printemps was actively wooed to attend many big parties, but she had not reached the eminence of being invited to the Principessa di Castiglione's bash which had been termed (by every other social columnist except *Joie de Printemps) The Party of The Year.*

None of this party of the year clamor was the Principessa's doing. She was known to loathe publicity and never spoke to journalists. In light of this, it was considered odd and even sinister that two journalists, both from The New York Times, *were actually at the party. One was Jane Atchison, of the* Times *society staff, who was one of the twenty-six dead. The other was Alvin Feinberg, an assistant foreign editor of the* Times, *and everyone was asking what on earth a foreign editor was doing at so glittering and so trivial a function as The Party of The Year.*

Feinberg, a veteran of twelve wars, including Indochina before it was called Vietnam, had survived because he had combat sense enough to keep his head down until the firing stopped. When he got back to the Times *city room, covered with the blood of others, he was acclaimed as a hero by his fellow journalists, not because he had survived the affray but because he had managed to crash the party in the first place. He refused to say how.*

The Times *editorial the next day was superbly unequivocal. Something Should Be Done. "How did the terrorists get into the best-guarded apartment building in New York? Besides its elaborate security apparatus, which had been designed by Israeli experts to prevent just this kind of thing, the Windletop was guarded last night by an extra detail of forty New York patrolmen. It had been reliably reported that both the CIA and the FBI had advance word that the Red Wind would attempt a coup. Why wasn't something done about it? How did the Red Wind get into the building, and how did it get out?"*

Questions everyone was asking. Because he had been on the scene and because he'd known the Principessa many years earlier, Feinberg's was easily the best newspaper recital of them all, but even his story was full of holes, as Feinberg was first to admit.

"Only Cassidy knows the whole story," said Feinberg to his editors, "and he won't tell."

·1·

Cassidy approached through the park, skirting the lower lake where ducks swam and children whooped. On the other side of the lake was the bronze horse and naked rider by Horloge, and there the Windletop sprang into his view. Fifty-five stories of black glass—severe, funereal, ultra-modern—surrounding a stone fortress that had been built originally in the 1920s. Sunshine splashing off the polished surface like sparks.

Impregnable. Cassidy bared his yellow teeth in a ferocity of a grin. My ass. Impregnable was a mockery of a word. Unmusical. Almost unsayable. Calling anything impregnable was simply an invitation to pregnate it. Cassidy stood chewing his lip, hands thrust deep in the worn black coat, looking at the Windletop's topmost story, his mind ablaze with imagery.

The walls at Acre had been 100 feet high. Impregnable. Like the Maginot Line. The Saracens had stormed Acre, blue and gold pennants flying in the air, the great ram horns sounding—killed every Christian knight in the city, sold the women and children into slavery—and that had ended the thing after 300 years.

Cassidy crossed Fifth Avenue, scowling.

"He's crossing," reported Security 1 on the Telefax. "A peeper."

Peepers were not considered to be menaces. Just nuisances. Everyone wanted to get into the Windletop. Just to say they'd done it.

Security 1 resumed his post at second floor control which had a clear sweep of Fifth Avenue from north to south.

"A scarecrow," observed Security 2, watching Cassidy through the black glass which rose from floor to ceiling, imprisoning the warmth. Impermeable to outside stares. Or bullets.

"Whom do you wish to see?" asked the Front in his even-tempered British voice which harbored neither welcome nor hostility. The Front stood almost eight feet tall if you counted his immense, cockaded top hat, and you could hardly fail to count it since it loomed over intruders like a portcullis.

He stood under the canopy, barring the way. Visitors had to explain themselves to the Front before they were admitted even to the lobby.

"Princess di Castiglione," barked Cassidy through yellow teeth.

The great name bounced off the doorman as if unspoken. He stared at Cassidy, sizing him up. That overcoat must be twenty years old. Spotless but threadbare. The man thin as a blade. Bony face, fierce and watchful.

"The Principessa di Castiglione," murmured the Front, putting her in the right country. (The Windletop had a Principessa, two plain Princesses, and one Princesse—highest ranking of all—from France.)

"Whom shall I say is calling?"

"Cassidy. *Professor* Cassidy."

Much good it did. The Front picked up the Telefax and relayed the title as if it were a curse.

"A Professor Cassidy to see the Principessa."

"Not *a* Professor Cassidy," Cassidy snarled. "*The* Professor Cassidy. The academic world does not teem with Professor Cassidys. There's only one, my good man, and I am himself in person."

"Indeed," murmured the Front. He had been imported from England especially for his attitude and impassivity, but also because he could say "indeed" as if he meant it.

Cassidy was inspecting the setup professionally. He was still outside, standing next to bronze doors probably backed by steel. You couldn't even look in to case the place. When the click came, opening the bronze door, Cassidy and the Front entered a small vestibule shielded from the lobby by plate glass Cassidy guessed was at least four inches thick, proof against anything up to .50 caliber. The terrorists hadn't got quite to .50 caliber yet.

Trapped in the vestibule between the bronze outside doors and plate glass inside, Cassidy was inspected by a man called the Desk, a solemn, pince-nezed fellow surrounded by all the latest wizardry—audio-visuals, teledynes, Comptoflax—that would be outdated in five years by later wizardry. The desk itself was of black marble and stood in an acre of mirrored, marbled carpeted lobby.

"If you'd just state your name again, for the Voice Printer," said the Front politely.

"Professor Cassidy," barked Cassidy, "to see the Principessa di Castiglione."

The plate glass swung open, and the Front marched Cassidy past the Desk to the elevator which was oval like the President's Office, wainscoted with curved mirrors on its rear walls, and curved red plush seats for those too weary to stand during the elevator ride.

"The Principessa is on the forty-ninth," said the Front and pushed the proper button, as if Cassidy might get it wrong. He withdrew. The door closed and Cassidy shot up alone, staring at himself resentfully in the curved mirror. A face to frighten horses, he was thinking.

There was no corridor. The elevator sprang open at the forty-ninth floor, directly into the Principessa's apartment.

That will have to be changed, thought Cassidy.

The butler was Italian, ivoried with age, a man of immense courtesy, deep set, wide-sad eyes, wearing blue and yellow livery with authority. He was standing—clearly forewarned and waiting—just inside a small exquisite entrance hall, oval like the elevator, with fuchsia walls and a frescoed ceiling in which pink angels in blue robes blew gold trumpets.

The butler inclined his head in not quite a bow, his hands clasped before his liveried chest. "The Principessa is on the telephone," he said, giving the statement importance, as Europeans do to small matters.

"I think you had better wait in the Conservatory." This statement invited Cassidy's compliance. He was not being told where he must go; he was being asked if this were agreeable.

They proceeded down a huge corridor (wide enough, Cassidy noted, to house his entire apartment), their heels clanging sharply on black and white marble floors, past the library (books to the ceiling, leather bound, looking unread and unreadable), the sitting room (vast and huge with tapestries; who had tapestries any more?), a dining room of stately dimensions with crystal sconces set in walls of painted red and gold wood. The corridor inside was hung with paintings of Italian aristocrats and their hunting dogs standing on idealized landscapes that clearly showed the palazzo in the background, Flemish paintings of serving girls bearing milk pitchers, and a few English portraits that looked Gainsborough. The long hall was full of furniture—Directoire tables bearing ormolu clocks over which hung gilt mirrors that looked French eighteenth-century, great chests of lacquered wood with Japanese scenes painted on them, and one bronze David, naked except for his hat and sword, standing one foot on Goliath's head, looking pensive, as if wondering: After this, what's left?

The place looked like Sotheby's—before a big sale.

The Conservatory was something else. Sunshine blazed through windows that ran from floor to ceiling. Plants gushed from everywhere, the ceiling, the floor, the walls—in bronze pots, oak casks, wicker baskets, copper receptacles. Unlike the rest of the apartment, it was informal. The wicker chairs, painted and scuffed, looked as if they had been actually sat in. A wicker table was covered with plant trimmings, seedlings, and a scissors.

The butler took Cassidy firmly by the arm and guided him to a white wicker chair with green pillows. Also a footrest. "This is the most comfortable chair in the house, sir," he said and seated him into it with his long slender hands which looked not unlike those hands in the paintings outside.

"Some coffee, sir." Breath whiffling out of him like wind on silk. He spoke excellent English.

"Nothing, thank you." It was better not to have anything in your hands. It spoiled the posture.

"The Principessa will be along presently," said the butler. "She takes rather a long time on the telephone." He smiled a crafty old man's smile, the face breaking into a thousand fine lines, and bowed himself out.

Cassidy decided he liked him very much.

Eyes roaming the plant room for cues. Green plants, with few blooms and those of discreet heliotrope and lavender. No orchids. Mostly forest plants of strong character. That should tell him something about the owner. Nothing so flighty as a flower.

Far back in the corridor one of the ormolu clocks struck ten. The hour of the appointment. Cassidy could hear no other sound. Where was the child? Why wasn't she making a noise? Laughing? Crying?

It was getting too warm in the conservatory and Cassidy rose from the chair and removed his black coat, dangling it from his wrist flamboyantly. There was a little flamboyance in all his movements, even alone. Especially alone. In the long run—so thought Cassidy—acting was striking a pose against the Fates themselves and one hardly needed an audience for that.

Cassidy walked on the balls of his feet, holding the coat negligently in his right hand and wrist, to the wall of glass and tried to look straight down. Impossible. He could see out across the park and down Fifth Avenue but the sidewalk below him was concealed by the building itself.

I know too much about fortification, Cassidy was thinking. A weakness. You stopped learning when you knew too much, and the situation was always changing.

"You're older than I thought."

Like a shot across his bow.

Cassidy directed his scowl straight down forty-nine stories, his back firmly to the voice. American voice. Principessa, my ass. Let her wait.

He transferred his worn black coat from right to left wrist and from his front to his back, then pivoted on the balls of his feet, gracefully and slowly (he'd seen Osgood Perkins do this bit once and never forgotten), finally bending his searching gaze on her as if she were applying for a job, rather than the other way around. The kind of arrogance that had got him fired more than once—including the last time.

The Principessa wore blue and gold Chinese trousers, tunic, and slippers, everything matching. Slim as a rod. Pale gold hair in a long swept-back bun. Wideset eyes like Lillian Gish's. (Another man might have said Lauren Bacall, but Cassidy reached farther back than that for his images. Who but himself even remembered Osgood Perkins who was Anthony Perkin's father and a much better actor than his son?)

She gazed at him out of radiant violet eyes set in a masklike face of indeterminate age, unmoved—untouched even—by his brusqueness. She was, Cassidy conceded, beautiful. Or had been beautiful. He found it hard to know what tense to use with the Principessa.

"I think you're *too* old." American rich, that accent. New York born. English cadences but Yankee timbre.

"Then I'd better leave." Cassidy was insouciant. (He barely had the subway fare back to Greenwich Village, and he bloody well couldn't afford insouciance, but it was at times like this it gave him greatest pleasure.) He swung the ancient black coat around his shoulders and would have performed his best Alfred Lunt exit (The one Lunt had done so magnificently in *Reunion in Vienna*.)

She was blocking the door.

"So sit down, Professor Cassidy," she said, firm as a rock in face of his truculence. "In that white wicker chair, the most comfortable chair in the place. Lorenzo must have liked you very much, or he wouldn't have put you in this room. When he doesn't like visitors, he puts them in the sitting room directly under the air-conditioning where they catch a chill. When he despises them, he leaves them standing in the foyer—sometimes for hours. Do sit down."

"After you, Madame." Cassidy turned on the Irish charm following the Irish bellicosity. He could be as changeable as she was.

She sat on the white wicker settee, tucking her legs under her, the violet eyes thoughtful. "You come highly recommended." The voice was dry now, skeptical.

"You've been talking to the wrong people," said Cassidy harshly. "I've been fired from my last three jobs."

"Why?" Absently.

"For tellin' the truth though that's not what they'd say." Facing her, the black coat hanging down in front of him straight, like a shield.

"What are you a professor of?" she asked unexpectedly.

"Medieval literature."

"Where?"

"Currently unemployed. New York is awash with unemployed professors of medieval literature."

"Medieval literature," said the Principessa dryly, "is almost the only subject my daughter doesn't need. She's already steeped in it. Can you teach anything else?"

Cassidy turned on the Irish charm again. He needed the job, dammit. "Anything you can name, Madame, Greek, Latin, grammar, logic...."

"Logic? An Irishman?"

Cassidy gave her his pixie scowl: "We learn it, Madame, like an elephant learns to stand on his hind legs. Awkwardly, but well enough to open the circus."

The Principessa smiled faintly: "If I may ask a rude question, why is such an all-around *wunderkind* unemployed?"

Cassidy snorted right back: "If I may ask an even ruder one, why don't you send the child to school?"

The Principessa withdrew into herself, her personality diminishing into a faint absence, like the Cheshire cat. "I'll answer your question if you answer mine," she said after a silence.

Cassidy considered. He had many answers to that question (which was frequently asked). "Employers object to my...visibility," he said finally. Visibility was a nice word for it.

"Oh," said the Principessa, amused, "*visibility. Not* alcohol, or embezzlement, or rape. Well, I don't pretend to understand my daughter, Professor. She has ferocious likes and dislikes—like any child—except the thing she likes you'd expect her to loathe—and vice versa."

Silence in the plant room, smelling of verdure and ozone.

"Why don't you send her to school?" Saying it gently this time.

"I'm afraid."

The Principessa rose from the chair and busied herself with a green fern, lifting it from its brass potholder and setting it on the wicker table, where she picked up the scissors and cut off the brown tendrils, talking meanwhile in her dry tone: "They kidnapped my husband—and killed him."

"I read," said Cassidy. Almost impossible to avoid reading. Even in the *Times*.

"They killed him after we paid the ransom. Seven and a half million dollars. They're killing my friends in Italy—one by one—or kidnapping them. Now do you understand?"

"No," said Cassidy bluntly. "You're not in Italy now. This is New York. We've had none of that here."

"Well, *that* is the situation, Professor." Clipping the words off and spitting them at him like bullets. The blue eyes glittered like sapphires, and the Principessa got much older, hard as cement: "I don't propose to waste away with worry while the child is at school. That's why you're here, Professor, why I summoned you above all others. I wanted not only an instructor but a protector. You had special qualifications the others didn't have. Your work in the CIA...."

"Who told you that?"

"I have sources of information."

The monied always had sources of information. That's why they're monied.

Cassidy bared his teeth: "You're quite rich enough to hire *two* people, Principessa—one to instruct, one to protect. What you need is some lout like that eight-foot doorman to protect. And a dormouse to instruct."

The Principessa put down the scissors and faced him, arms across her chest, imperious as a Chinese empress. "I wish you'd stop telling me what I need and what I don't need. I want one man for both jobs because it's going to be hard enough for Lucia to accept even one man. She's a willful, stubborn, dreamy child—much like her father. She would not abide either a dormouse or an eight-foot lout. The big question is—will she like you?"

Cassidy rubbed his nose and shifted his tactics. Quite unexpectedly the job was inviting. He wanted it badly. Neither twelve-year-old girls nor protection were his specialties, but the combination of the two things he found appealing. He turned on all his Irish charm and swept the Principessa a low bow like Douglas Fairbanks in *The Three Musketeers*—all gallantry and grace. "Well, there's only one way to find out, Madame. Let's go ask the young lady."

·2·

After the brilliant sunshine of the conservatory, the nursery was dark and cheerless, its curtains drawn tight. The only light came from a bedside lamp which cast most of the room into deep shadow.

"*Ecce,*" hissed the Principessa, suddenly very European. She drew the curtains, letting in the north light. A big room with wallpaper of butterflies and birds and trees in soft colors. In that north light they'd never see the sunshine, Cassidy noted.

Lucia sat cross-legged on the floor before a huge replica of a medieval castle, moat, turrets, drawbridge, and all. In her right hand the child held a belted knight in armor with the shield of de Lessey, white plumes surrounding a boar's head. The coat of arms Cassidy knew well.

"Why is this room always so *gloomy?*" cried the Principessa.

"We're playing nighttime, Mama."

Lucia was dark-haired, unsmiling, plain, and withdrawn. Thin as a willow.

"Titi, playing nighttime, you must not let her do it."

"Sorr-ee, Principessa."

The Nanny was crouched before the castle on all fours like a dog. She was dark complected and wore a bright red scarf on her head, peasant style, and the rest of her was encased in jeans and a sweater. Cassidy had expected a proper English nanny—tweeds, middle-aged, thin-lipped disapproval—like the other rich kids. This one looked no more than eighteen. Untamed as a beast of the forest. She sounded not at all sorr-ee. The two of them, Cassidy guessed, in league against the Principessa.

"Lucia, this is Professor Cassidy. I'm trying to persuade him to be your tutor."

That was stretching the facts a bit. Never mind. Cassidy's eyes were on the girl.

A look of anger and stubborn pride crossed the plain face and disappeared into one of resignation. The girl scrambled to her feet and bobbed a curtsey—swift, practiced, totally unselfconscious, as European children do. Eyes on the floor, avoiding his. This wasn't going to be easy, thought Cassidy.

"How old are you, Lucia?" he asked, feeling like something out of Charles Dickens.

"Twelve, sir."

Lolita's age. Nothing but trouble.

"The age of awakening," he said mellifluously. (Playing Charles Laughton now.)

"Lucia awakened the day she was born," commented her mother dryly. "She's her father's child. Every inch." The Principessa plucked the belted knight from the girl's hand. "As I told you, medieval literature is one subject she doesn't need. Her head is already too full of it. You must teach her to live in the present like the rest of us." The Principessa sounded defiant as if she found the present not much to her liking either.

She handed the belted knight to Cassidy peremptorily. "Titi, come along. We'll leave them alone."

The girl didn't like the command. She rose from all fours reluctantly, and skulked out, glowering.

The door closed behind the Principessa and Nanny, leaving Cassidy and the girl facing one another.

Not a situation of his choosing.

The girl stood there, still as a mountain lake and as deep. What do I know of twelve-year-old girls, Cassidy was thinking. Nothing. He was dismayed at his nervousness and even more at her lack of it. He was out of his area.

"How many languages do you speak, Lucia?"

"Four." Negligently.

"English and Italian and what else?"

"French and German."

Doesn't everyone? Cassidy was losing this contest.

"No Spanish?"

"Oh, *Spanish*." Scornfully. "I can get along in Spanish."

Spanish was not a language to be taken seriously. Two falls to nothing, Cassidy was thinking.

"Latin?"

"I *hate* Latin."

Aha, thought Cassidy, pinning her. "You will never truly understand this knight"—holding up the lead soldier—"without some Latin in your little skull because he is a true descendant of the Roman Empire—and so are you with that Latin nose and Mediterranean eye." Then, bellicose. "Not me. We Celts have stayed out of reach of the Romans to this very day. We are poets first and bridge builders second." If at all. Had any Irish bridge ever withstood the first snowfall?

She had nothing to say to that but the tilt of her head suggested defiance. I displease her, he thought. Good. He took pleasure in her displeasure like the connoisseur that he was. If she'd been all dimples he'd have been bored.

He was on his knees now next to the castle. "Where did you get this thing?"

"Mama bought it. At F.A.O. Schwarz."

So. Mama disapproved the Middle Ages but bought her child medieval fortresses at F.A.O. Schwarz.

"It's not very good, you know," said Cassidy, trying her out. "The curtain walls are too thin and the bailey is much too low. The Saracens would overrun such a thing in half an hour."

She wasn't buying it. "You're too old to be my tutor," she said, plunging it into his heart like a stiletto, the face rigid with dislike.

Cassidy rose from his knees, awkward as a camel, and bent a wintry smile on the mutinous child. "How many tutors have there been, miss?"

"I'm not a miss. I'm a contessa."

Cassidy's wintry smile grew broader: "How many?"

She sniffed an aristocratic sniff at that and set her jaw.

"They all left," said Cassidy, "because they wouldn't put up with you, eh?" He was hunching into his worn black coat now, using it as a prop to cover his exit.

"Haven't you got a nicer coat than that?" she asked.

"That's an impertinent question, miss."

"I'm not a miss. I'm a contessa."

The Principessa was in the plant room, watering the ferns. "I'll take the job," said Cassidy.

"I haven't offered it yet."

"You will," said Cassidy. "Not many others will put up with her. I'll want two thousand a month—one thousand as instructor, one thousand as protector."

"Fifteen hundred for both," said the Principessa, not even looking up from her plant. "And room and board. You'll have to live here, you know."

"I'll want fifteen hundred in advance, and tomorrow is the earliest I can move." He bowed, heavy hearted. Why was it every time he landed a job he wanted to run? At his age he hadn't the breath left to run. "You didn't tell me the child was a contessa, Madame. That makes it harder to civilize her."

"Oh," said the Principessa. "Every other child in Italy is a contessa. Lucia has other liabilities—much worse than that."

"Like what?"

The Principessa eyed him malevolently: "She's rich. Filthy rich."

·3·

Cassidy took the Lexington Avenue subway at Eighty-sixth, huddling in his black coat, eyeing the svelte black girls lustfully. These last ten years the blacks had got so elegant—and so visible—where once their complaint had been invisibility. Now it was the rich who craved invisibility to keep from being kidnapped or murdered. Visibility had changed hands.

I am a discordant note in that household, thought Cassidy bleakly. Why me? "I have sources." Alison? Alison had thrown him bones in the past not altogether out of fondness. Alison's moves were always dictated by something a little more self-serving than affection. Wanted to keep Cassidy occupied, probably. Prevent him from getting into mischief. Like writing books about the CIA, which everyone else was doing.

At Times Square, Cassidy slipped a dime in the pay phone and called Robins in the *Times* library. "I'm a block away. Can I come up?"

A hesitation. "We're pretty full, Horatio. How long will it take?"

"di Castiglione. The whole family."

"Jesus, Horatio! The murder alone is four folders thick."

"I'll be quick," said Cassidy and hung up immediately so Robins wouldn't have a chance to say no. The CIA was no longer popular in newspaper offices. Once they'd had the run of the place from the publisher right down to the office boys. Not any more. He wasn't even in the Company now, which made him less welcome.

Robins had the di Castiglione files clutched in his arms when Cassidy walked into the *Times* library. A little ferret of a man who'd covered City Hall until an ulcer forced him into desk work.

"Why do you want to rake up the di Castiglione thing?" said Robins, the ferret eyes gleaming with pure curiosity, strong as whiskey.

"That is classified information," said Cassidy.

"A crock of shit. You're not with the outfit any more."

"I've been hired as nursemaid," cried Cassidy harshly. "The little di Castiglione girl. Age twelve."

"Jesus," said Robins, his voice full of pity. He handed over the thick folders. "Take your time."

Cassidy took four hours, poring over each clipping, taking no notes, arranging the thing in his head. He lingered longest over the Principessa's clippings. Schoon was her maiden name. One of the old Dutch families. Elsa Schoon. Brearley School, Wellesley, cotillions, Southampton. All the usual upper class watering holes. Later a working girl. Was the family down on its luck? The Schoons hadn't been heard from in years, though they'd once been rich, powerful, and very social.

The marriages had been a string of disasters. First Horace P. Loring IV, polo player and drunk. Two car crashes, three drunken brawls, had made the papers which meant there had been lots of ones that hadn't. Eight years married to Loring. No children. Then Gregory Forge, cowboy star. Four years for that marriage, which was probably two more years than it had really worked. No children.

Finally the Prince di Castiglione, one of the great names. Rich, too. Why? The Italian aristocracy didn't marry Americans unless they were broke. The Prince was as rich as they come, and Cassidy doubted Elsa Schoon had any money at all. Perhaps she was a great lay. No. Italian aristocrats didn't marry the great lays. Wives were for breeding purposes.

There was no mention of Lucia in the clippings until the kidnapping and murder, after which her name and photograph made the papers often. Lucia, head lowered, ducking out of her Rolls-Royce (bullet proof) and into her *palazzo* in Rome. Lucia running the gauntlet of press photographers to get to school— until she'd been taken out of school. Lucia arriving in New York—always head down, face averted.

Cassidy went over the kidnapping and murder, clipping by clipping, separating the crap from the real with experienced skill. A vicious killing never explained, though many had tried. The Red Wind had wanted publicity, which it had got. It had wanted money, which it also got. Why kill the Prince, casting an unpopular playboy into the role of martyr? It didn't make sense.

Many photographs of the Prince. A beautiful Italian. No other word for it. He looked, in fact, like some of those paintings of Italian landed aristocracy in the di Castiglione hall. A man with a scornful eye and sensual lip, over all the physiognomy a sort of imperious sadness. Just like the Donatello David. What's left? Is this all there is? Or perhaps I'm reading a little more into the Prince than is there, Cassidy thought. The Prince was not generally admired. At Oxford, he'd played with the richest and most useless English. In Rome he'd led *La Dolce Vita* conspicuously and wastefully. Finally he'd been kidnapped and killed. Not much to admire there but apparently some had. His parties and presence were legendary and had been sorely missed.

Cassidy bundled up the clips and took them back to Robins. "Let me do something for you some time," he said with his expansive smile. (Because who knows when he'd need Robins again?)

"Yeah," said Robins skeptically. "Get me an invitation to one of the Principessa's parties."

"Parties?" said Cassidy. "Does the Principessa have parties?"

"The press is not invited. Not even the *Times*."

Cassidy went up the backstairs in order to avoid the dragonfly who guarded the editorial offices at the front. The foreign desk was behind a glass screen, sheltering the deep thinkers there from the more ordinary scribblers who covered ship sinkings and horticultural shows. Feinberg was editing a wire story when Cassidy slipped into the seat next to him.

"Cassidy," said Cassidy mellifluously, as if announcing the entrance of the Pope.

Feinberg, an orotund intellectual, with gold-rimmed glasses that emphasized the enormous intelligence behind his eyes, looked at Cassidy with total absence of welcome.

"We met in Beirut in 1954," said Cassidy, overflowing with

Irish bonhomie. "At the Ambassador's cocktail party for Nehru. An affair brimful of explosive implications which you wrote about with such prescience and self-confidence."

Feinberg was not amused. "Where did you come from just now? Through the roof?"

"The floor. You don't remember?"

"My God, a cocktail party over twenty years ago. Oh, wait. Yes! You were...cultural attaché or some such malarkey which was just a cover for...."

"I'm not with that group any more," said Cassidy, his arm describing an arabesque in the air, wiping out the CIA altogether. "My role in life has seriously diminished since those days. You might say I'm operating on a more human scale. To put it in a nutshell...." Cassidy scratched his head and made a clown face and shrugged, all at once. (Only Jack Lemmon could get away with all those gestures at the same time.) "I'm running security for a certain Contessa di Castiglione who—I think—you once knew."

"Never laid eyes on her. I knew her mother and father."

"I need information. You covered the kidnapping."

"It's all in the clips," Feinberg sat erect in his creaky swivel chair impatiently.

"There were a lot of rumors that didn't make the papers."

"Oh rumors," said Feinberg. He took off his gold-rimmed glasses and polished them on his shirt ends. "If you wanted all the rumors about Nicky and Elsa di Castiglione you'd be here a week—and I haven't time. The scandals about those two—sexual, financial, social—ran the gamut. Much of it crap. Some people even said he arranged his own kidnapping and it went wrong and he got himself killed by accident. Wild stuff like that."

"You covered the kidnapping and murder. What did you think about those rumors?"

"Look," said Feinberg impatiently, "you were in the information business yourself. You know rumors. They're never all wrong or all right. The di Castigliones were rich and glamorous and beautiful. Sexually they were both swingers. Stories grew like weeds even before the kidnapping."

"You knew them well."

"I wouldn't say that. I went to their parties—but in those

days that wasn't hard. Everyone went to their parties. You ran into them at other parties, too, and they glanced off you like—sunshine. They were a dazzling pair, beautiful and rich and witty and bright, though, God knows, not very useful."

Feinberg rubbed his nearsighted eyes, remembering: "He was a physical fitness freak. Did karate and things like that. He could throw you on your back with a twist of his wrist. That kind of thing. Did it to me once."

Cassidy bored in here: "There was rumors the Mafia wound up with the kidnap money. Took it away from the Red Wind."

"Rumors," said Feinberg dismissing it. "I even heard the opposite—that the Mafia kidnapped the Prince and the Red Wind stole the money from *them*. In Rome you can hear anything."

"Do you see the Principessa now?"

Feinberg shook his head: "She won't talk to newspapermen any more. She blames us for the whole thing, as if it was our fault they were so conspicuous. I haven't laid eyes on Elsa di Castiglione for six years."

Cassidy leaned forward diffidently: "One last question. Did you like him—the Prince?"

"Yes, I did," said Feinberg smiling. "Everyone liked him. He was thoroughly reprehensible and thoroughly likable."

"Thanks," said Cassidy and rose abruptly.

"Wait," said Feinberg. "How about a little something in return. If you're going to live at the Windletop, we'd appreciate a little information about that damned building. Nobody has been able to get past all those guards...." The telephone rang. "Feinberg. Yeah, I'll be right up." He hung up and swung his swivel chair around. "We'd like to get a line...."

Cassidy had gone.

·4·

"The wardship of rich little girls was much sought after,"
Cassidy grimaced, clownlike in the privacy of his own room.
"One wealthy three-months-old orphan was fought over by no
less than two English kings. Abbot Samson contested his right to
nurture the young lady (and her fortune) against Henry II.
Richard the Lionhearted continued the struggle for the
wardship of the little orphan when he became king and was
finally bought off by the gift of hunting dogs and horses."

Cassidy lay on his unmade bed, feeling sorry for the little
highnesses. Greed in the thirteenth century was no different
from the twentieth but the arithmetic was. You couldn't buy
people off quite so cheaply. "The girl was later kidnapped by her
godfather, his way of getting into her fortune. The Abbot then
sold his claim for $100 to the Archbishop of Canterbury, and he
promptly sold it to the brother of the King's Chamberlain for
$333."

What happened to the girl after that? Did she grow up and
marry a few fortune hunters who looted her like the others?
History didn't say.

Which brought him to Lucia, a rich little girl, whose father
had been kidnapped and then, unnecessarily, murdered. It stuck
in his craw—that unnecessary murder.

Cassidy rose from the bed and returned the book to its special
shelf next to the *Chronicle of Richard of Tours 1217, Chanson de
Roland,* the *Castellan de Courcy,* the *Contes de Severin,* the
Annals of Dunstable, and all the other lays and legends.

The Chamber, Cassidy called it, because the word *room* was
inadequate. It was too spacious, too high-ceilinged, too grand
with its fourteen-foot windows on West Thirteenth Street to be

called a room. A true chamber with its own towering personality. Cassidy had clung to it even when the Company had sent him to Tangier for three years and to Belgrade for seven. Each time he'd had to evict his subtenants when he returned from abroad because the tenants clung like barnacles having become as fond of the Chamber as he was.

Cassidy crossed the room to the highboy desk next to the shuttered windows that kept the place in perpetual twilight. What was the point any more? Who'd want to look at an aged Irish—ex-CIA, ex-academic, ex-husband, ex-everything? Force of habit, that's why. All my habits are outworn like myself.

Cassidy picked up a pile of bills held together by a rubber band. Twelve hundred dollars worth. "I can pay them off in a month," he said aloud, addressing himself to his dead wife, whose photograph stood on the desk. "I'll soak up the Principessa's light and heat and pay the bills, in a month's time." He picked up the photograph and blew the dust off it. "I've been looking for work," he explained apologetically. "I've not had the time," explaining the dust. I'd be a much better husband now than then. "I had ambitions then," he said to the pretty, roguish dead face, "a husband with ambitions is too self-centered to pay proper heed. Today I'd be at your feet all day long. You'd be bored to death." He put the framed photograph back on the desk tenderly, skeptical of his own sentimentality. Maria had been dead fourteen years, and he distrusted the memory of happiness as probably bogus. Maria had died of leukemia at thirty-eight. He remembered the pain. Not the marriage. I had a wife when I didn't need one, and now I need one I haven't one. My timing is wrong, all the way down the line.

Cassidy tossed the pile of bills into his aged portmanteau which lay open on the floor. It already contained his three shirts, his four pair of socks, his two cardigans.

Now, . . . books. Cassidy pulled off the shelves the *Chronicle of Behemund*, the *Conte de Brabant*, the *Chanson de Passim*—bloody tales of villainy, treachery, and greed for the edification of a twelve-year-old contessa. As Groucho Marx had once said, they have to learn sometime.

Cassidy mounted the teak ladder which ran on rails clear round the chamber and propelled himself half the length of the room. From the second highest shelf, just under the ceiling,

Cassidy took out three pamphlets—Caetano's *Red Fascism* (the best book on Italian terrorism yet written), Sylvester Guardi's *Mafia in Italy*, and a very private highly classified document he'd stolen from the CIA on personal protection procedures in Israel. Outdated, but the best he had.

The Middle Ages were for the education of Lucia. These books were for his own edification.

Cassidy pushed the ladder, himself on it, to the corner of the room where he reached behind the books to bring out his silenced .22. Very portable but not much at stopping a man in his tracks. For that he pulled out the .38, which could shatter the head of a crocodile. Cassidy hated it because it was so noisy.

He dropped the two guns in the portmanteau (real Brabazon leather which smelled of the nineteenth century) next to the books, and closed the bag.

Mounting the ladder once again, he propelled himself to the far corner of the room and pulled out a large volume of French medieval songs. The letter was just inside the cover.

> Horatio:
> I did what I could but in the current climate of Presbyterianism around here it didn't help. The black bag job was a pretext as you know. We all did them in the old days and when I authorized yours, I couldn't foresee Watergate, could I?
> Keep in touch.
>
> Hugh

Then at the bottom under the signature on the plain paper: *Please Ds.*

Cassidy smiled. Trust Alison to put a Ds on a letter that had self-destructed twelve hours after he got it. (But not before Cassidy had carefully Xeroxed it, knowing Alison.)

Cassidy tucked the letter back into the book, not just inside the cover this time but deep inside.

On the way out, he double-locked the door and put the telltale in place overhead. As always, he felt bereavement. Half my life, he thought savagely, I've spent away from this place for the sole purpose of earning enough money to pay the rent. It was self-defeating. There must be some aim in life higher than this—

to hang on to the latch key of a one-room apartment I'm hardly ever allowed to live in.

He picked his way down the brownstone steps past the garbage cans and let himself into the Spumi, the little Italian restaurant in the basement underneath his apartment.

Henry was behind the bar laying out slices of lemon, olives, and triangles of lime for the luncheon crowd. Without a word, Henry poured out a shot glass full of Wild Turkey. Cassidy threw it down his gullet in one motion.

"I'll call in, Henry, if you'd be so kind."

The Spumi had taken his phone calls for years.

"Want to leave a number?" Henry was Swiss. He liked to write it all down in his little book.

"No," said Cassidy. "Anyone calls. Get the number. I'll call them."

"Suppose Sophy drops by."

Cassidy sighed and rubbed his ear. "Tell her I'm in Turkestan."

Henry blinked. So it was like that, was it? He didn't comment, wise bartender that he was. "You want to pay a little on the bill?" Very gently. He and Cassidy had been friends for thirty years.

"I'll pay it all in a couple of days," said Cassidy harshly.

"No hurry," said Henry, polishing a glass. "I just thought . . . well, Turkestan is a long way."

"I'm not leaving the city this time, Henry."

"It's a big city. Don't get lost."

"I'm expecting a call sometime this evening. Just get the name and number. It's important."

Henry nodded. When he looked up from his polishing, Cassidy had gone. Henry racked up another ninety-five cents on the tally sheet next to the register.

·5·

"Every single resident of the Windletop fears kidnapping," said the Security Chief in tones so emotionless they vanished from the mind seconds later—as if unspoken. What was he—German? A round smooth face on which nothing was imprinted except caution. Very good English but not the kind picked up at mother's knee.

"That's why we must insist on these annoying procedures."

"Life is just a bowl of annoying procedures," said Cassidy.

None of the staff had names. They were known as Security 1, Security 2, the Front, the Desk. All this, it was explained, so their own wives or children couldn't be held hostage as a way to gain entry to the Windletop. Many of them seemed European, men with few home ties or ties to anything. (Like me, thought Cassidy.)

"You were in the CIA—in covert operations," said the Security Chief tonelessly.

"Who told you that?"

Security Chief smiled faintly, a trace smile for purposes of showing he'd heard a question he had no intention of answering: "Of course, you have *left* the Company—as they all say they have." Security Chief leaned back in his leather armchair and contemplated the ceiling, fingertips together as if praying: "One wonders..." speaking to the ceiling. Or to God. "...whether anyone ever actually *leaves* the CIA or the Mossad or MI5 or the KGB."

"One is paid to wonder these things, isn't one," said Cassidy evilly. "Well, for your information, people do get fired from the CIA. The KGB kills theirs; the English rusticate them; the

Israelis parachute them into places they never come back from. We all have our national idiosyncrasies."

The Security Chief smiled as if enjoying the sarcasm. "For a very high price the Windletop provides shelter—in the fullest sense of the word—not only from the wind and rain but from all the vicious social currents that so *bedevil* the lives of the rich and the powerful in all the western world."

Bedevil, thought Cassidy. Lovely word. I must use it in a sentence sometime. Aloud he said: "I'd like a list of all the residents."

"Well, you won't get it." Again that whisper of an apologetic smile. The Security Chief leaned forward, his glossy black hair (A wig? Dyed?) glinting in the overhead light. "If you must know, Mr. Cassidy, I don't know the real identities of all of them. We have people here who I'm sure are not using their real names and even their fake names are secret. Of course, everyone knows a few identities like the di Castigliones and a few others who are so rich and well known we've not been able to keep it out of the papers." The Security Chief played with his pencil. "If you live here, you'll hear rumors. Oh, my God, the rumors!" Security ran his fingers lightly through his glossy black hair. "We have the Pope here, deposed kings, the Mafia." Security smiled a weary smile: "I'd disregard the rumors if I were you. About the only thing you can say of our residents without being hopelessly wrong is that all of them are rich. And afraid."

Cassidy spoke harshly: "What kind of security is that? If you don't know who the residents are? They could be anyone—Red Wind, Symbionese Liberation Army, PLO, Japanese Red Army."

"Oh, I don't think so," said Security lightly. "*I* don't vet the residents. But believe me they are *vetted* by the toughest security check in the world. After all, Mr. Cassidy, if a single resident were kidnapped—or assassinated, the Windletop would empty out in three days. As it is, we are 100 percent occupied."

The Security Chief rose and picked up a large ring of keys. "At the Windletop, we have nothing so flimsy as identification badges which can be easily forged. We operate entirely on faces and voices which are difficult to duplicate—though not impossible. Total security is, ... " he spoke with the impersonality of a scientist explaining the diffraction of light "... is not possible. A dream. We play the percentages. After you."

Showing him the door with the professional courtesy of a hotel clerk. The office was on the second floor directly over Control where Security 1 and 2 kept watch. Security pushed the elevator button. "There are twelve elevators in this building, Professor Cassidy—a security nightmare—but one of the glories of the Windletop is the fact that elevators are never crowded because there are so many of them. This building—as you must know—was built in 1928, the last extravagance before the roof fell in in 1929. It was completely gutted, remodeled and faced with glass in 1974." The word "glass" came out of him with a distinct hiss like escaping steam. There was no doubt that he regretted the remodeling of the Windletop, conceivably even the entire last half century.

The elevator door opened at the basement. "I'm showing you around the services. We provide all services," said Security, smooth as a fish, "except undertakings for which there has been no demand. Yet."

The services were lit indirectly by lights concealed in enormous bronze urns, another extravagance left over from the 1920s. The two men strolled the length of the corridor, past a beauty shop with a flaming pink door, a flower shop where a Japanese girl arranged violets as delicate as herself, Buccellati's jewelry shop where an emerald ring in the window was $12,000 (appalling, thought Cassidy, the medievalist whose own taste ran to the blazing simplicity of Saracen goldsmiths), a leather shop (Barthelme's of Paris whose prices were even more rarified than Gucci's), a boutique where the salesgirls were all sisters in linen suits and sold blouses that were silk and Italian and explosively colored. The delicatessen displayed cheeses from France, caviar from Russia, bonbons from Belgium. Across from it was a fur boutique displaying sable and marten and otter (nothing so ordinary as mink). Laundry and dry cleaning were tucked out of sight beyond a series of double doors.

"As you see," said Security Chief with silky good nature, "we could withstand a siege just like your medieval castles."

My medieval castles, thought Cassidy. Security was showing off just how well informed he was. Cassidy didn't rise to the bait. Instead, he said: "Have you vetted all the service people?"

"Yes, indeed," said Security Chief softly. "Some of them will be around much longer than yourself, Mr. Cassidy. The turnover of tutors up at the forty-ninth floor is quite high. The Contessa has already fired two...."

The *Contessa* fires them? Not Mama?

Cassidy didn't feel like rising to that either. Instead he said: "This isn't the lowest floor in the Windletop. There must be some guts to this building where garbage and sewage and all those unpleasant things are taken care of. There has got to be another exit. I'd like to see it."

"We don't allow anyone below this floor, Mr. Cassidy." Velvety voice, very firm. "One of our annoying procedures."

"Very annoying, too," agreed Cassidy.

"When you tire of ogling that Japanese girl—who is quite unavailable; she's been spoken for by one of the Windletop's richest and most lustful residents—I'll show you the Windletop Club."

"Will they allow either of us in?"

The Windletop Club was an anomaly, a relic of the past, so exclusive that many of the residents, while sufficiently rich and presentable to gain occupancy of the Windletop itself were *not* good enough for the Windletop Club. Most of the Club members didn't live in the Windletop and many of them—Cassidy had got this out of the *Times* clips—openly scorned many of the Windletop's newer residents, especially those who had moved in for security reasons.

To get to the Windletop Club, they had to descend to the main lobby, go out the bronze doors and around the corner where the Club had its own quite separate canopy and door and lobby. To say nothing of its own elevator. As they shot up to the roof, the Security Chief said casually: "This elevator makes only one stop—the Club on the roof. Club members can't wander around the rest of the Windletop. Or vice versa."

The Club restaurant was small, elegant, and hushed. Great plate-glass windows overlooking Manhattan were softened and given shape by heavy drapes in soft autumnal colors, the same pattern as the tablecloths on the oval tables. The restaurant floor was a series of giant steps which made for many embrasures and landings and changes of elevation, all in curved shapes. Through the plate-glass windows Manhattan was spread out below like a table of hors d'oeuvres, shining in the sunlight. Waiters were setting the tables for lunch—silver, brown napkins, wine glasses, fresh flowers—making it a sacerdotal rite like altar boys. There was a small dance floor with a ceiling of antiqued mirrors.

"This is Robert," introduced the Security Chief, using the French pronunciation (Roe-bear), "the maitre d'. Professor Cassidy will be accompanying the little di Castiglione girl on her monthly luncheons, Robert. Do take good care of him inasmuch as he may not be with us very long. The last tutor, you'll recall, lasted three days."

"I'll try to hang on a little longer," said Cassidy. Robert was eying his suit with the sort of horror his clothes always aroused in headwaiters. In retaliation, Cassidy said: "This restaurant is too small to break even. How much do you lose a week, Robert?"

Robert examined his fingernails for small flaws and said nothing.

The Security Chief leapt into the silence. "The restaurant doesn't depend on luncheon altogether. It has many private parties. The place is booked solid through Easter."

"Including a big party to be given by the Principessa," murmured Robert.

"Am I invited?" asked Cassidy.

"Only if you last that long," said the Security Chief, taking his elbow. "And the odds on that are not very high."

The Security Chief led him firmly back to the elevator, chatting away almost to himself. "Aah, the dreams they had in the 1920s, so much more *nourishing* than the ones we have now." He pushed the button for the elevator. "Did you know this building actually had a railroad station built below it for the private railroad cars of the residents? The Depression ended all that and private railroad cars vanished from the possessions of the rich—even our rich who are very rich indeed."

"Now they have Lear jets which are even more expensive," said Cassidy.

"But it can't deliver you to your own doorstep," said Security with infinite regret for a vanished age.

The two men were back in the lobby.

"You may call me Alfred," said Security with a small private smile. "It's not my name but it's my handle in this place. Behind my back the staff call me Alfred the Great. They think I don't know, but there is little goes on in this place I don't know."

·6·

"We are a mélange," murmured Lorenzo.

The butler wore a leather apron over his livery. He was polishing a silver and gold coffee urn of gigantic size which had a sea nymph's face in gold for a spout. The nymph's arms, gracefully pulled back from the hips, were handles. A great clamshell with gold flutings was the base of the urn, the sea nymph's fish-scaled body reposing on the clamshell.

The aged butler looked like a deposed Pope, the face a mixture of taciturn wisdom with deep sadness. With the soft polishing cloth, he caressed the nymph's face, making love to the object, mouth moving as if framing unspoken endearments.

They were in the pantry, Cassidy sipping coffee which Lorenzo had laid before him with such deference it seemed actually to improve the taste. One does not sip coffee lightly that is so elegantly presented, Cassidy was thinking. He was trying to draw Lorenzo out on the subject of Titi.

"She is a whim of the Contessa," said Lorenzo, his cloth burnishing the sea nymph's ears.

"Where is this whim from?"

Lorenzo smiled his hooded Florentine smile (looking, Cassidy noted, like one of the paintings of the Doges of Venice—crafty, all-knowing, and benign): "She is a little peasant girl from one of the di Castiglione estates, a little forest creature full of innocence and evil, about equally mixed."

Cassidy sipped his coffee. "Is the Contessa always permitted these whims?"

Taciturnity closed down Lorenzo's exquisitely lined face. "I think, signor, you should find out some of these things yourself."

"I stand rebuked," said Cassidy.

"Admonished, sir" the old man corrected him. "You must reach your own conclusions in this household. I don't wish to...lead you astray." Lorenzo held up the heavy coffee urn, inspecting every crevice, each golden fish scale, eyes aglow.

"Tell me about the coffee urn," said Cassidy.

Lorenzo pursed his lips. A long silence. Finally he said almost brusquely: "It is by Fironi, the di Castiglione's silversmith in the seventeenth century. In those days each family had its own silversmith."

Cassidy probed gently because the old man didn't like too much curiosity: "The staff seems to have shrunk quite a bit since then. We are a rather small mélange—yourself, Titi, me. Who else?"

"The two maids are Irish. I picked them myself. The secretary is Miss Cass. English. Neither she nor the maids live in."

"No cook?"

Lorenzo smiled his fine Italian smile: "Like so many people the world over we are looking for a cook. The earth was once agog with cooks. They have all become lawyers. Eventually we shall all starve surrounded by lawyers making out our wills. This is called upward mobility."

They both smiled.

Cassidy was aching to ask questions about the dead Prince, but he didn't dare. Lorenzo shut him up, with embarrassing finality when he felt like it. He rose from the pantry table.

"Well, to my duties. To bring the light of civilization to the Contessa's twelve-year-old mind."

"I wish you good fortune, signor," said Lorenzo, uttering the antique sentiment as unself-consciously as hello. "I think sometimes the Contessa suffers from perhaps too much civilization. One of the great tasks of future educators will be to devise some system, not for putting things into little heads, but taking things out."

Lorenzo said this absently. He was using his polishing cloth on a silver cup in the shape of a conch held by a mermaid whose hair was solid gold. Treasures of the di Castiglione family. The Red Wind wouldn't call them that. Treasures of the Italian people, they'd say, stolen by this American upstart of a wife and smuggled out of Italy. That's what they'd say. If they knew.

Cassidy walked down the corridor from the kitchen, past the fifteenth-century Perugia painting of a di Castiglione Cardinal, past the Donatello bronze of David, mounted on its pilaster of red marble (Donatello had done a good many Davids, not all of them in museums), past the door to the Principessa's bedroom where she lay asleep, past the seigneurial armor in silver edged with gold (which meant it had not been intended for serious fighting), finally to the nursery door.

Not a sound. There should be sounds coming from a nursery, thought Cassidy. Laughter. Chatter. Some kind of outcry.

Cassidy opened the door. Lucia was gazing at herself in the mirror with hauteur, upstaging her own image. Titi was on the floor next to her.

Lucia was wearing a man's shirt of English poplin which hung down over her little flat behind clear to her knees. She had nothing else on.

"*E troppo grande,*" murmured Titi.

"*Mi piace troppo grande,*" retorted Lucia.

"It's too old for you," commented Cassidy. "When you're fifteen is time enough to wear boy's shirts."

He'd caught them unaware, and they didn't like it. They looked violated, their young bodies drooping like flowers. Both stared at the floor, shrinking from him emotionally to such a degree it left a hole in the air.

"I thought the shirt would please you, Professor," said Lucia eyes downcast.

Meekness, thought Cassidy. I'm being savaged by meekness Italian girls know all the feminine wiles at birth. "Time for your first lesson, Lucia," he said.

"Oh!" cried Lucia, a lament that has run down the ages from 100 generations of schoolchildren.

Cassidy turned on the Irish charm, bowing from the waist: "Might you be persuaded, Contessa, to slip on a pair of blue jeans."

She underplayed him skillfully. "Might I wear the shirt with the jeans?"

"Well," said Cassidy. The first of probably many surrenders. "Would you leave us, Titi?"

"Oh!"

A piercing strangulated cry from Lucia. She does that well thought Cassidy, the actor in him admiring it, the professor in him loathing it.

"Titi has no education, Professor." Lucia had turned on him her black eyes full of pleading. "It would be enriching for her to experience your English vocabulary."

And what can I say to that, thought Cassidy. Deny my splendid vocabulary to this poor, deprived, peasant girl. I'd be violating at least twelve anti-poverty laws. I'm being diddled up the ass with marshmallows.

Cassidy walked to the window and stared out stonily. "If you'll put on the blue jeans, we'll start." Not surrendering this time, just sidestepping.

When he turned around—a good five minutes later (If she disobeys me about the blue jeans, I'm going to paddle her little Contessan ass, he was thinking)—he found her dressed in blue jeans (bare feet to preserve a sliver of rebellion). She was seated cross-legged on the floor, eyes fixed demurely on him. The peasant girl sat next to her, eyes bright with laughter as if they'd shared some secret pantomime joke behind his back. I'm to be a figure of fun, am I? thought Cassidy furiously.

"Let us begin at the beginning," snarled Cassidy, "with the assumption you know nothing at all." A gambit he'd employed with great success at Brandeis University (before they'd discovered the CIA connection and tossed him out.) "This planet, demoiselles, . . . " giving them a fierce grimace of a smile, "is roughly four billion years old, an accident of cosmic dust and gravity, wholly unimportant in the mechanics of the universe. The human race has glorified and despoiled this little *ball*, . . . " forming a little ball with his hands, peering down at it hunchbacked like God looking at his creation, a bit of play acting he'd stolen from Bronowski's TV show which always slayed the girls at Brandeis, "for a million years or—if you lean toward the Leakeys and their discoveries at Olduvai Gorge, perhaps four million years—a blink in the vastness of eternity. I bring it all up because you must never forget two things—the glory of human accomplishment and its total irrelevance in the larger cosmic scheme—if the word scheme is not too demeaning for the cosmos. As humans, we are splendid but *temporary*."

Titi's eyes were beginning to glaze. He had enriched her vocabulary to the point of putting her to sleep. Lucia's eyes on the other hand were bright with astonishment. Cassidy was deliberately flattering her twelve-year-old ego with college intelligence.

"I'm endeavoring, Contessa, to arouse your wonder at the modern world and your skepticism in the hereafter. If you are ever to be truly educated, if in this dangerous world you are even to *survive*, you must not look to God. There is none."

"I am a good Catholic," piped Lucia, eyes gleaming with...what? Fear? Anger?

"So am I," bellowed Cassidy. "An Irish Catholic—the best or worst kind of Catholic, depending on the point of view. I entreat you, Contessa, banish these medieval superstitions."

The girl's black eyes stared back at him frozen. Mutinous?

Titi's face meanwhile had sunk into a sullen apathy.

Cassidy sank, cross-legged to the floor facing Lucia and bent his fierce face to hers. "What do you know," he whispered, "about Sumer? About Crete? About the Mediterranean civilizations that gave birth to your black eyes and your long Roman nose?"

"Nothing," said Lucia defiantly, glaring back at him.

"What in hell," bellowed Cassidy, "did they teach you in those four languages?"

"Manners," shot out the girl.

"Banish them," said Cassidy.

"I'm to discard my God and my manners?" said Lucia disbelieving.

"*Banish* was the word. Not discard. Hang God and your manners in the closet like habilments to be worn when occasion demands. When you are learning, you must put these *impediments*," spitting the word out, "aside and open your mind to *facts* as opposed to superstitions, prejudices, and myths. If you have been taught that God made the world in six days and on the seventh day he rested, forget it. He didn't. Let us now briefly explore the beginning of civilization as it *really* happened...."

For an hour he held forth conceding nothing to her twelve years, delivering the same lecture he'd given college students twice her age. The black eyes stared back, smouldering. Cassidy hadn't the faintest notion whether she even understood. There was nothing writ on the plain withdrawn face except consciousness. She was definitely awake. (Titi wasn't. She'd fallen asleep, head on her chest.)

After an hour, Cassidy stopped abruptly. "Quite enough for today," he barked.

He rose, tall, emaciated, towering over her like an overeducated crow. "Tomorrow," he said, "we take up Egypt whose five thousand year death wish has done great damage to civilized thought ever since." He bowed to Lucia, sulkily, because she gave him no idea how well—or poorly—he had been received.

He closed the door behind him and leaned against it for support, exhausted as if he'd been playing football, breath whiffling out of him.

Lorenzo appeared soundlessly, bearing a breakfast tray. "The Principessa would like a word with you, Professor. Follow me if you would be so kind."

•7•

The Principessa rested against an extravagance of pillows, four of them, all immense, square, and edged with Belgian lace. Before her was an elaborately carved bed table with mirror in which she was doing her face. *Finishing* her face, actually, because the face was young and radiant—and youth and radiance were not, Cassidy thought, part of her natural equipment any longer. The Principessa was working now on the upper left eyelid with great care. She'd never have let me watch the earlier, uglier stages, thought Cassidy.

The two of them, Lorenzo and Cassidy, stood at the foot of the great painted bed (cool green with autumnal brown shadows), Lorenzo holding the heavy, silver, breakfast tray until the Principessa deigned to pay attention. Meanwhile, holding them hostage.

Lorenzo was used to it. Cassidy wasn't. He examined the breakfast tray, a work of art. It contained little nourishment—coffee and two rolls with butter and marmalade. But what a profusion of china, silver, and linen: The china and silver was emblazoned with the di Castiglione crest, a crenelated castle with prancing unicorns on each side (facing the camera, as it were). There was an extraordinary amount of silver—separate knives for butter and marmalade, separate spoons for sugar bowl and for stirring the sugar in the coffee, each of quite different design and filigree. The plates were delicate, primarily white and red and gold design at center and were used only for breakfast, never for any other meal. Cassidy felt a twinge of sympathy for revolutionists everywhere.

The Principessa finished work on her upper left eyelid and snapped the mirror down on her bed table, transforming it into a breakfast table. Without a word, Lorenzo lay the tray on it. On Cassidy she turned a smile of such brilliance that Cassidy thought: Someone made love to her last night.

"Some coffee, Professor?"

"Thank you, no," said Cassidy, dryly.

"All right, Lorenzo," said the Principessa dismissing him. No smile.

I get a smile. He doesn't. What should I deduce from that? Nothing, thought Cassidy.

"Sit down, Professor, won't you." Indicating a chair by her bedside. She was tucking into her breakfast with good appetite, her white teeth biting into the roll, after slashing it with butter and marmalade, pouring herself coffee, stirring in sugar and cream—and talking. Lorenzo had vanished.

"I heard your first lesson," she said crisply.

"How did you manage to do that?" Himself dismayed.

The Principessa flipped a lever next to her on a box-like device. Immediately the voices of the two girls filled the room chattering Italian.

"Sometimes they talk French," said the Principessa. "It amuses Lucia to teach Titi all her languages." She snapped the device off. "A nursery device, Professor." All the while chewing on her roll, sipping coffee, glancing at him out of her heavily made eyelashes (if they were her own). Terribly busy, she was, for a woman in bed. "One puts these things in the nursery to listen for coughs and bad dreams when they're tiny and one keeps them there...for other reasons. I do hope you'll forgive me."

"I'm not sure I will, Principessa," said Cassidy harshly. In his CIA days he'd eavesdropped shamelessly. He found it unforgiveable in others. "I cannot instruct your daughter if the walls have ears."

"The walls won't have ears for very long," she said, amused. "I have no intention of listening to all your lessons, Professor, fascinating as they undoubtedly are." (Laughing at me, the bitch! thought Cassidy.)

"It just occurred to me..." Now she was crooning, caressing him with her magnificent eyes, softening him up "...that just possibly, Professor, your superb lecture was a *trifle* advanced for my daughter. She's only twelve."

"The greatest age of all," cried Cassidy, becoming very

mellifluous and Irish. "Our advanced aptitude tests have shown, Madame, that the age of twelve is the magic time when more can be imparted than at any other year of life." A lie from beginning to end. Cassidy was making it up as he went along. "There is in the twelve-year-old—on the very brink of puberty—the receptiveness of innocence without the grievous self-interest of sexuality that so shrivels the learning process later."

The Principessa munched her roll thoughtfully. "Innocence," she murmured, "is something no one has ever accused Lucia of. She was born wise as a serpent."

She leaned back into her pillow, eyes closed, the face beautiful and ageless like a death mask of a Pharaoh. Cassidy felt abandoned. After a moment she opened her eyes and fixed on him a blue, transparent, and infinitely seductive gaze: "I must explain to you—and it will come as a surprise—that I am not your employer. You are in the employ of the trustees of the di Castiglione fortune. I hired you as I hired all the others at their insistence, but they pay your salary and their wishes must be heeded."

She smiled a weary smile: "They are terrified of Lucia being kidnapped, not because they are fond of the child but because it would cost a great deal of money to get her back," the Principessa bit her lip pensively. "They'd pay billions to get her back. If I were kidnapped, they wouldn't pay a single lira."

Now why did she say that, wondered Cassidy. Bid for sympathy? Not likely from so self-possessed a woman. She was, he decided, giving him information. He arched an eyebrow, signifying nothing much except that he was listening.

"There may be no God, Professor," she said dryly, "but there *are* trustees. They wouldn't like you teaching anything remotely subversive to my daughter."

"My purpose, Madame, is *not* to subvert her but to teach her self-reliance. If she looks to God for protection in these most troubled times, she'll be eaten alive by wolves."

"I doubt they'd look at it quite that way."

"Madame," said Cassidy scowling, "if you'd remove that listening device, they'd have no way of knowing what I teach your daughter."

"Oh, Professor," making a face at him. "*I'm* not their source of information. I don't know how they find out what's going on in the nursery. Perhaps an old hand at intelligence like yourself could tell *me*."

·8·

In the perpetual gloom of the Spumi, Cassidy counted out the money, $180 in $20 bills, on the dark mahogany surface of the bar. Henry rang it up and lay a dollar and eight cents change down. He poured Cassidy another Wild Turkey. "On the house," he said, disconsolate. Henry had never understood the curious American custom of giving away drinks. For Alison he poured another glass of white wine. For himself, a little Old Kentucky.

Cassidy held up the Wild Turkey to the multicolored chandelier. "To your continuing prosperity, Hugh," he said, and drank the bourbon in a single gulp. First time in three years he'd paid the whole bar bill.

"Have the *fettucine*," he suggested. "Henry's old lady makes it. My treat."

"No," said Alison, bent over the menu. "I'll put you on the expense account."

The expense account, thought Cassidy. Alison would be asking something in return for getting him the job.

Alison put the menu on the bar and turned his smooth round WASP face to Henry: "Do you think I might have just a very large shrimp salad with a crabmeat cocktail with no dressing at all to start. Might that be possible?" Alison had been station chief in England for two years, and he'd picked up the might-that-be-possible routine there. To Cassidy he said: "Iodine rich."

"Oh, yes," said Cassidy gravely, "Iodine rich." Alison always embraced the latest diets before anyone else had even heard of them and abandoned them before the hoi polloi got there.

"Always the needle," complained Alison.

"Needle?"

"To my continuing prosperity," said Alison, his round pink face aggrieved. "Now that was a needle, Horatio. You know it was."

"I was toasting your success," murmured Cassidy. Alison's uninterrupted climb to the corridors of power in the Company, his four-hundred-dollar suits, his Ferraris (or whatever was his latest hot car), his rich wife (who bought the Ferraris), his diets, had always been targets of ridicule tinged with envy. Alison, the joke had been, could give lessons to a chameleon. In his day he'd been a Roosevelt liberal, a Truman pragmatist, a Kennedy idealist, a Lyndon Johnson hardnose, changing his spots, his ideology, principles, prose style, even the way he wore his hats to whatever wind blew at the moment.

He left no trail and no incriminating documents. It was impossible to pin down how he'd stood on the Bay of Pigs, the Tet Offensive, the Castro assassination plot, or anything else because it was impossible to remember exactly what he'd said twenty minutes later. He never signed anything except in disappearing ink. The complete modern public servant, changing his ethos with his underwear, and with every administration.

"The *fettucine*," said Cassidy to Henry, putting down the menu. To Alison, he said: "I'm already so iodine-rich I glow in the dark."

"Always the needle," complained Alison. "How does the Principessa put up with it?"

"We don't see that much of each other."

"And the little Contessa?"

Cassidy didn't want to discuss Lucia with him. There was a point beyond which you didn't return favors. "Lucia's all right—if you like twelve-year-old girls."

The restaurant was empty of all but waiters and themselves. Alison had specified early lunch because he had to get back to Washington. They sat at Alison's favorite table at the back wall.

"Tea for two is it?" asked Cassidy pleasantly.

"No jokes," said Alison. "Not even here."

Tea was for Terror which was where it was all at in the CIA these days. Covert was out. The fashionable department was

Terror and Alison was Number 2 man. He hated being number two. Tea for two was a very unfunny joke to Alison.

"We'd like a little help with the Windletop," said Alison.

"Everyone wants a little help with the Windletop," said Cassidy. "*The New York Times*, the CIA. Any day now I expect a call from the President. Can I get him invited to the Principessa's party—and I doubt it."

"How impregnable is it really?"

"Nothing's impregnable. You know that, Hugh. It depends on how badly they want to get in."

"They want to get in very badly."

Alison threw it out between bites so casually that Cassidy knew that's why he'd come. All the way from Washington. Well. Well. It would give him bargaining power. He ate in silence, letting Alison run with the ball.

"They've done it to themselves," said Alison bitterly. "The damned place has such a reputation for impregnability. The guerillas know it was just rebuilt to keep them out—and that's like waving a red flag at a bull. Some of the biggest sons of bitches in the whole wide world live there—Kaspar, that German swine who owns half the coal mines in the Ruhr. The di Castigliones who own the Vatican and most of Rome. That prick from Peru who owns the Andes. These people cry out for kidnapping. Or assassination. Asking for it. If you were the Red Wind, wouldn't you?"

"Speculation," said Cassidy, dismissing it.

"We've got to speculate. We can't just let it happen like the Olympics. Anyway, it's not just speculation."

"Hard rock."

"Hard sand."

Cassidy doubted it. The intelligence organizations of the world—German, Japanese, American, Israeli (not the British who had more sense)—had tried hard to infiltrate the terror organizations, which had just got a lot of good agents (frequently the best) killed. So far as Cassidy knew (and he knew a lot) no one had managed even a toehold.

"New York," Alison was saying, "is ceasing to be an American city. It's the capitalist headquarters of the world—French money, Belgian money, Italian money, British money, Arab money. All the white Americans have left New York."

"I haven't left yet. But then I have a black grandmother. She runs a whorehouse in Harlem. One-legged lesbians are the specialty of the house."

"Horatio!" protested Alison.

"What do you want of me, Hugh? Let it all hang out."

"McGregor is on my ass to find a weakness in the building."

McGregor was Number 1 in Tea.

"Steal the plans."

"We already have. The parts we want to know about are missing—for very good reasons."

"I'm confined to quarters," said Cassidy. "I'm not only the little girl's tutor, I'm a bodyguard; that doesn't leave much time."

Alison laid down his fork, creating a meaningful silence. "Horatio you are the greatest scholar of medieval fortifications in the western world."

"Bullshit," said the scholar.

"The Windletop,..." Alison leveled his pale eyes at him, "has all the trappings—the walls, portcullis, the inner fortifications, the self-sufficiency. The place is a medieval castle. It has everything but a moat."

Cassidy grunted: "Chivalry it also hasn't got."

Alison looked annoyed: "These people—the Italian Red Brigade, the Japanese Red Army, the Red Faction of Germany, even the American wildeyes like the Weathermen—have all been trained in Lebanon by Palestinian terrorists whose ancestors were Saracens."

"Jupiter," said Cassidy. He didn't think Alison had that much imagination. "That's very good, Hugh. Very good."

"If you were training a terrorist how to take the Windletop, what would you teach them?" Alison whispered it.

It was all in the books. Alison might just have done a bit of reading—but that was less nourishing than an expense account luncheon. Cassidy leaned across the table conspiratorially: "I'll want a little something in return."

"Like what?" asked Alison suspiciously. Cassidy had an awe-inspiring reputation as a scrounger.

"Files on some guys."

Reluctantly: "Well, okay."

"And four thousand dollars."

"Oh, for God's sake, Horatio...."

"Out of your contingency fund. It's not very much and it's not for me. I want to get Fingertips to do a little legwork because I haven't time. Fingertips can't handle it alone so I'll need the Gypper to help out."

"I'm not running an employment bureau for all your old pals."

The Gypper and Cassidy had been friends and colleagues in the Company for thirty years. The locales of their capers ranged from Bulgaria to Korea. Fingertips had been involved in, not all, but some.

"Maybe even Jacoby and Freddie if the operation gets out of hand." Cassidy used the well-known ploy of expanding his demands to win quick acceptance of a lower earlier demand. "After all, I'm up to my ass in the nursery, Hugh, I can't go running around town."

"Four thousand. No more."

Only then did Cassidy tell Alison some stories—how invaders had broken into Richard the Lionhearted's Chateau Gaillard through its weakest point, the toilet; how Count Baldwin's men disguised themselves as peddlers to get inside two gates where they stuck knives into the guards; how Edward I's spies found out Simon de Montfort's warriors planned a night on the town and surprised them in bed with the girls—bare-assed and unarmed—medieval tales of duplicity and wickedness which Alison listened to, frowning.

"I'm disappointed in the Middle Ages," said Alison. "We've done all those tricks ourselves. Every last one."

"They invented most of them. We haven't improved on them."

Alison lit a Romeo y Julieta (the CIA always had the best Cuban cigars). "I've got to write a position paper, Horatio. Give me your best thinking."

"You wouldn't know what to do with my best thinking, Hugh. It's so high minded as to be impractical. I'll give you my second best thinking—low cunning."

Alison let it pass. "If you were to try to take the Windletop, how would you go about it?"

Cassidy turned on his most spacious Irish smile: "Treachery is quickest, cheapest, most effective, and most reliable."

"Reliable treachery. Only you would think of something like that, Horatio."

"Oh, no," said Cassidy. "I'm sure they have, too."

"That widens the field quite a lot."

"Very wide field—treachery," agreed Cassidy. "There's a lot of it around." Treachery wasn't the whole of it. You had to combine it with tactics and those he kept to himself. After all, he had to keep a little for future bargaining with Alison.

On the way out Henry called Cassidy to the bar and confided. "Sophy called. I told her you were in Brazil."

"Brazil's nice," said Cassidy. "Tell her I got eaten by the piranha."

"I only tell Sophy good constructive lies. I'll tell her you sent your love all the way from Brazil."

"She'll never believe that. Sophy only believes bad destructive lies."

·9·

"If you're worrying about how well I sleep at night...." The Principessa was in ribbons and flounces and ruffles covered by spring flowers in pastel colors. The dress soft and pliant covering the hard slim body and steely mind. "I should rather toss and turn than yield my fuchsia walls and my Tiepolo ceiling...."

"Tiepolo!" Cassidy was flummoxed, eyes darting upward. Tiepolo! Damned if it wasn't! The di Castiglione's had somehow smuggled out of Italy this masterpiece of late Renaissance fresco and affixed it to the ceiling of the entrance hall. Probably worth half a million.

That was the issue—the entrance hall. The elevator opened directly into the apartment, once a status symbol, one's very own elevator, now a security risk. Gunmen could pour out of the elevator, shooting.

"My dear Professor, "the voice trilling with exasperation, "security is *downstairs*, out of sight. That is where security belongs. That is why I am in this building—so I can decorate my flat as I damned well please."

"Madame," Cassidy pulled at his earlobe, standing straight, head slightly bent, face El Greco-esque which is to say stylistic or decorative agony as opposed to the real McCoy, "doing what you please is not possible in the climate of modern terror. Particularly for the rich."

Orchestrating his argument slowly and carefully. He had a big finish, and he intended to build to it through a series of steadily mounting climaxes.

The Principessa's eyes were on the ceiling: "I selected this ceiling, this particular Tiepolo—one of four in the palazzo in

Rome—for this foyer." She turned her violet eyes (with their magnificent makeup) on Cassidy, caressing his angularities with her soft glance like moonlight on hard stone. "This entrance hall, Professor, sets the tone for the whole flat." (Anglicisms like *flat* crept into her speech as did words and phrases of Spanish, French, and Italian—the international rich contributing little flecks of color to each other's vocabularies.)

"The mood of the visitor is ineradicably set the moment he steps off the elevator by these fuchsia walls, the exquisite modeling of those angels with their slightly underripe reds and purples—topped off by that splendidly rococo and altogether marvelous settee."

Cassidy cracked his knuckles: "The question, Madame, is your daughter's safety next to which the *mood* of the visitors—especially considering we never have any visitors...."

He trailed off, thinking he'd gone too far.

In the month he'd been there, there had been no visitors or anyway, none he was supposed to know about. No child or adult visitor entered the closed world of the Principessa, the Contessa, Lorenzo, Titi, and Cassidy in the daytime. Nighttime was something else. The Principessa had a hyperactive social schedule. She went out every single night—never, so far as Cassidy could make out—wearing the same thing twice. Sometimes she was in a superbly simple long evening dress, sometimes in informal cottons, once even in jeans to some disco or other where jeans were what was worn and the Principessa, always in tune, wore them.

She returned long after everyone else was in bed. Cassidy, a light sleeper, heard the murmurings, the laughter, and wryly noted the time—2 A.M., 3 A.M., 5 A.M. He had no idea who her companions were. Lover? Or lovers? She had a monumental reputation as a swinger even at her age, but one never knew how accurate the gossip was. Anyway, he was not supposed to know about these things. To cover up his slip, he threw in quickly: "We need a second line of defense, Principessa. Maybe even a third and fourth."

Her glance had hardened and grown thoughtful. She hadn't liked that crack about no visitors.

"In a medieval castle," said Cassidy, "the invaders had to fight their way through one defense after another—the barbican, the portcullis, the bailey, the keep, the inner castle itself."

"This is not a medieval castle, Professor." The voice just short of exasperation. "It's a very sophisticated modern building. By turning a key in that elevator, it's impossible for anyone to make it stop on this floor."

"Impossible for jewel thieves perhaps, Madame. Not for well-heeled modern terrorists. They have their own electronic experts who could neutralize that elevator in twelve minutes. Then they would be inside this apartment. What I'm trying to provide is a second line of defense to slow them, not necessarily stop them. In the Middle Ages, despite insurmountable defenses, castles *were* taken and its knights seized and imprisoned and later, if they were lucky, ransomed. Just like today."

She regarded him with passionate dislike. "Professor, you are not seriously asking me to replace my fuchsia walls with steel gates?"

Cassidy smiled: "You can paint the steel fuchsia, Madame."

"My soul revolts at the thought of *steel* in my foyer. I will not have it."

"Then, Madame," Cassidy strode to the double doors which led from the foyer to the rest of the apartment and flung them open, one with each hand, then pivoting on his heels to face her, "hire someone else to protect your daughter. I resign."

He bowed. His short bow, not his big courtly bow. A rapier thrust slap-in-the-face sort of bow like those John Barrymore did in some of his more foolish costume movies. Then he turned his back and swaggered off toward his room. His big finish.

It was a risk, and a week earlier he'd not have been so inflexible. He'd have left some avenue of retreat open for her. But the time had come to make a stand. Anyway he was fairly sure of his ground. He had divined from things she'd said and Lorenzo had said that the Principessa intensely disliked changing tutors. Lucia had forced her hand on the other two. (Why? That he didn't know, but he intended to find out.) She would lean over backward to avoid having to find another tutor (and protector, the job being what it was) but whether to the extent of losing her Tiepolo. . . . He hadn't realized Tiepolo would get into this.

"Oh, come *on*, Professor!" The Principessa's voice fluted up the scale. "*Must* we have these theatrics!"

Cassidy paused in his flight. She's as theatrical as I am, he was thinking, but of a different, more naturalist, school. He swung around and gave her his sidewise glance from under heavy lids. (Walter Matthau used that look with stunning effectiveness having stolen it from Rex Harrison who stole it from Alfred Lunt who taught the whole lot of them.)

"How much will it cost?" asked the lady.

"A great deal," said Cassidy.

In the nursery, the problems ran deeper. Cassidy was groping in the darkness, feeling his way in the jungle of child psychology. He'd never been a father (why hadn't Maria managed a child to fill his long absences?) and sometimes felt he'd never even been a child. I must have had a childhood, he said to himself in the mirror while shaving. It's been stolen from me like Peter Pan's shadow.

In his single month, Cassidy had progressed from the Pleistocene through Babylon and into Greece. "You must know man's chronology," he said to Lucia, "or you will understand nothing."

The two girls sat cross-legged before him as he paced back and forth, doing what he called his deposed archduke bit, hands behind his back, face working, stressing each syllable, pounding it into her little skull, Lucia's eyes black as ink and as unfathomable. Was he getting through? Titi sat next to her, dark and vengeful. Titi had begun by falling asleep at his lectures (which Lucia never did), but lately had stayed awake. This was worse because she was a disturbing force.

"All mankind's great leaps forward have been accidents over which he had little control and almost no understanding. We have evolved upward, as thinkers and as civilized human beings, through a series of blunders that can be understood only in the long clear light of history."

Then came the explosion, most unexpectedly, out of Titi. "Erragh!"

Or words to that effect. A sound that was derisive, angry, scatological, and very, very positive. That alone—that positivism—stopped Cassidy in his tracks. It revealed in Titi an editorial sense he didn't know she had. This little forest creature was supposed to be learning vocabulary, not expressing opinion.

"Cose, Titi? *Cose?"* exclaimed Lucia, angrily.

Italian poured out of Titi like molten lava. That's what these two did to him when they wanted to talk behind his back, talk Italian at great speed where they lost him entirely.

"Taci! Taci!" said Lucia, shutting her up. *"Voglio sentire!"*

Titi subsided into a sullen mass, eyes on the floor. It threw Cassidy off stride, the whole outburst. He strode to the window and stared out, collecting himself. It had all been disturbingly illuminating. First, that Titi had the will to disagree even if she didn't know what she was disagreeing with. (She barely understood English.) Even more that *"Voglio sentire."* In his month there Cassidy had never known whether or not Lucia wanted to listen or whether she was submitting because she had no choice.

Voglio sentire! I want to listen! Well! Well!

"Let us proceed," said Cassidy. He turned from the window to face a new situation. Lucia still sat cross-legged in the center of the floor her black eyes fixed on him. Titi had deserted stage center and was crouching in the corner of the nursery over the medieval castle, glowering, raising the drawbridge and lowering it, raising it and lowering it.

"Reason," crooned Cassidy, eyes on Titi, "has intruded on man's progress only occasionally and then at long intervals— Greece, the Renaissance, the eighteenth century, all fleeting moments of sanity in the general lunacy of history."

Here Cassidy squatted on his haunches next to Lucia. "The paradox we must live with is this: Mankind has reached his highest pinnacle at moments of most extreme irrationality—the times that try men's souls bring out the best, the worst, the greatest, the most profound illumination."

"What about *women's* souls?" asked Lucia scowling right back at him.

"Jupiter," exclaimed Cassidy. "A feminist!"

"I'm a woman."

"You're a twelve-year-old girl." Still, he was absurdly pleased with the interruption. She was listening, evaluating. He wasn't just dropping the stuff down a well. "Women's souls as well," he said. "In the high Middle Ages, women's souls and their bodies and their minds were tried to a degree never known before. Women were left in charge of the castles when their knights went off to the Crusades. They ran the castles, led troops in battle, were tortured, imprisoned, enslaved, and slaughtered with great equality."

"Just like now," said Lucia, eyes shining.

"Yes, just like now," said Cassidy. He was delighted. It was better that the pupil make the deduction than it be made for him.

"*This* place is a prison!" hissed Lucia.

"Yes," said Cassidy. "It is." He sat next to her. "In the Middle Ages, the highborn spent much of their lives in captivity, just like now. Richard the Lionhearted spent most of his reign as King of England in various prisons waiting to be ransomed."

Dangerous territory—talk of ransom. It was meant to be.

"My father was kidnapped," said Lucia passionately. "We paid the ransom and they killed him anyway."

It was the first mention of the Prince di Castiglione since he'd moved into the apartment. Lucia's mouth hung open, her eyes furious, body tense, a volcano about to erupt.

"They killed him because he was too smart to be left alive," she cried. "If they'd left him alive, he'd have caught them and got the money back and *killed* them."

Cassidy was impressed by her ferocity.

Then he noticed the Principessa, standing very straight beside the door. Dressed in a gray wool suit with a little toque on the blonde hair. How long had she been standing there?

"Mama!" cried Lucia. She sprang to her feet and rushed into her mother's arms where she burst into tears. The Principessa enfolded her in her gray skirt, her eyes on Cassidy coldly.

"Rather emotional, the lesson today, Professor?" said the Principessa.

Accusingly.

My fault! What have I done?

The Principessa and the Contessa had gone, leaving Cassidy alone with Titi who sat crouched in the corner playing with the medieval castle.

Cassidy rolled over on his stomach and contemplated Titi thoughtfully. Titi kept playing with the medieval castle and its knights and horsemen as if he weren't there.

"How do you suppose a woman with such beautiful violet eyes managed to have a child with eyes as black as ink, Titi?" asked Cassidy softly.

She said nothing, as if the question had never been asked.

·10·

There was a cocoon within a larger cocoon, spotless, air-conditioned, smelling always a little of furniture polish. In his black, threadbare suit, Cassidy moved down waxed floors catching glimpses through half open doors of the Irish maids polishing the mahogany and rosewood and satinwood surfaces of chairs that were never sat in and breakfront cabinets that were never touched by any hands but their own. Outside, shimmering in the sunshine, lay New York, dirty, noisy, and dangerous. Inside the cocoon they breathed air redolent of flowers and furniture polish. The raucous sounds of New York came through a kind of anesthetic hum. Once in a while Cassidy could catch sight of his scarecrow frame in one of the innumerable mirrors which everywhere cast reflections—one room mirroring another, making the whole place look endless—and he'd make a face at himself—baring his teeth, grimacing, scowling, crossing his eyes. "The only thing that looks out of place in this place is himself, namely me," he'd say to himself in a sort of parody of his Irishness.

The Principessa caught him doing this one day: "Your face will grow like that, if you're not careful," she said as if reproving a child.

They lived in a kind of hush; shuttered, twilighted, compartmented, and enclosed. In the long corridors Cassidy would catch sight of a figure ahead of him—Titi, Lucia, the Principessa, Lorenzo—and when he got there the person had vanished into some room or other and closed the door. Doors were always kept closed. The Principessa's bedroom door, the nursery door, the doors into Lorenzo's room, the kitchen. Lorenzo lived back of his own kitchen in a little servant's wing which contained two bedrooms. Cassidy never so much as caught a peek into it. Lorenzo was a private person.

Once in a while he flattered himself that he caught a glimpse into Lorenzo's soul—but he couldn't be sure. It was like the mirrored surfaces of the apartment, beckoning one into distant recesses that did not really exist.

Once after a battle with the Principessa over the foyer, he remarked to Lorenzo: "She'll stick a knife into me one day."

"She doesn't use knives, signor," said Lorenzo. "She has other weapons, more powerful, more subtle and...more *interesting*." It was the way he said *"Interesting"* that caught Cassidy's attention. A gleam of a smile, sardonic, almost satanic, as if being *"interesting"* was at the heart of the matter.

Lorenzo lay deep within layers and layers and more layers of reserve, each layer containing a century of experience beyond mortal comprehension. Cassidy loved to watch the very way he polished—he was forever polishing—the amber look in his eye as he ran his fingers over three-hundred-year-old silver candelabra, as if feeling each century in his fingertips, drawing sustenance and, yes, wisdom from it.

Relations between Lorenzo and Titi were fragile and mysterious, something only caught out of the corner of his eye, or at the end of a corridor. Lorenzo, his tall, beautifully proportioned frame bent respectfully down over the little peasant listening as she chattered, himself saying little, but according her that immense courtesy which flowed out of him in waves. She wasn't all that courteous in return, the little wild forest beast that she was, and sometimes her chatter crackled angrily, dark eyes flashing, Lorenzo unruffled.

Cassidy tried and tried to draw Lorenzo out about himself to be met with a gleaming smile, and little else. He had little luck drawing him out about anything. About the dead Prince, Lorenzo was reserved, respectful, almost worshipful—but underneath it all, disapproving. One day, Cassidy repeated a few things he'd heard about the Prince (or read)—a wit, connoisseur, good shot, great horseman, et cetera, et cetera.

"Superbly talented," agreed Lorenzo in his engraved English whose accent was like perfume, "all of it wasted."

He thereupon shut up, and Cassidy couldn't for the life of him find out if he meant the Prince had wasted his talents on frivolity or that the murder had wasted the man—as the current phrase went.

That night he got tired of waiting any longer, and he called Alison in Washington. Alison wasn't glad to hear from him. "I told you not to use this number except in emergency, Horatio."

"I was worried about your welfare, Hugh. Rumor in the underground they'd trashed you and dumped the body in the Gowanus Canal." Hugh would hate being found in the Gowanus Canal, a very unfashionable spot to be caught dead.

"What do you want, Horatio?"

"I sent you the prints a week ago."

He'd got Alfred the Great to look at some photographs of prospective cooks. Good prints they were.

There was a pause on the other end—and Cassidy could read Alison's pauses like a book. He didn't like this pause at all. "Nothing at all, Horatio," said Alison smoothly.

"I'll try the FBI then," said Cassidy instantly. "They owe me a couple from long ago...."

"Horatio!" A bleat of rage. "We want him left alone and we don't want any interference from the Bureau."

"What's his name, Hugh?"

"He's a handle, a good handle, into the building."

"I thought I was the handle."

"We can use all the handles we can get."

"I'll call the Bureau in the morning."

A long pause. Pressure building up as in a steam kettle.

"Hugo Dorn." said Alison sullenly. "SS."

"Jupiter," said Cassidy. "I can't believe it. He's too young."

"Facelift. Dyed hair. You can never tell with these old Nazis. We flushed one out of Ecuador the other day looked thirty-five. What you must bear in mind, Horatio—and I mean this sincerely—is that even if he is old SS it doesn't mean he isn't on our side. Hugo was put in there by the people who rebuilt that building. All Fascist money. We know that."

"We do?" said Cassidy. "Whose side did you say we were on again, Hugh?"

"They're not the enemy any more," said Alison sharply. "That was forty years ago. Hugo is a good Nazi."

"A good Nazi, how nice," murmured Cassidy, and hung up. He put the phone off his lap back on the night table and stood up. Then he saw her standing quietly in her nightie, black eyes enormous. "I heard all that," said Lucia.

"Why aren't you in bed, little monster. It's long past midnight," blazed Cassidy who hated being eavesdropped.

"*Je n'aime qu'on m'appelle monstre*," said Lucia demurely. Always demure in European languages, Cassidy decided. In English she was a different personality altogether.

"I had a terrible dream." Lucia sat on his bed and pulled her skinny legs up under her nightie. "About...frogs. Do you ever dream about frogs?"

Cassidy sat next to her carefully. "No, I don't think so. Frogs?"

"A roomful of frogs. It was very frightening." Looking at him soberly out of the black eyes. "I went to Mama's room. She's not there."

Mama didn't come home that early.

"Do you have bad dreams often, Lucia?"

She shook her head. "No, but when I do...." She played with her nightdress. "Papa used to come into my room when I had bad dreams and comfort me with lullabies. He had a lovely voice, my father."

A whole new aspect of the Prince.

"Do you know any lullabies, Professor."

She's having me on, the vixen, thought Cassidy. Childless academics are barren of lullabies.

"I know a song your mother wouldn't approve of, Contessa."

Lucia's eyes gleamed. Anything the Principessa didn't approve had the enchantment of the illicit.

"Sing it," she said.

In a high harsh falsetto, he sang her a song from the Middle Ages:

> Peace delights me not.
> War—be thou my lot.
> Law I do not know
> Save a right good blow.
> I crave no meat or drink beside
> The cry On! On! from throats that crack,
> A riderless and frantic pack,

And set the forest ringing.
The cries Help! Help!—the warriors laid
Beside the moat with brows that fade to grass and
    stubble clinging.
And then the bodies past all aid
Still pierced with broken spear and blade.
Come, Barons, haste ye, bringing
Your vassals for the daring raid.
Risk all—and let the game be played.

"What a bloodthirsty song!" exclaimed Lucia, eyes like black holes.

"It was written 700 years ago by a noble troubador named Bertrand de Born. Great pal of Richard the Lionhearted. No more vicious than some of the pop songs today."

He picked her up—she weighed nothing at all—and carried her out the door and down the corridor toward her room.

"Who was the nice Nazi?" asked Lucia face in his chest.

She doesn't miss a trick, this kid, thought Cassidy. "Nice Nazis," said Cassidy, "are like unicorns. Mythological beasts."

At the doorway to the nursery, they ran square into the Principessa. She was dressed in a long, gold lamé dress, carrying an ermine wrap, and she was cold with fury.

"I'll take Lucia, Professor!" she snapped, each word a pistol shot.

"Mama!" cried Lucia eagerly. "You're home!"

The little body was transferred from Cassidy's arms to her mother's as if she were contraband, the Principessa's eyes narrowed to slits.

"She had a bad dream," explained Cassidy.

The Principessa said nothing. She bore Lucia into the nursery, in her arms, her whole body stiff with anger. The light was on in the nursery, and Cassidy caught a glimpse of Titi standing in the middle of the room, hands clasped. She, too, looked furious, but then she always did when Cassidy was around.

·11·

Meals in the di Castiglione household were largely solitary.

The Principessa had breakfast in bed. For luncheon and dinner she was invariably out. (A large part of her day was devoted to dressing, exquisitely, for these repasts.) Titi prepared Lucia's lunch and supper—salad, chops, spaghetti—of which Lucia ate little, Titi hovering over her like an evil genie. Titi's own lunch and dinner, if they could be called that, she took standing up beside the big refrigerator in the kitchen, stuffing bread and hardboiled eggs into herself as if stoking her inner fires. Lorenzo prepared lunch and dinner for Cassidy and served them with his exquisite deference that made Cassidy very nervous. Try as he would he could not make Lorenzo sit down and have a meal with him. In part this might have been because the meals themselves were pretty bad. Lorenzo's cooking was not nearly as good as his manners. Cassidy rarely saw Lorenzo take food and even more rarely sit down.

Meanwhile the search for a cook went on.

"Why do we need a cook?" expostulated Cassidy. "Nobody eats here."

The Principessa gave him an ivoried glance full of disapproval, as if to indicate he was getting into areas that were none of his business. It was the morning after she'd taken Lucia from him, he was standing at the foot of her bed with Lorenzo while the Principessa ate her breakfast.

"I speak in the interest only of security, Madame," said Cassidy magniloquently. "Another servant, another security risk."

Forcing her to explain herself which she liked not at all.

"We must have a cook to take the burden off Lorenzo," said

the Principessa, marmalading her toast. "Also I want someone to cook for Titi and Lucia in the nursery. Titi is terrible. She boils the vegetables into jelly."

"The agency has sent the name of a German woman," said Lorenzo.

"The best cooks are men," said the Principessa.

Why do we need the *best* cook? Cassidy was wondering, for a household that doesn't eat.

Meanwhile the work on the front hall proceeded. The Tiepolo was removed (Cassidy had recommended covering it but was overruled by the Principessa) by Joseph Grant Ltd. from London, England, who were fearfully expensive but the world's acknowledged experts on removing priceless frescoes from ceilings. Where the Tiepolo went, Cassidy had no idea.

He was too preoccupied with the steel doors which Newcastle Safe and Lock installed in front of the elevator. It took two days because the bolts holding the frame had to be sunk into solid concrete which meant removing plaster and wood in between door and wall—an operation that filled the apartment with fine dust and the Principessa with cold rage.

The moment the job was finished and the dust cleared by Lorenzo (who worked days polishing the whole apartment and everything in it), Cassidy was convinced the steel doors would never be needed and were a total waste of time. And just as equally convinced that if the work had not been done, the doors *would* have been needed and it would have been a fatal error not to have constructed them.

"Security," he snarled at Lorenzo in the pantry, "is a mug's game. There is no such thing."

Lorenzo said: "The agency has sent in the name of a cook. Jefferson Lee. He's black."

"Jefferson Lee sounds like a high school," said Cassidy. "No black man calls himself Jefferson Lee any more unless he's making jokes."

He met Fingertips at Ariadne's, a little Greenwich Village bar, under street level at Flame Street. "You're always beneath street level, Cassidy," said Fingertips, giving his dreamy smile as if he were stoned out of his skull which he probably was. "Am I to conclude you're hiding something?"

"I'm living on the forty-ninth floor now, Fingertips," said Cassidy. "Half a mile straight up and it's addling my wits." He told Fingertips what he wanted.

"Relations," said Fingertips with his bland smile. "You've been swept out to sea by *Roots*."

"I just want to know what the Schoons were up to recently—that's Elsa Schoon's sister and brother—and the early marriages. I already know more than I want to know about the ancestry."

"This is relevant to guarding the little girl?" inquired Fingertips with his bland smile that took the edge off this kind of impertinence. (That was why he was so good at investigation. He could ask the most intimate questions as if he were talking about the time of day.)

"I don't know anything, Fingertips," said Cassidy, "Except something is very fishy. Who have you got in Italy?"

"Fabrizio. In spite of that name he hails from Brooklyn. Returning to the land of his ancestors."

Cassidy explained what he wanted to find out.

"Rumors about a playboy are likely to be wishful," said Fingertips. "You'll hear what you want to hear."

"I can check them with the facts I have. I'm not so much interested in what is true as in what isn't. A lot of what I've been told makes no sense. You understand?"

"No," said Fingertips.

"Good. Let's keep it that way."

Jefferson Lee was produced by Lorenzo two days later. He was superbly muscled, impassive as a bronze statue and he looked, thought Cassidy, as if his name ought to be Malcolm X, not Jefferson Lee.

Cassidy marched him in to see the Principessa who was in bed doing her prebreakfast face which Cassidy found most beautiful of all her faces. The finished face was a little too studied.

"Mmm," said the Principessa, glancing at Jefferson Lee's muscular outline. "Where have you cooked?"

The atmosphere reeked of sexuality.

"Mr. and Mrs. Halford in Savannah, Georgia. Faw yeahs."
He spoke pure molasses candy, and Cassidy distrusted that as
well as everything else. "Real nice people, the Halfords."

A real tame nigger, thought Cassidy. I thought they'd been
repealed by the Race Relations Act.

"Then I was in Washington with the Flemings. He was in
the Commerce Department, economic assistance, somethin' like
that, but he's gone back to Iowa."

"Where in Iowa?" asked Cassidy flatly.

The Principessa smiled her waxen smile: "The Professor
likes to know all the details."

"Hornung," said Jefferson Lee immediately.

"Shall we try Mr. Lee on an experimental basis, Professor?"
asked the Principessa, working with the eyebrow pencil on the
left eyelid.

The question was not meant to be answered, just assented to.

Cassidy spent an hour on the telephone that night. There
were no Halfords in Savannah, information told him. As to
whether there had ever been any Halfords in Savannah, she
didn't have that kind of information. "We have fourteen
Flemings in the book," said information in Hornung, Iowa.
Cassidy tried them all. Yes, there had been a Fleming who had
worked for the Commerce Department and was now in India for
OECD. He got this from a cousin. No, he couldn't be reached by
telephone.

Alison was very interested in Jefferson Lee. "Get a
photograph and some prints. We think he's a live one."

"If he is, we want him out of there," said Cassidy.

"We'll keep an eye on him," said Alison smoothly. "See who
he sees."

"I've got a twelve-year-old to protect," explained Cassidy.
"Suppose he puts a gun to her head, holds her hostage?"

·"That's what you're there to prevent," said Alison. And
hung up.

Cassidy was left sitting on the edge of his bed with a dead
telephone in his hand. "The son of a bitch is also a lousy cook,"
said Cassidy into the dead telephone.

Noon the next day, Cassidy found the Principessa pouring a thin stream of water on the hyacinths in the conservatory.

"His credentials are bogus, and he's a lousy cook," said Cassidy.

"Those are not grounds for dismissal any more," said the Principessa.

She looked radiant—and sad. A peculiar combination. But very becoming, thought Cassidy.

"Have you tried firing a black man in New York State recently," said the Principessa. "It's against the law."

"Even if he's a terrorist?"

"Come, come, Professor," said the Principessa wearily. "What evidence for that could you give the Equal Opportunities Board, to say nothing of the Race Relations Commission and the NAACP. The first two would investigate me, and the last would file suit."

"He's a liar," said Cassidy. "There are no Halfords in Savannah."

"They've moved to Europe," said the Principessa, snipping a dry leaf from the hyacinth.

"Where did you learn *that*, Madame?"

"Jefferson told me."

Jefferson. Cassidy had been there a month and a half, and he'd never been addressed by his first name.

"You've been doing your own security, have you, Madame?"

The Principessa put down the watering can and turned her violet eyes on him. Large, luminous, and furious. He'd overstepped his bounds. But then so had she. She had no damned business discussing his security checks with the cook. If he was a cook.

Cassidy strode back through the apartment—through the enormous sitting room in which no one ever sat, through the music room with its burnished satinwood piano no one ever played, through the stately library stuffed with books no one read, past Donatello's David....

Which wasn't there.

Cassidy brought his cadaverous frame to a swift halt. The red marble pillar stood in its accustomed spot but the bronze statue was gone. Cassidy rubbed his cheek sardonically. In his mind's eye he saw the rippling black muscles on the David and they brought to mind Jefferson Lee's superb musculature. Perhaps Jefferson Lee didn't like the competition.

In the nursery Lucia was playing gin rummy with a sullen Titi, a poor gin player who always lost.

"We'll go to the park," said Cassidy.

"Did Mama say we could?"

Cassidy scowled at his hands (like Lady Macbeth in the sleepwalking scene) and sidestepped the question. "Titi," he barked, "this nursery is a disgrace to western civilization. Clean it up."

Titi threw him a look of purest malevolence. She's brighter than she makes out, thought Cassidy. Malevolence of that order requires a bit of brain.

"You *didn't* get Mama's permission," stated Lucia with a quiet smile. "Oho!"

She got her new, gray, fall coat out of the closet and put it on.

"You're the first tutor I've had who has faced up to Mama," she said.

·12·

The elevator was driven by Security 3 who was Welsh and taciturn to the degree that Cassidy wondered if his tongue hadn't been torn out altogether. Cassidy and Lucia were the only occupants until the thirty-fifth floor. Then the elevator stopped to take on the Comtesse de Lourdes, a formidable French lady, whom Lucia called the Countess of Smell because she had founded and run a perfume empire, first from Paris, later from New York, where the big money was. With her was her bodyguard, a beefy redneck from Georgia.

Cassidy nodded at him and he nodded back. All the bodyguards were on a nodding acquaintance. They recognized each other instantly by their clothes, their watchful air of unease, the bulges under their armpits. Above all they spotted the stigmata of the unmonied. In the old days, the poor stank of poverty. In more recent times, the rich had the smells—leather and tweed and good perfume—above all cleanliness and newness. The unmonied reeked of the absence of money.

On the twenty-sixth floor, the elevator stopped again, this time for a square cut Belgian industrialist and his bodyguard, another Belgian. Nobody spoke and nobody except Lucia sat on the red plush seat under the mirror. Lucia lounged on the plush with the insolence of childhood, staring boldly at the adults who hadn't the temerity to stare back. Everyone else took refuge in looking at the back of Security 3's neck.

In the lobby, they lined up dutifully and waited to be cleared like airplanes. From the mezzanine watch post Security 1 and 2 scanned Fifth Avenue for suspicious cars or people who had been loitering too long without clear purpose. If there was to be a snatch, this was the time, close to the entrance the moment they stepped out from the protection of the bulletproof glass. Security 1 looked north, Security 2 south; then the Windletop rich were escorted quickly one at a time by the Front to the waiting limousines which whisked them off (changing routes every day as the manual dictated).

There was no waiting limousine for Cassidy or Lucia. "My protection," Cassidy told Alfred the Great (alias Hugo Dorn, the Good Nazi), "is Werner Heisenberg's uncertainty principle. Never the same day, hour, or weather." Alfred hated the absence of plan.

Cassidy and Lucia strolled out the door, ducked across Fifth, and then ambled down the parkside footpath south under the big plane trees.

Half a block from the Windletop was a large metal obstruction bearing a sign which Lucia read aloud: "A new crosstown subway is being constructed in this area. When completed this new line will be a vital link in the MTA's overall program, adding over forty miles of new subway to better serve New Yorkers. It's signed by the Mayor."

"Which Mayor?," grunted Cassidy. "They've been digging that subway for years. It was started several Mayors ago and it'll outlast the present one and perhaps the next one after that before they get it open."

"I've never been in a subway," said Lucia wistfully. "Will you take me on a subway some time?"

"If we wait for that one, you'll be an old lady."

They stopped for a little while to ogle the Temple of Dendur in its new glass cage at the end of the Metropolitan Museum. Then Lucia took Cassidy by the hand and led him to the great bronze sculpture by Barzini of a lion leaping on a terrified horse, her favorite statue in the whole park. It wasn't Cassidy's favorite because there were too many bushes which could conceal terrorists. He inspected each of them before sitting next to Lucia. The two sat a moment enjoying the sunshine and the freedom.

"Titi hates you," said Lucia primly.

"I know," said Cassidy.

"Jefferson Lee hates you, too."

"Jefferson Lee hates all white people, including you."

"I don't think he hates Mama," said Lucia thoughtfully.

"On the other hand, I *think* Mama hates you. That leaves only me who doesn't hate you."

"Why don't you make it unanimous?" asked Cassidy.

"Because you're the first tutor I've had who is more interested in me than in Mama."

Cassidy chewed on that bit of information in silence.

"Mama says you're not really interested in me. You just want an audience to prance around in front of."

"Prance?" said Cassidy. "Did she say prance?"

"Yes, she said prance."

"Well, perhaps she's right." He grimaced. "I'm trying, in my prancing fashion, to teach you a set of rules to live by which is all that education can do. But the rules are changing so fast that it's difficult for a man of my age to teach one of yours with any degree of confidence that the rules of civilized behavior have not already changed.

"In the Middle Ages, the lords of the manor had all the privileges, and this was never questioned. When a knight went hunting—which they did all the time when not at war—they trampled over the peasant's garden, trampling down the foodstuff that was to keep him alive. If the peasant complained about this, it was the peasant who was considered barbarous rather than the knight destroying the man's livelihood. This was fashionable behavior for hundreds of years.

"But morality is accelerating. When the Americans colonized the west, they shot Indians as you might shoot wolves. In my lifetime, one of these settlers has remarked openly that he didn't know shooting Indians was wrong. We are very close to a time when duck hunters will proclaim they didn't know shooting ducks was wrong and by the time they say it, shooting ducks will be considered as barbarous as shooting Indians. Eating ducks is already considered immoral by some vegetarians."

There were ducks on the lake below the ledge on which they sat. A small boy and his mother were tearing up a loaf of bread and scattering it on the water for the ducks who were already too overfed to care.

"It won't end with the ducks," said Cassidy. "Being rich will be considered as immoral as shooting Indians—in fact, it already is. You are an endangered species, Contessa, an over-privileged child."

"Over-privileged?" said Lucia sadly. "I haven't even a bicycle."

"Where would you ride it—in the corridors?"

"Why not here? In the park?"

It was out of the question, a security risk he didn't dare take.

"I haven't even a *friend*."

"You have Titi."

"Like having a pet mouse," said Lucia contemptuously.

Not quite, thought Cassidy. Titi was not anyone's pet mouse.

"My father was kidnapped and killed because he was . . . *over-privileged*, and I, an over-privileged child, have no Papa."

They came back through the rear entrance, an unobtrusive opening between two towering buildings on Madison Avenue marked *Service, Windletop*. A steep ramp led to a little rear courtyard where the delivery vans from Bendel's and Van Cleef and Arpels and Bergdorf's deposited their expensive packages. When the Windletop had been remodeled for the modern age of fear, an immensely expensive gate of filigreed steel had been added to bar the entrance way.

Cassidy and Lucia stood in front of the gate to be inspected by the TV monitors, after which the filigreed steel vanished upward. They walked down the ramp, the steel gate closing behind them.

"Enjoyin' the splendid sunshine," sang out Rooftop from his glass booth. "How very nice!"

No one on earth was less suited to his occupation than Rooftop. He loved letting people into the building and hated keeping them out which, as Cassidy pointed out to Alfred the Great, was not the right attitude for his profession. Love of his fellow man was a fatal weakness in a guard, and Rooftop overflowed with it.

"How's your mother, Rooftop?" asked Lucia, who was very fond of the black man (as was everyone).

Rooftop's mother was a chronic invalid, and Rooftop shared his concern about her health with one and all. "She's up and down. Up and down," caroled Rooftop. "One day this, the next that. Ah don't know what to say."

He had already clicked open the door at the foot of a flight of steps leading into the building. Theoretically Rooftop was supposed to inspect his visitors one more time before admitting them. If he suspected trouble, he had a button on his cubicle wall which sounded the alarm at the Holmes Protection Agency. An even more sinister device was in his pocket—a little box the size of a cigarette pack which was connected to the nearest police station by radio. A push of the button in his pocket, and the radio cars would race over to see what was the matter.

All very foolproof except for Rooftop's indefatigably sunny good nature. Already he was halfway out of his bullet-proof cubicle, his white teeth gleaming with welcome. If I were a Red Wind I could shoot him through my pocket from here, thought Cassidy gloomily.

Rooftop personally escorted them up the concrete steps to the rear elevator—one of the four rear elevators in this preposterously over-equipped building. Standing there waiting for the elevator was the most beautiful young boy Cassidy had ever seen. Huge blue eyes firmly fixed on the floor, behind long curly eyelashes.

Cassidy, Lucia, and the beautiful boy, who looked about fourteen, stepped into the elevator. Lucia stared at the young man so intensely that a slow flush crept up his neck and suffused his entire beautiful face.

At the thirty-ninth floor, the elevator door opened, and the young man got out. The elevator door had scarcely swung shut when Lucia cried gleefully: "Struthers is at it again!"

Struthers had a reputation for liking beautiful young boys. Had them shipped in from Sweden—so the word went—and delivered to his backdoor like bonbons, a different one each week. It was one of the more lurid sex scandals of the building, which had many.

"Who told you that?" asked Cassidy.

"Titi. She heard it in the laundry. What does Mr. Struthers do to them exactly? I mean how does he...."

"Never mind," said Cassidy.

"You keep saying I have to learn sometime," argued Lucia. "You tell me terrible things about Jesus Christ and Karl Marx, and yet you clam up on sex."

It was true.

"Titi says he sticks it in their mouth, or they stick in in his mouth...."

"Titi ought to get her mouth washed out with soap," said Cassidy.

Lucia burst into giggles. "You're a *prude*, Professor," leveling her finger at him and giggling. Cassidy scowling.

That's how they entered the backdoor, Cassidy opening it with his key—Lucia having a fit of giggles, Cassidy's mouth drawn down like the tragedy mask in Greek Theater.

Gathered in the kitchen were all the others—the Principessa, Jefferson Lee, Titi, and Lorenzo. The atmosphere was thunderous.

"Where have you been?" asked the Principessa in tones of purest ice water.

"We've just taken a walk in the park, Mama!"

"You might have told someone. We were very worried."

"Titi knew!" protested Lucia.

"Titi says she wasn't told anything. You spoke English and you know very well Titi's English is not very good."

Titi's English wasn't all that bad, thought Cassidy. But he couldn't say anything like that. Instead he said: "I'm sorry, Principessa."

All this in front of the others. Jefferson Lee leaned against the great stove, arms folded, his chef's hat jauntily over one ear. Lorenzo stood, head bowed, his fingertips pressed judiciously together, eyes averted, as if pondering some deep legal problem. Titi wore her customary sullen look, eyes on Cassidy.

"Lucia, go to your room," said the Principessa. "Professor, I would like a word with you." Biting off each word.

In the conservatory, they faced off like duelists. The onslaught came from an unexpected direction: "What three men have caused more suffering and murdered more people than any others?" spat out the Principessa.

Jupiter, thought Cassidy. So that's what's making her mad!

"You told my daughter the three most destructive men in history were Jesus Christ, Karl Marx, and Sigmund Freud. What kind of thing is that to teach a twelve-year-old child?"

"I was trying to make her think, Madame," said Cassidy. "I was trying to get some answer to that question a little less brainless than Attila the Hun, Genghis Khan, and Adolf Hitler. I was trying to show that ideas were more murderous than swords and they lasted longer. I am still *endeavoring,...*" coming down hard on that word to shut off the Principessa in whom he could see protest rising, "to teach your daughter self-reliance in these dangerous times. God will *not* take care of rich little girls nor will socialism nor will psychiatry. She must look to herself for salvation and survival."

"You're turning my child into a monster."

"An educated and self-sufficient monster, Madame."

It was hot in the conservatory, the sunshine pouring in through the heavy plate glass. The place smelled of ozone and damp earth. The Principessa was wearing an oriental costume, trousers and tunic with heavily stitched scenes of parrots and poppies and trees in brilliant red, green, and gold which fitted her taut little body as if embroidered there. She was expressionless, only the molten eyes betraying the anger. Underneath the anger, Cassidy thought he detected despair. So many tutors. Nothing worked. She had never looked more beautiful nor more frightening. He wished she'd scowl just once but she never did. Cassidy wondered if perhaps she'd had so many facelifts she couldn't.

"I think, Professor Cassidy," she was hissing a little like a goose, "you and I have reached the end of the line. If you care to resubmit your resignation...."

That's as far as she got.

"No! no! no! no! no! no! no!" A wilderness of noes from Lucia who had been standing at the conservatory entrance for God knows how long. "No! No! No! No!" a ferocity of noes. A whole new aspect of Lucia, this ferocity, this determination, this fury. "No! Mama! No! No! No!"

Mother and child faced each other now, both blazing.

Cassidy felt superfluous. He was the issue, but he had no voice in the matter. Both mother and child were acting as if he weren't there, and that being so, Cassidy quietly made himself scarce.

The storm between mother and child broke as he crept down the corridor, but they were speaking Italian. Cassidy couldn't understand Italian spoken at that speed.

Where had the Principessa learned what he was teaching

Lucia? Cassidy had long since closed down the little gadget that eavesdropped on the nursery. That left only Titi who claimed to know so little English she couldn't understand they were going to the park but managed to comprehend a question about Marx, Freud, and Christ.

Not only comprehend the question but get mad about it to such a degree she reported it to the Principessa. Cassidy had questioned the divinity of three great names—Jesus Christ, Karl Marx, and Sigmund Freud. Which one of the three was so sacred to Titi that she went bellowing to the Principessa about it? Certainly not Freud.

Christ?

Or Karl Marx?

Cassidy sat on the edge of his bed and ran his fingertips over his brow, trying to sort it all out. Who called the tune in the di Castiglione household anyway? The Principessa said it was the trustees without whom she could do nothing. But it was she who had passed on him and could easily have passed him over. Lucia stood in awe of her mother and in most things was scared to death of her. Yet it was Lucia—so everyone said—who had seen to it those two tutors were fired, and it was Lucia who was now forcibly intervening to prevent his being fired.

Why was she doing that? Cassidy was deeply pleased, and he knew he shouldn't be. I'm getting emotionally involved with these people—and not only with Lucia but also Lorenzo, Titi, and the Principessa—and that was very dangerous because it interfered with a clear cold assessment of the situation. Anyway, it was self-defeating. When the job was over, it was over.

·13·

FIRONI SILVER BRINGS $185,000

Cassidy didn't usually read the auction news, but the headline had caught his eye. Fironi?

He was alone in the kitchen with the *Times* and his breakfast coffee.

Fironi?

> A silver and gold coffee urn made by the seventeenth-century Italian silversmith Fironi brought the top price of $185,000 yesterday at an auction of silver at Sotheby's. This is one of the highest prices ever paid for silver in this country.
>
> The Fironi urn is a massive bit of silver and gold ware with a spout carved into the shape of a mermaid. The mermaid's arms are the handles. The base of the urn is a clamshell with gold flutings....

Oh! *That's* where he'd heard it.

Cassidy rose from the table, ears cocked for Lorenzo who was last seen in the sitting room polishing furniture and Jefferson Lee who spent most of his time in his room looking at color television. No sound.

The silver was kept at the rear of the huge pantry in its own cedar cupboard, which was lined in green baize. Each of the big silver pieces had its own niche in the green baize. The Fironi urn wasn't there.

Cassidy closed the cupboard swiftly and went back to his coffee.

Lorenzo had entered the pantry wearing his leather apron over the di Castiglione livery, carrying his polishing cloth.

Cassidy sat down at the pantry table, picked up the *Times* and turned the page, folding the auction news out of sight.

Lorenzo was divesting himself of his furniture polish and cloth.

"Do you miss Italy, Lorenzo?"

This provoked so long a silence that Cassidy looked up from the *Times* to see if Lorenzo was still in the room. He was standing before the drawer where the polishes were kept contemplating Cassidy with his finely etched smile, thinking it over. Lorenzo was not one to rush into things.

When he spoke, the voice was far away: "I am sometimes dismayed by how *little* I miss Italy. I tell myself this is a betrayal, and yet I do not convince myself this is so. Italians are so Italian, signor, they don't *need* Italy—they *are* Italy. Italians in America are more Italian than they are at home."

"Do you have many Italian friends here?"

Lorenzo's hands described a parabola: "A man needs only *one* friend."

Lorenzo's comings and goings were a mystery to everyone. He left the apartment Thursday after noon and returned Friday at 10 A.M. That was his day off. Where he went, no one knew. Anyway, Cassidy didn't.

He hadn't a clue about Lorenzo's politics either: "Italy is being torn apart by terrorists," said Cassidy, to see what that would produce.

The response was immediate: "No, signor, it is *not* being torn apart. Italy is much tougher than you Americans have ever realized."

"Aldo Moro...," said Cassidy.

"...is dead," finished Lorenzo. "Many others will die before it is over. Sometimes it is necessary to die in order to live."

Whatever that meant.

Cassidy went back to his room down the long corridor past the Gabrieli painting of Henry IV (a distant cousin of the di Castigliones), past the bronze head of Cardinal Constant (a di Castiglione on his mother's side). Would these treasures follow the Donatello and the Fironi? Cassidy doubted that the Donatello had been sold at auction. That would have caused an international uproar.

In his room Cassidy dialled Henry at the Spumi. "Two messages. One guy don't leave no name. He just says Brandy, makes me repeat it—Brandy—and hangs up, says you'll know."

Alison playing games. Damn! He'd have to go to the oak tree in the park where the drop was. Why didn't Alison send a letter? Because he loved all the paraphernalia of espionage, that's why—the mystique, the cloak-and-dagger symbolism. A drop meant a courier from Washington. Very expensive—and that was half the fun.

Or perhaps he was being unkind. For all his love of trappings, Alison was a good agent. He was up to his ass in Terror, and just maybe he knew something that could be conveyed safely no other way.

"The other guy," said Henry "was a character named Feinberg—wants you to call please."

"Anything else?" asked Cassidy.

"Sophy was in. I sent your love all the way from Brazil."

"I'm not in Brazil any more. I went back to Turkestan." He hung up and called *The New York Times.*

"I want an invitation to the Principessa's party," said Feinberg.

Cassidy exploded: "Jupiter Jehoshaphat! The man who interviewed Adolf Hitler, the first man to figure out what a shit Chiang Kai-shek was and what a great man Mao was—now a social climber. Aren't you ashamed?"

"It's not for myself," said Feinberg in tones of deepest courtesy. (Feinberg was always at his most dangerous, someone had said, when he got very polite.) "We are very anxious to cover this party for many reasons."

Cassidy's nostrils flared like a rutting stallion: "What reasons?"

Feinberg sidestepped: "We have a girl in Society as highborn as any of those wastrels invited to the Principessa's party. Her name is Atchison like Atchison, Topeka and Santa Fe."

"Impossible," said Cassidy. "Sometimes I do the impossible, but the price is always very high."

"Would you like to know *why* Prince di Castiglione was killed," said Feinberg silkily. "And how?"

"I'll be right down," said Cassidy.

"Don't forget that invitation," said Feinberg.

The invitations were in the Principessa's Venetian desk with the bronze claw feet and the inlaid rosewood, a gem of late eighteenth-century furniture that rested in the library. Two hundred and twenty-five people were coming to the Principessa's party, all invited on beautifully engraved stiff white cards with gold edges bearing, also in gold, the di Castiglione crest. Cassidy had already protested to the Principessa that she was a bit careless with those precious bits of cardboard which ought to be locked up. He pointed out they were a pass into the Windletop.

"Only to the Windletop Club," the Principessa had said absently.

She had been seated at the desk on the high-backed Tuscan chair with its glowing red and gold painted arms, making out invitations to her friends, who all seemed to have nicknames like Dee Dee and Poo Poo and Gigi and Jojo. They were a tight little group of mixed nationalities—Spanish, French, English, Italian, American, Peruvian, Bolivian—all of whom seemed to have houses in Cap Ferrat and Paris and London and New York and sometimes Venice, too, and who fluttered like birds of passage from one house to another depending on the seasons— June in London, August in Deauville, October in New York for the parties and the plays, November in Madrid for the shooting.

The Principessa was having a dinner for eight in her own dining room in the apartment, after which they would join the others at the rooftop restaurant for the ball and midnight supper and much later breakfast at 5 A.M. for those who lasted. Oh, it was going to be a very good party, as well it ought to be, thought Cassidy savagely, considering that the guests were flying in from Buenos Aires, Paris, Rome, Rio de Janeiro, and Hong Kong. A long way to come for scrambled eggs at 5 A.M., but then that was a large part of the mystique of the di Castiglione party—the distances people traveled to dance till dawn.

On the edge of the precipice, as it were.

Always there were parties, Cassidy the historian reflected, before the cataclysm. The ball at Waterloo the night before the engagement. The one at Moscow, the courier interrupting the waltz to say Napoleon had crossed the frontier. To horse! To horse! The Count de Castellone's great feast, the servants parading the roast peacocks at the very moment the ram's horn had sounded the alarm, signaling that Henry II's men had stormed the barbican and were racing to the moat. To arms! To arms!

Why did the *Times* want to attend so frivolous an affair as the Principessa's party? Unless the *Times* knew something....

Cassidy skulked down the hall, feeling his criminality to his very toes. He'd done his share of black bag jobs, but he'd never succeeded in enjoying the work (as so many others did). The Principessa was asleep. (She had come home at 4 A.M. Cassidy had checked on his watch, had listened to the distant laughter, the murmur, the silences.) Lorenzo was in the pantry, Jefferson Lee in his bedroom, Titi? He hoped she was in the nursery, but you could never tell with that imp. She slithered around the apartment on her little cat's feet to pop up in most unexpected places.

Cassidy tiptoed into the library. Quickly because it was always best to do these things quickly. The beautiful desk with its yellow and green lacquered rolltop stood next to one of the great windows. Cassidy pushed up the rolltop and felt in the mahogany alcove where he'd last seen them. They weren't there.

He opened the beautifully curved desk drawer with its bronze handles shaped like acanthus leaves. The stiff white cards were scattered carelessly all over the drawer. Cassidy slipped one into his pocket, closed the drawer, and rolled down the top. He turned around....

Lucia was standing at the entrance door, very straight, very solemn.

"I saw you," she proclaimed.

"There's very little you don't see," complained Cassidy. "Are you spying on me, Contessa?"

Trying to throw her on the defensive. It didn't work.

"You don't have to steal invitations to Mama's party. She's going to insist you be there anyway. She told me so."

Cassidy chewed on the side of his cheek: "You don't eat enough, Contessa. Everything about you is undernourished—except your eyes."

"What are you going to do with that invitation?"

"Invitation?" said Cassidy. He plucked it from his side pocket, held it with the left hand while doing the Baskt flourish with his right hand, leading Lucia's dazzled eyes astray. Then the old Ferraldi switch—and the white card disappeared.

She giggled. "Do it again!"

"Let's take a walk in the park before your mother wakes up," said Cassidy.

"Goody!" said Lucia. "I'll get my coat."

In his room, Cassidy slipped the invitation out from his sleeve, wrote Jane Atchison in bold script across the upper face and put it in his inside breast pocket. He pulled the silencer .22 from under the mattress and slipped it in his side pocket, just beating her entrance.

"Come on," said Cassidy.

·14·

The oak was in the northernmost thicket of the park, an area so dense even the rapists avoided it. Cassidy walked rapidly, forcing Lucia into a run to keep up. "Why must we go so *fast?*" wailed Lucia. "I'm dying."

"You're *living,*" corrected Cassidy. "Have I told you of the vigil demanded of your squires before they became knights?"

"Every *day!*" squealed Lucia. "I'm *bored* with that story! Anyway, I'm not a squire, I'm a girl."

"You're a contessa, and therefore I demand more of you." Cassidy picked up the pace, provoking a thin squeal of outrage from Lucia. What he was trying to do was lose her, if only for a moment, to get the letter out of the oak before she got there.

He didn't succeed. She was still at his side, panting, but in better shape than he was when he reached the oak. Cassidy leaned against the tree, blowing like a whale. She leaned against him, laughing triumphantly. "You were trying to get rid of me. I know! You were running away so I'd get lost and die of hunger and thirst in this wild forest."

Cassidy wrapped his long arms around the bony body: "I wouldn't do a thing like that, Contessa. Your Mama would dock my pay if I lost you."

"*Money!* That's all you're interested in!" The lament of rich little girls since the beginning of time.

"Look there," said Cassidy. "A hawk." Pointing south. "In that big tree."

"Where?" said Lucia who had very good eyes.

Because there was no hawk.

Cassidy had already reached into the oak and got the letter. "It's gone."

"It was never *there*," said Lucia, loving the game. "You were tricking me." Wrestling now, her little hands all over him. "You got something out of that tree." Rapturous with the adventure, little hands feeling every inch of him.

"Contessa! Contessa!" Cassidy was fighting her off as best he could, but he was still winded and off balance. "What will people say?"

He tripped and fell over, Lucia on top of him, laughing like the child she so rarely was, the hands exploring him, looking for the letter.

She didn't find the letter. She found the silenced .22.

"Golly," said Lucia, a new expression for her. (Usually it was *Ecce*.) She held the long weapon in her hand, eyes round as basketballs. "Is it real? Does it go off?" She pointed it at a tree.

Cassidy took it away from her.

Lucia turned beet red, her mouth sagged open, and the round eyes were terrified. "You're going to kidnap me! You're going to kill me!" Little screams followed by an outburst of tears. She struggled in his arms like a demented ape, biting his wrists. "Murderer! Murderer!"

Cassidy wrapped her up in a Murphy, his left arm over her mouth.

"Silence, you idiot child!" he hissed into her ear. "I'm your protector! Your bodyguard! My job is to *prevent* you from being kidnapped!"

Lucia went limp as a cloth doll. Her eyes were forlorn, exhausted.

Neither of them said anything for a very long time. Sunshine filtered through the leaves in hot splashes. Three joggers in blue wool sweat suits huffed and puffed down a distant footpath. The city sounds were muffled and far away.

The terror of her, Cassidy was thinking. He had never seen a truly terrified child before. There were deeps in her terror beyond adult imagining. The terror of her was itself terrifying.

"Bodyguard!" said Lucia, making it contemptible. "I thought you were my teacher."

"I'm both—teacher and protector."

"Mama's idea, I suppose."

Cassidy said nothing.

"Bodyguard! Like that fat nitwit who guards that awful Belgian!"

She looked at him with solemn eyes: "You're much too intelligent to be a proper bodyguard. I bet you've never fired a gun in your life."

She had to be reassured about that. Cassidy didn't want to see the terror in those black eyes ever again. Without a word, he rolled over on his stomach and leveled the silenced .22 at a smooth-barked plane tree. He squeezed off nine shots, the bullets forming a slightly wobbly L. With a flourish of arm and hand, a magician seeking applause, he presented the feat to Lucia "Anyone can carve his girl's initials with a knife. It's more difficult with a gun."

Lucia was enchanted. "Do it again!"

"The Park Department wouldn't like it." Cassidy loaded the weapon again and put it away in his sidepocket. He took Lucia's little pointed chin in his hands and looked deep into her black eyes. "Lucia, no one should ever be as frightened as you were about anything at all."

"Sorry," said Lucia. As if she'd been found wanting.

"I want you to be careful but not *fearful*." Asking a lot of a girl whose father had been kidnapped and killed and who had been brought up in the climate of modern terror. "Fear will eat your life up in little bites. You must die only once, not every day."

He pulled her to her feet. "I'll take you home now."

"I don't want to go home now," said Lucia. "If you're going to protect me, protect me." She was being willful now, chattering gaily, as if the terror had never happened.

"I've got an appointment, Lucia. It's very important."

"It has something to do with that invitation you stole from Mama's desk, hasn't it?"

"You're not invited, and polite little girls don't go where they are not invited."

"I'll tell Mama what you did!"

"Blackmailer!" said Cassidy scowling.

"Thief!" said Lucia.

Standing straight as a pole and expressionless as a wax dummy (he'd seen Albert Finney do this bit in a curious Spanish play the National Theater had done in London), Cassidy performed the introductions.

"Contessa, this is Alvin Feinberg, once one of the most

distinguished foreign correspondents in the whole world, now reduced to excising adverbs from other men's reportage. Mr. Feinberg, this is the Contessa di Castiglione."

They were in Feinberg's little glass-enclosed cubicle, Cassidy in his worn, black coat, Lucia in her new, gray, fall coat. "How do you do, Mr. Feinberg," said Lucia, round-eyed. She dropped a curtsy, well brought up European child that she was.

Feinberg was flummoxed as Cassidy intended him to be. He leaned back in his creaky swivel chair and scratched his bald spot, staring through the gold-rimmed glasses as if the little girl was some kind of freak show. "I hadn't expected the Contessa."

"I'll bet you hadn't," said Cassidy rubbing his nose, flaring his eloquent eyebrows, holding back on the argument until he got full attention: "I thought you should meet the girl whose safety..." his voice rising with the big speeches, singing them really like Olivier, "you are *endangering* so thoughtlessly in pursuit of a news story," the voice dropping to a whisper now, "which—besides being a *flagrant* intrusion on privacy—is also of such *blithering* triviality as to be totally beneath the dignity of *The New York Times*." Straightening up for his big finish, voice ringing like a bell. "And, for *that*, you would imperil the life of this poor child!"

"Oh, for Christ's sake, Cassidy," Feinberg's fist hitting the desk. "I don't give a damn about the party!"

"Why do you want an invitation?"

"*They* want it!" Jabbing his thumb straight down. "Downstairs. *They* want it because the *Washington Post* already has a big story on it." Feinberg threw the paper at Cassidy: "Don't you read the papers?"

"Not this one." Cassidy was horrified. Three columns spread all over Page 3. INTERNATIONAL JET SET WILL CONVERGE ON MYSTERY APARTMENT said the headline. Followed by two thousand words on how rich and useless and altogether socially fascinating was this little group of partygoers who flew from continent to continent in the private jets (while millions went hungry). What made this particular jet set party intriguing (said the *Post*) was that it was taking place in the Windletop, the mystery building about which little was known but much suspected. The writer laid out in full rich prose all that was suspected, while disavowing most of it. The story, Cassidy noted sourly, mongered scandal, rumor, and class consciousness while radiating social disapproval.

"Hypocrisy," roared Cassidy, "thy name is journalism."

Feinberg ignored this (though he found it hard to disagree with). "I'm being pressured because I once knew the di Castigliones. I can't persuade anyone down there that I have not laid eyes on Elsa di Castiglione since she moved to New York. *They* want to cover the story because—and *only* because—they're afraid the *Post* will be there. Otherwise they wouldn't touch it if the Principessa went down on her knees and *begged* them to come."

"The *Post* is *not* going to be there. I went over those invitations myself."

"You can't tell which one of those creeps is a source. A big party like this gets to be news, and then everyone leaks—the guests, the waiters. We can't afford to stay away. That's the way things are."

Cassidy knew. A story had been created out of nothing. These international parties happened all the time in a dozen countries. This one had been singled out by a famous newspaper because it was taking place at the Windletop, which was a fortress for the rich and highborn. That gave the party an extra glamour. Now that the *Post* had waded in they'd all have stories—the *Post*, *The Daily News*, the foreign press—full of speculation, gossip, scandal, each trying to outdo the others—the whoppers getting bigger as the great day approached—and it was still three weeks away.

An open invitation to terrorists to come in and share the limelight, which they treasured above the collected works of Lenin.

Cassidy laid the invitation on Feinberg's desk. He was standing behind Lucia and therefore concealed it from her. He jabbed his thumb down in the direction of her head, shaking his own head at the same time, indicating they couldn't talk under the circumstances. "Put it in a letter," he barked. "At the old address."

"The old address?"

Cassidy gave him the address of the Spumi.

"Come on, Contessa," said Cassidy. "I'll take you to the Aquarium. They have a fish there that glows in the dark all red and green like a Christmas tree."

"Will you take me on a subway?"

"That, too. We'll be as irresponsible as seagulls."

Feinberg blinked his round intelligent eyes behind the gold-rimmed glasses. Cassidy had, after all, once been chief of station in Belgrade. Anyway, he owed him one for that crack about excising adverbs.

"You do this sort of thing for a living now, Cassidy?" he asked sweetly.

Cassidy was already at the entrance of the cubicle. "A higher calling than yours, you ink-stained *society columnist*."

·15·

Cassidy was reading Alison's letter in his room with the door locked. Feet up on the bed. Two A.M.

> ...the terrorists import hit men from all over the place for specific assignments totally unrelated to their own grievances. The Lod massacre was done by Japanese Red Army people for the PLO which would have had trouble getting in there. The thing that ended at Entebbe was pulled off by a conglomerate of terrorists—Baader-Meinhof, Carlos and his bunch, the PFLP with unofficial help from Libya, Uganda, and even South Yemen, all of whose Palestinian interests were tenuous.

Cassidy farted—a form of protest. This was old stuff. When was Alison going to get to the point?

> We were very happy to get the prints of Jefferson Lee. The FBI's prints, taken by Chicago Police after the uproar at the Democratic National Convention of 1968, accompanied the name of Tancred O. The FBI says he's a member of the 6th of July movement, a splinter of the Weather Underground who were altogether white (though they deny racism, of course). We think 6th of July has links in Amsterdam with Baader-Meinhof, Japanese Red Brigade, Red Army Faction. If so, Jefferson Lee's an advance man. The Windletop is definitely a target, though of undetermined priority. Anyhow we're very anxious to keep an eye on Jefferson Lee so don't rock the boat. He's the only link we have

That's as far as Cassidy got. The scream split the still night air—E over High C, a child's scream—coming from the direction of the Principessa's bedroom.

It kept coming, a high sustained screech that Cassidy, galloping down the corridor now in his pajamas and bare feet, the .38 in his fist, past the Pope Constant painting, past the empty pedestal where the Donatello had once stood, divined as a scream of fury, not one of fear.

Reassuring but not so reassuring that Cassidy didn't burst into the Principessa's bedroom without knocking (feeling, even in this moment of high emergency, unmannered and out of costume so powerful are the social embarrassments grained into us by the rich and powerful).

The overhead light was on in the painted, mirrored, intensely rococo bedroom, and that in itself was peculiar because the Principessa rarely used the overhead light. Lucia—her face contorted with rage—was astride her beautiful mother on the bed, beating her with her little fists, screeching pure outrage, pure in the sense it contained no words in any of her four languages, simply animal sounds.

Her mother was fending her off without expression, routinely, as if this sort of thing had happened before, perhaps many times, the little girl's fists landing on the Principessa's hands, her elbows, everywhere except her beautiful face.

The Principessa was wearing very little, but she was covered by a sheet of blue percale with the di Castiglione crest in white lace, under which the thin muscular body writhed and strained in this combat, sensual as a bit of pornographic film.

Cassidy tossed the .38 into the winged armchair—the same one he'd been invited to sit in by the Principessa—and grasped the child by both shoulders, pulling her backward away from the Principessa. Lucia was in her woolen nightie with forest scenes of bears and deer and birds imprinted in soft autumnal colors—its innocence almost obscene next to her mother's nakedness.

"Lucia! Lucia!" Cassidy was astounded at the pain in his own voice.

He pulled her off the Principessa and picked her up into his arms, trying to deflect the fury toward himself. There was no need. The rage had ended. Lucia burst into tears flooding his shoulder with wetness, burrowing her face into his chest.

It was an intimacy he didn't want, not with the Principessa

looking at him that way, the violet eyes furious. She wasn't angry with her daughter, she was angry with *him*—for being there, for witnessing this humiliation. Relieved of her daughter, she had slithered under the blue sheet like a snake taking cover in forest leaves, still gazing at him as if this terrible scene was all his fault.

"I'll take her back to her bed," said Cassidy.

The Principessa said nothing.

Cassidy turned toward the bedroom door, and there he found Lorenzo, in a long dressing gown that reached to his heels, impassive as an Indian. Next to him was Titi in her wool bathrobe, saturnine as always.

Everyone but me, thought Cassidy, took time out to put on something before chasing down the hall. I'm just a boor. Or perhaps not. Perhaps this scene has happened before so often these people don't take Lucia's screams very seriously any more.

Lucia still sobbing against his chest.

"You forgot your gun," said Lorenzo. The butler retrieved the gun from the winged chair and put it into Cassidy's right hand protruding from underneath Lucia's buttocks.

Where was Jefferson Lee? Everyone in the household was there but him.

It was a long walk from the Principessa's bedroom past the paintings, the sculpture, the objets d'art to the nursery, and long before he got there, the sobs had stopped. When Cassidy laid Lucia in her bed, she was already asleep, face washed clear of ferocity, innocent as a fawn.

As he stared down at her, Titi crept in and put herself in her own bed, malevolent as a spider.

Cassidy didn't return to his room immediately. Instead, he went into the immense unused sitting room, his eyes going from one object to another, cataloguing, counting. The silver and crystal chandelier from a sixteenth-century Medici palace was in its place. So was the Fabergé egg with the little lapis lazuli door that sprang open revealing the sadfaced Tsarina painted on ivory inside (an Easter present from the Tsar). It was in its glass case against the wall alongside of the enameled armband from an eighth century Holy Roman Emperor, the carved ivory fan from the Tsu dynasty—everything in its place....

No, not everything.

The little ten-inch-high four-thousand-year-old urn from Carthage, with its incredible perfection of symmetry—Cassidy's favorite of all the di Castiglione treasures—was missing. It normally stood in the place of honor (as well it should) in the very center of the glass case.

The di Castiglione loot of four centuries was slipping away. The best pieces, too. Cassidy bared his teeth in his satyr grin. All very appropriate—the looters looted—and none of his business really since he was there solely to guard Lucia.

Still, what was Lucia *doing* in her mother's room at that hour?

Feeling the richness of the blue and gold Aubusson under his barefeet. Then the cold marble of the corridor.

Alison's letter lay on the floor where he'd dropped it. He picked it up and read on:

> Much of the financing of the left wing terrorists now comes from East Germany and even the Soviet Union. Many of these commandos are trained in East Germany by—knowing you, you'll find this droll—ex-Nazis. We have no information that Hugo Dorn is in any way involved, but a lot of these ex-Nazis know one another. Therefore, he's vulnerable to blackmail. What makes this situation dangerous is that not only are the various terrorist groups—PLO, Red Army Faction, Weather Underground, and all the rest—sharing arms, money, training, et cetera—but also information. They are putting together the germ of their own CIA—and it's worldwide.
> Destroy.

Cassidy cut the letter into small pieces with his nail scissors and flushed them down the toilet of Orosco marble with finely veined red traceries. Too good for excretion, Cassidy was thinking. I ought to hang my ass out the window and shit straight down forty-nine stories.

He brushed his teeth in a bowl of the same marble as the toilet, with gold faucets in the shape of dolphins, wondering if corruption was infectious like disease, if he could catch it by touch.

He went to bed and through his brain flashed the image of a lovely Principessa struggling expressionlessly with her furious child. In a flash of afterglow long after the event, it struck him that the very absence of emotion was itself a kind of despair beyond the ability of facial muscles to express.

He thought about that for a long time. Then he thought about Alison. Why was Alison telling him all this? Alison never did anything that didn't, in some way, push the career and good fortune of Alison ahead to some minute degree. He was not trying to tell him something but to sell him something.

·16·

Eleven A.M.

Sun streaming through the Venetian blinds, all over the brilliant blues and reds of the Persian carpet. Cassidy hunched himself out of bed dismayed at the hour and hurtled into his clothes. Eleven A.M. Damn!

In the corridor outside his room, he encountered the Principessa, fully dressed, an event of such magnitude it stopped him in his tracks. It was the first time ever she'd been up ahead of himself.

She was in a gray wool suit, not so tight-fitting as most of her clothes, and she was putting on a little gray, matching, cloche hat, looking at herself in the gilt Louis XV mirror that hung over a small marble-topped table. Their eyes met in the mirror, Cassidy's and the Principessa's. Just for a moment a smile hovered on the Principessa's face, like a sunbeam.

This was so unlikely that Cassidy didn't know what to make of it. She never failed to rattle him, he was thinking, because always she did the unexpected. A smile!

"A bit late, Professor, aren't you?" The voice mocking and playful (which was the last mood in the world he expected her to be in after the scene of the night before). She looked fresh as a teenager and Cassidy, catching a glimpse of himself in the gilt mirror, thought himself looked a hundred and two.

"I've been neglecting m' duties," said Cassidy. He swept her his d'Artagnan bow, the one Douglas Fairbanks, Sr., did in *The Three Musketeers*. "I'm very sorry."

"You apologize charmingly, Professor," said the Principessa. Then very lightly to take the sting out. "But underneath all your apologies I always detect some intention or other quite at variance with what you're apologizing for."

Yes, and underneath all your smiling banter is always some intention quite contrary to what you're sayin', said Cassidy to himself. Aloud, he said: "Charm, Madame, is a weakness of the Irish. They mistake it for integrity."

"Good heavens!" said the Principessa. "Aphorisms so early in the morning!"

She passed down the hall in the direction of the foyer (with its new steel doors guarding the elevator), her back to him as carefree as a sparrow.

Cassidy took himself to the kitchen where he found Lorenzo in a light overcoat, slipping on a pair of leather gloves. At sight of Cassidy, Lorenzo's face crinkled into its leathery Florentine smile. "Signor, I am desolate, but I must leave you. Might you get your own breakfast this morning?"

Everyone going out. Very peculiar.

"Where's Jefferson Lee?" asked Cassidy.

"Gone," said Lorenzo, working the leather gloves with his fingers to see that they lay on his fingers totally straight. "Dismissed," working out a wrinkle with great care, "you might say."

Jupiter, thought Cassidy. Alison will be furious. He'll say it's my fault.

"The Principessa thought Jefferson Lee's cooking lacked *esprit*," said Lorenzo mildly.

"I recognize the Principessa's prose style," said Cassidy pleasantly. But what happened to all those reasons for *not* firing Jefferson Lee—the Equal Opportunity Commission, NAACP, and all the rest of it? Aloud, he said: "I just ran into the Principessa in the corridor. I've never known her to be up and dressed so early before."

Lorenzo's smile was purest Florentine silk: "The Principessa is going to confession, Signor. Always on Thursday."

Cassidy puffed out his cheeks ruefully. No wonder she was in such a good mood. She was going to lay her baroque, ultra chic sins at the feet of the proper authorities who would take them off her hands and mind and soul.

"Who hears the Principessa's confession, Lorenzo?"

"The Cardinal, Signor. He is an old friend from Italy."

Confessing to a Cardinal was even better than having a Titian in the back hall, as status symbols went.

"What do you suppose they talk about, Lorenzo? Not *sin*."

"Oh, no!" said the Lorenzo with his fine smile. "The aristocracy doesn't sin, signor. It makes mistakes."

"Has the Principessa made any lately?"

The hooded look closed down on Lorenzo's remarkable face: "I bid you good morning, sir." He went out the rear door, which lead to the rear stairs and elevator in the Windletop, closing the door behind him.

Cassidy made himself a cup of coffee, chewed on a stale croissant left over from the Principessa's breakfast, and thought about Jefferson Lee.

Later he poked his nose into the nursery. Lucia was taking her piano lesson from the formidable French lady named Madame Frontenac. The child was playing a Chopin *Étude* savagely—which was not how Chopin intended it to be played. "*Pas de tout!*" the French lady was saying. Cassidy caught a sidewise glimpse of Lucia's face. That was all he wanted—a glimpse. She looked triumphant, like an Amazon who has just chopped off a head.

Cassidy closed the door without anyone seeing him. Twenty minutes later he was on a bar stool at the Spumi reading Feinberg's letter.

Don't ask me where I got this because if I told you I'd never get any more. I can't even vouch for its authenticity beyond saying it fits the facts, as I know them, and came from someone who is not unimpeachable (who is?) but very intelligent and knowing, especially about Nicki.

Nicki di Castiglione was—as so many of the people in his thoroughly depraved circles were—bisexual, but his real inclinations ran to men. When he did it with women, he frequently did it with another man watching or sharing. Nicki was also deeply masochistic, and it was whispered among his sexual companions (which numbered, as I say, both men and women) that the act of marrying Elsa itself was a form of masochism. She resembles a whip in many ways, and she could both be one and use one. So it was said. Her infidelities, which were legion, were not only forgiven by Nicki but actually demanded by him as Masoch who gave his name to the game did with both his wives.

Cassidy put down the letter at that point and tossed the Wild Turkey down his gullet to help digest the information he had just read. He sat there a moment, feeling the whiskey, keeping his mind open. It was a quarter to twelve, his favorite hour at the Spumi. No one was there but Henry and the waiters. The tables were neatly laid, and the place smelled of fresh flowers and cleanliness. Restaurants, he was thinking, were at their best before the customers wrecked the place with their eating and drinking and smoking and noise.

He read on.

As you know, Nicki was kidnapped and kept prisoner for many months while the ransom demands were haggled over by his sister Clothilde. During this time his captors indulged Nicki's sexual tastes. Bondage itself Nicki found to be sexually gratifying—and right here I should say the information becomes a little suspect. One wonders who got all these details, but they were given to me with such positiveness as to carry weight. Anyhow....

Nicki adored being tied up and constantly requested new and different bondages, positions that were very painful, being suspended upside down, the whole bit. One day his captors went too far. They tied him in some complicated way and left him—because part of the thrill was being tied up and abandoned—and when they returned, Nicki had strangled himself. Inadvertently.

With seven and a half million dollars at stake, naturally they carried on with the negotiations and, when the demands were met, delivered a dead body. Aah, but you say, Nicki wasn't strangled, he was shot. Here comes the black comedy. The kidnappers were—as you know—radical ideological terrorists kidnapping rich folk for lofty revolutionary groups, who are very puritanical about sex, especially such decadent bourgeois sexual perversions as practiced by Nicki di Castiglione. If it had become noised around the radical underground that they had indulged Nicki's curious sexual habits, the kidnappers would have lost face and perhaps even been tossed out of the lodge altogether. Therefore they shot the dead body and left it on the city dump. This was a perfectly respectable radical revolutionary deed, just as allowing him to strangle himself in pursuit of perverse sexual pleasure was a thoroughly disreputable, counter-revolutionary and therefore utterly impermissible deed.

I hope you relish the joke as much as I do.

Cassidy was not amused. A good joke—but on who? Self-strangulation of that kind was a Mafia trick and the Mafia was not left wing but very right wing. Someone had infiltrated the left-wing revolutionary kidnapping and just possibly turned it into a right-wing old-fashioned kidnapping and murder for fun and money. Very funny indeed but the joke was on Feinberg. Someone had sold him a bill of goods.

"You look awful," commented Henry. "Your liver?"

Like a lot of Europeans of his age Henry traced everything to the liver.

"I never discuss my liver in public, Henry," said Cassidy gently, "because of the biofeedback, you know."

Henry let it go. "Sophy was in. She's terrified about you being in Turkestan. She says they got brigands there. That's what she said—brigands."

"They had brigands in the seventeenth century. Now they got hoodlums like everyone else."

Cassidy clambered off the bar stool and went up the brownstone steps to his apartment.

The place looked as if a hurricane had struck it. The books were piled four feet high on the floor, and the shelves were empty. The mattress had been slit open from top to bottom. The place had been ransacked from floor to ceiling.

Cassidy made a little clown face and did a slow clog dance—for the hidden cameras. You had to give them something. Afterward he sat on a pile of books and thought about things.

He was supposed to go directly to the hiding place to show the hidden cameras where it was. But Alison's letter was somewhere in that pile of books—and there were a lot of books. Anyway, he had another copy in the bank. If that's what they were after. . . .

Cassidy left the place just as it was, simply walking out the door and locking it behind him. If they wanted Alison's letter, let them find it themselves.

·17·

He awoke with dread, predecessor of fear. The room was almost black with only the faintest glow of light on the ceiling. Someone was in the room—*that* he knew—while pretending sleep, breathing slowly, regularly, trying to control the heartbeat.

Rustlings of pure silk against flesh. An exhalation light as a butterfly's wing. Cassidy clutched the silenced .22 underneath the pillow, but already he knew this peril lay beyond bullets. He was still wildly considering his course of action when he felt her lips against his, mocking, unmistakable, the two hands grasping his face, centering for the firm tongue which split his lips in short, sharp, stylish strokes.

"Principessa!" He got it out, all four indignant syllables, as best he could against those lips, that tongue, which dismayed speech at its source.

"Let's fuck, Professor. We can talk later."

The obscenity in the darkness loomed large. As Lucia had divined, Cassidy was a prude in matters sexual and especially in sexual language, a man to whom Jupiter Jehoshaphat was the strongest expletive allowable, an old-fashioned man. The Principessa seemed to have guessed it as well as Lucia and had used the pungent Anglo-Saxon word to stun him into immobility as she climbed into his sheets, her body—his protesting hands informing him—as naked as a moth's.

"No! No!" protested Cassidy, straining away from her, his mind seething with the implications.

"Hush, Professor," whispered the Principessa, laughter lurking in the whisper as if the joke were devilish—a joke on him as indeed *she* was on him rather than with him.

As he still pushed at the supple naked body, she delivered the fatal sting like a wasp paralyzing its victim. "Hush now! We wouldn't want to wake Lucia, would we?"

Wake Lucia!

Cassidy lay back robbed of volition. Wake Lucia! To find him in bed with her mother!

"Rape!" said Cassidy furiously—but softly so as not to wake Lucia.

"If you like!" Unbuttoning the pajama top, untying the pajama trouser cord, all very expertly and swiftly, as if having committed these invasions against how many couchant males while her husband watched hungrily?

"You don't leave a lady much choice, Professor." Laughter in the voice now thickening with naked lust.

"I'm old!" moaned Cassidy. "Too old for these games!"

"Oh, no, Cassidy, you're not too old at all!" Her tongue and hands fluttering all over his ancient nudity with the expertise of a confident aristocrat that harbored no sexual timidities. She played his maleness like a violin, teasing his reluctant body into a lechery that aroused and unmanned him simultaneously, because, in this affair, she was altogether the aggressor, taking possession of him as if by seigneurial right. She mounted him and—only after she had played with him with hands and tits and lips to the utmost of her extraordinary sexual gifts—fucked him with overpowering agility. Even as he was coming into her, he sensed the laughter in her as if laughter was her form of orgasm, her kind of release, as if sex was her revenge.

Cassidy dozed and dreamed. Of barbicans stormed and overrun. Of watch towers crumbling. Defeat, everywhere defeat, and himself left flat on the ground, stripped of his armor....

He awoke in the darkness, feeling her nakedness next to him. He could sense her awakeness like a current of electricity. He said nothing, testing if she was as aware of his awakeness as he was of hers. She was.

"Three A.M., Professor." The voice languorous and sad. "The hour of despair."

"Speak for yourself, Madame. I am not so familiar with the hour of 3 A.M. as you." A bitter remark. Actually Cassidy wasn't bitter but curious. She was not the kind of person who went about raping for no reason. She was a rapist with purpose. At least he thought so.

The Principessa's voice was reflective and gentle, lust and mockery gone. It made her sound wistful: "I stay up too late much too often to have company, Professor. I'm without a husband now. I don't like to be alone."

"Alone? With your legion of lovers?" Jeering at her, which he would never dare in the daylight.

She didn't get angry. Instead, she sounded amused: "Legions of lovers! At my age, a lady's escort kisses one on the cheek—and rings for the lift."

He didn't believe her. Still, it was best to play along if he were to learn anything. "So, Madame, it was the absence of alternatives that caused you to cast yourself on my ancient, wrinkled, reeking body."

That brought out her low throaty laugh: "It's just possible I take pleasure in ancient, wrinkled, reeking bodies. There are brothels in Paris that have only seventy-year-old whores, appealing to some tastes."

How far were her defenses down? "Someone is stealing the silver, Madame, and the statuary."

He heard a swift intake of breath. He'd penetrated the armor of her playfulness. Presently he felt the bed move, and she left him. In the darkness he could hear her slipping on whatever she had taken off earlier. The door to his bedroom opened, letting in a triangle of light from the corridor.

"Good night, Principessa." Trying her out. He wanted very much to test the tone of her response for anger of fear. The reply was none of those. It was dry and jeering: "*Buona notte,* my ancient, wrinkled, *reeking* lover!"

The door closed behind her.

He lay awake wondering. It wasn't the attraction of his body certainly. She was a woman of cool determination, whose every act seemed precisely reasoned (if not always reasonable), a woman of logic, order, and precision. She did few things on impulse, certainly nothing so demeaning as raping the servants.

It was all part of some cool calculation, and Cassidy felt he knew exactly what it was.

The next morning Cassidy ate his croissant, sipped his coffee, and then sprang it all on Lorenzo. He didn't really expect to get an answer out of Lorenzo, but he wanted to test the temperature of the water on the butler. You could find out a lot of things by a man's face.

He spoke harshly, positively: "Lucia caught Mama in bed with that black stud, Jefferson Lee, and that's why we had all that uproar in the middle of the night. That's also why those two tutors got fired—because Lucia won't stand Mama's going to bed with them."

Lorenzo said nothing. He was in his leather apron, polishing silver as always. He would, Cassidy felt sure, have protested eloquently, maybe even angrily if these accusations were pure libel. Instead the turtle eyes narrowed, the mouth pursed, the fine lines around the temples deepened. The atmosphere reeked of disapproval, not at the deeds themselves (Lorenzo's servitude was unquestioning: the actions of a mistress might be confusing or frightening, never wrong) but at voicing these actions. *That* was wrong, giving tongue to these dark deeds.

So.

She had slipped into bed with him because she feared his hold on the little girl. Any time she wanted to get rid of him she'd just have to let it be known in the nursery that an amorous relationship existed—and that would just be that. Lucia would scream in the night, beating her little fists on her mother's flawless features, while her mother held her off without expression, as if she'd arranged the whole thing—as indeed she had.

But how did she go about letting the news be known in the nursery? She certainly wouldn't go in there and announce it.

Titi?

·18·

Cassidy crept down the back stairs like a decrepit cat, joints creaking. At each landing he listened to the echoes of his own breathing. Severely purposive, these stairs. No marble or chrome. Cement and steel painted dull gray. Nobody was supposed to go on these stairs, according to the dictates of Alfred the Great (otherwise known as Hugo Dorn, the Good Nazi). If no one was supposed to use them, what were they for? The stairs at the Windletop, front and back, were put there by the dictates of the fire laws that had been superseded by the alarms of modern terrorism. Whether it was better to be burned alive in your bed—or massacred there—*that* was the question.

Cassidy was circling down, counting as he went—forty-nine, forty-eight, forty-seven, his footsteps sending hollow booms clear down the stairwell. He was thinking of those circular stone stairways in medieval castles—the last defense line of all. If the invaders got into the castle proper, the resident knight fought his way up the front stairs, then down the back stairs, each stairwell designed so as to favor his good right arm and hinder the good right arm of the invader.

Forty-six, forty-five, forty-four. . . .

At the thirty-ninth floor he ran square into the Security Chief (alias Alfred the Great, alias Hugo the Good)—clearly waiting for him, lips smiling disapproval.

"We've been following your descent on television," said Alfred almost apologetically.

Television.

Cassidy noticed—as he should have noticed much earlier—the round black bulges at the corner of each landing. The boob tube. Trust Alfred not to overlook TV monitors.

"One wonders," said Alfred negligently, "exactly what the Contessa's bodyguard is doing, tiptoeing down the backstairs."

Cassidy sat on the cement stairs and blew on his hands irritably. "Reconnoitering," he said harshly. Normally he didn't believe in telling the truth to good Nazis, but there were moments when you couldn't avoid it. "One wonders," said Cassidy, mimicking the Good Nazi, "where the exits are and how well guarded and so forth and so on. One is paid to wonder these things."

Alfred pulled at his earlobe thoughtfully. "Mr. Cassidy might I invite your attention to Windletop Security Regulation 522 forbidding personal use of these stairwells except in dire emergency."

"Might I invite your attention to the fire regulations of the city of New York which decree complete access and information about fire exits to every resident."

Alfred the Great studied his fingernails: "The Fire Commissioner and I have gone all over this, Mr. Cassidy. The Windletop is permitted certain exceptions in view of the extraordinary nature of its problems and its clientele."

"You mean the rich are exempt from the fire laws? Perhaps even fire itself?"

Alfred smiled a weary smile: "The elevator is right here, Mr. Cassidy. Might I put you on it? You'll find it easier than walking—at your age."

"Leave my age out of it," snarled Cassidy—and then let him have it right between the eyes. "*Hugo.*"

The name bounded down the stairwell—Hu-go, Hu-go, echoing away like a sound effect. Hugo's eyes went blank, and the silence in him deepened to infinity. He ran his fingers over his temples, as if smoothing the dyed hair into place.

"There are at least twenty-six Jewish residents of the Windletop who...."

That was as far as Cassidy got. He had meant to say "who would be interested in your true identity" but Hugo Dorn's hand brushed his mouth and shut it up. All done as if accidentally, brushing against him that way, the eyes indicating the black bulge in the stairwell.

Cassidy closed up. Blackmail wasn't any use if everyone knew it. He rose from the steps: "Let's walk down, shall we? A little exercise alters the point of view. After you...."

Alfred the Great, alias the Good Nazi, acceded gracefully. At least on the surface. What went on underneath, Cassidy would have given a pretty penny to know. But Hugo Dorn gave very little away.

A long way down and around, thirty-nine, thirty-eight, thirty-seven, and so forth and so on, as Cassidy liked to say. No words passed, but the atmosphere in the enclosed concrete space was explosive.

Down and around, down and around. Eighteen, seventeen, sixteen. The numbers were painted on the sides of the landings. Otherwise no landing was different from any other. Cassidy tried the doors at several landings. Locked. "Each resident has a key to his own floor and no other floor," said Hugo Dorn without looking back. "A resident can get off only at his own floor."

The obstruction was on the third floor, one landing beneath the private apartments. A solid concrete wall pierced by a triple plated steel door unmarred by anything so ordinary as a lock. "If they managed to breach the outer defenses," murmured the Security Chief, "there must be an inner line to fall back on. You know that, Professor Cassidy, expert that you are on fortifications."

"Open it," said Cassidy.

Hugo hesitated, mouth slightly open, eyes unfathomable. Examining his options, thought Cassidy. He kept himself loose and above the man.

A long silence. Hugo Dorn neither acceded nor demurred. He did nothing.

"Hugo,..." said Cassidy using the forbidden name like a whip.

Hugo's body sagged as if hit. With infinite reluctance, he drew from his breast pocket a rectangle roughly the size of a deck of cards. On its top was a series of numbers like those on a telephone. He pressed three numbers quickly (but not so quickly that Cassidy didn't note them; 8-6-2) and the device emitted three different bleeps.

The steel door sank silently into its concrete base.

"You go first...." Cassidy was turning *Hugo* into *You go* for the benefit of the listening devices "...and I'll precede. A genuine malapropism. Mrs. Malaprop actually said that one in Richard Brinsley Sheridan's *The Rivals*."

"A vastly overrated play," said Hugo Dorn.

Down and around, down and around....

"This is the basement," announced Hugo pleasantly. "We are back in the nineteenth century which in many ways was more ingenious than the twentieth."

They were in a huge room filled with ancient red pumps with copper fittings. It was stiflingly hot. "These marvelous machines pump hot water to the tank on the fiftieth floor where it descends by gravity to the various apartments beneath it," Hugo was saying. "This is a vacuum pump which pulls hot water up whenever the water cools up there so that in the Windletop you never have to run the water to get it hot. It's always hot."

He was preening himself on the Windletop as if he owned it. Now that the 1,000-year Reich had crumbled, what else was there? Hugo was showing off his sump pump, which operated mechanically when the water fell below a certain level—like a toilet bowl—as if electricity had never been invented. In the next room were the steam pipes from the New York Steam Company which heated the water for the radiators in the copper coils contained in great concrete tanks, machinery straight out of 1928 when the building went up.

Hugo was showing it all off too willingly. Cassidy was sure there was more.

"Where does that door lead?"

Hugo smiled his sad make-believe smile, sighed. He paused, thinking things over. After these preliminaries, the little rectangle came out of Hugo's pocket, and trilled their message. The numbers were 4-7-5. The steel door slid sidewise into the wall.

Behind them lay a broad stone staircase, leading down.

"You go first," said Hugo politely, "and I'll precede."

Cassidy stepped through the door just a second before his brain sent the *Tilt* message flashing though his skull. Never go down a staircase *ahead* of a Nazi, not even a Good Nazi! Do something! Cassidy stumbled—or pretended to—twisting his body around to face Hugo Dorn, both hands in front of his face, in the Dorrier Defense, the best he could come up with.

The switch blade snickered just an inch above his skull. Falling, Cassidy gripped the wrist that held the blade, pulling Hugo on down the stone steps with him, using the fall to pull

Hugo into the Harrison hammerlock. *Too old for these games! Not too old at all, the Principessa had said.*

Down they tumbled, first Cassidy on top, then Hugo, the blade held outward until the weight of the two bodies wrenched it out of Hugo's grasp.

It should have subdued the Good Nazi, but it didn't. They had fallen now the full flight of stairs into an open space where Hugo knuckled Cassidy in the balls, slipping out of the Harrison hammerlock as the pain struck. Flat on his back, Cassidy, his knees cocked back on his chest, fired them against Hugo's jaw, hurtling him against the wall. That stunned Hugo just enough for Cassidy to spin Hugo around and put a knee into his kidney.

"Whoof," exclaimed Hugo, his muscles turning to water.

Cassidy kneeled on the man's back, holding Hugo's crossed arms by each wrist. For a half minute, no one spoke.

"It was forty years ago!" said Cassidy, unbelieving. "You must be in your late sixties."

"Seventy-two," said Hugo Dorn, snapping it out like a salute, preening himself on his age.

Slowly Cassidy removed his knees from Hugo's kidneys. You couldn't kneel on a man's kidneys when he was seventy-two years old.

In place of the knee, he pulled out the silenced .22 and leveled it at Hugo's face after rolling him over.

"You were going to kill me, Hugo," said Cassidy, a flat statement, "a form of displeasure so extreme that I feel you're trying to *tell* me something in your own Teutonic way. It'd be less painful for both of us if you just put it into words."

Hugo smiled his tired European smile—and said nothing.

Cassidy searched him carefully from head to toe—feeling inside the shoes, under the armpits, in the crotch, behind the knees. Afterwards he poked him with the gun to get him to stand up.

"This time you go first, I'll precede."

"The joke is getting a little tired," said Hugo. "It wasn't ever a very good joke."

Cassidy was inspecting the room he'd fallen into. Quite a change from the basement just above it. Each of the four walls was lined with electronic equipment. Dials flickered. Spools of tape slowly revolved in the very latest computers. On one wall was a large console with three blank TV-faced monitor screens. Buttons of all colors bearing numbers, letters and symbols, crawled the length of the console.

It was a control room, exactly duplicating the one outside Hugo's second floor office. A *second* control room, which could probably supersede the first one, just in case terrorists overran the first one. Cassidy felt exhausted and enraged by the expense and elaborateness of all this electronic machinery which probably wouldn't work. Oh, the futility of it all! Just for a second, he closed his eyes in exasperation.

That was time enough. Hugo's boot caught him in the center of the wrist, a beautifully timed shot which sent the silenced .22 spinning lazily across the room. Cassidy went over backward swiftly to avoid the other boot, aimed at his face, which whistled after it, Hugo leaping like a high jumper rolling over the bar, landing crouched and ready. Cassidy came up hard against the gray console in sitting position as Hugo came for him, fingers outthrust in one of the nastiest sortileges in the book. Also one that took the quickest reflexes and, at seventy-two, Hugo wasn't quite up to it. Cassidy took the thrusting fingers on the top of his skull rather than the eye sockets where they were aimed. At the same time he threw a knee into Hugo's face and came up with his .38.

"You don't think I'd go down a dark stairway with you with only one gun, do you, Hugo?"

Both men flat on the floor, panting like spent runners.

"You come very well armed, Professor." Hugo smiled painfully. "But you haven't the proper motivation to use that gun, have you?"

He sprang straight at the gun, testing. Cassidy clubbed him briskly on the temple with the muzzle of the gun. As he rolled over on his back, Hugo's eyes glazed.

"Motivation, is it?" chattered Cassidy cheerfully. He felt marvelous, bruised but full of macho juices that made his eyes bright. "I can always summon up a little motivation when the need arises." He was slipping out of his jacket, rolling up his sleeves. "Somebody has got hold of you, Hugo, and I aim to find out who. After that I'm going to turn you around."

Hugo was in some pain but it was a matter of principle for

him to voice defiance. "You haven't the absence of scruple, Cassidy. Or the dedication."

Cassidy had Hugo's switchblade knife in his hand, testing the blade on the ball of his thumb. "Oh, haven't I now? For dedication to the absence of scruple, there's nothing like a lapsed Catholic, me boyo."

He thrust Hugo into a chair and tied him there with his own shirt—an old Company trick.

"Don't worry about your face lift, Hugo. I won't leave any marks. Now what I want to know is: How do you get out of this place? You wouldn't plan all this electronic wizardry unless you knew a way to get into it and a way to get out of it in a hurry."

He opened with a Duvalier, that interesting little torment devised by the French in Algeria, and worked up slowly and with enormous reluctance to the Vivaldi.

He hated using the Vivaldi, even on old Nazis, because no one—neither torturer nor torturee—was ever quite the same afterwards.

·19·

"We are accustomed to thinking of Renaissance man as complete in that he was artist, thinker, philosopher, lover, swordsman, diplomat, architect, all that...." Cassidy was prowling back and forth, hands behind his back—his Austrian archduke act.

Lucia was standing on her head, a new wrinkle in Cassidy's training. Brought oxygen to the head, Cassidy told her. Also forced concentration and relaxation.

"You have a nasty bruise on your cheek, Professor," said Lucia, upside down but observant.

Cassidy ignored this: "However, the completeness of Renaissance man was not perceived except retroactively—about 200 years later. Now let us consider how future man—say, 200 years from today—will regard *modern* man."

"To say nothing of modern woman," said Lucia severely.

"In retrospect we will be seen to be fully as versatile as Renaissance man—fighting our way through the jungle of modern cities while building shopping centers that will be seen in the light of 200 years as models of ingenuity and beauty, driving our cars, jogging, doing our own carpentry and plumbing because we can't find people to do it for us—and at the same time engaging in endless political, social, psychological discourse on all manner of subjects. Oh, modern man is required to cope with more social problems of greater complexity than anything Renaissance man dreamt of in his philosophy."

After the lecture came the fencing. Cassidy had insisted on thrusting both ballet and fencing down Lucia's unwilling throat. "She has no natural skill at all," said the fencing instructor, a small, thin, unsmiling man named Guiseppe Sforzi (whom Lucia called the Little Wop. "I can call him that because I'm a little Wop, too"). Cassidy would watch the two of them doing their highly formalized arabesques counting "One, two, three...point." After each session, the Little Wop would shake his head and mutter that he'd never known anyone so devoid in natural aptitude.

"Why," yelled Lucia, "must I do something I don't like and do badly?"

"You can't spend your life," snarled Cassidy, "just doing things you do well. You must learn quickness of response—both physical and mental. It might save you from assassination."

"I'm not important enough to be assassinated!" said Lucia glumly. "I'd just get killed."

"My job is to *prevent* you from being killed. You will be only thirty-four when the twenty-first century arrives. Ahead of you lie upheavals and cataclysms unparalleled in the history of rich little girls. I want you to be ready. What is the square root of 79,865? Quickly! Quickly! Quickness of response is everything."

Always there was combat between them. She wanted to know the why of everything, and he was secretly delighted that she wanted to know why. Meanwhile, the disciplines rained down—declensions, square roots, participles and gerunds, new math (and old math), past conditional as well as future derivative, hyperfunctional and post historical.

At supper Lorenzo said: "No tutor has ever treated the Contessa so harshly before, and none has lasted as long as you."

Cassidy said: "Where is the Principessa?"

He had not laid eyes on her since the night she'd slipped into bed with him.

"Italy, Signor."

"Why?"

Lorenzo laid the grilled sole before Cassidy like a priest laying a burnt offering before his deity. "Trustees. They make business."

That night, after days of constant calls, Cassidy got through to Alison on the private line. Cassidy's first words were: *"Agent provocateur!"*

"How can you *say* such a thing?" said Alison, aghast. "Especially on the *phone!*"

They were taping everything at Langley these days. It made a nice weapon against Alison, whose memory of conversations was unreliable.

"The Spumi," said Cassidy. "Noon tomorrow."

Alison would show up if only to prevent him blabbing any more on the telephone. He did—right on time.

"You shouldn't have leaned on Hugo so *hard,* Horatio," said Alison deeply aggrieved. "You've intimidated him."

"A good timid Nazi," said Cassidy, "is like fairies at the bottom of the garden."

Alison was feeling under the table. "You sure this place is okay...."

"Nobody would bug the Spumi. I'm the most important person who's ever eaten here, and you know how important that is."

"It wasn't a rattrap, Horatio. I promise you. Just a little fishing expedition. We've got to throw a little bread on the water to lure these cookies out into the open sea."

"The little bread on the water is a twelve-year-old girl who is under my protection. Jefferson Lee now has the whole setup, the keys...."

"Change the locks."

"I've already changed the locks—but he knows where everything is, the Contessa, the Principessa, me. He knows the building, the procedures. I ought to go to MacGregor with the whole story. In the present climate of opinion you'd get dumped on your capacious ass."

Alison went cold as a dead fish. Cassidy didn't like it. You could push Alison only so far. Then he got dangerous.

"What do you want, Horatio?" said Alison coldly.

Cassidy smiled his biggest Irish smile and turned on all the charm. His answer was was so unexpected Alison's mouth fell open—just like in the movies. "I want an art expert—and I know you got some over there. I want an art expert dressed up as a locksmith delivered at my front door no later than next Tuesday."

Cassidy walked to Flame Street, a longish walk from Thirteenth, down Sixth Avenue crossing Eighth Street, then kitty corner into the jumble of streets at Christopher. Very good exercise not only for himself but for his tail whoever that was. He'd picked up a tail when he left the Spumi. Or maybe had him all day and hadn't spotted him.

Alison had jumped into a taxi, and Cassidy had walked down Sixth, window-shopping, trying to get a glimpse in the glass. Whoever it was, he was very good. Time and again Cassidy caught a movement, but that was all he caught—not a frame or a face. He tried all the tricks—stopping, ducking into arcades and out the other end, circling around the block. He didn't want to lose the tail; he wanted to nail the tail—if only to belt him one for trashing his flat. (If it was the same guy.)

At Rucker Street, Cassidy ducked into a drugstore and jumped quickly into the phone booth. The sensible thing for the tail to do in these circumstances was to wait, if it took three days. But Cassidy counted on the man's ignorance of the terrain. He'd have to come in to find out if there were a rear entrance.

It wasn't a he, it was a she—a small, dark girl with huge black glasses. She saw his glance and shot out of the drugstore like a rabbit.

Titi.

"Don't apologize," said Fingertips, smiling his cherubic Peter Lorre smile when Cassidy arrived very late at Ariadne's. "I have been sitting here quite pleasantly, wondering what it's all about. I mean life itself. Do you ever wonder what it is all about, Cassidy?"

"Not unless I'm paid," said Cassidy. "Have you got the stuff?"

"Yes, and very boring," said Fingertips. He laid the envelope in Cassidy's hand. It was so dark in the Ariadne people had to feel for each other even when they sat next to one another. "Elsa is the only contemporary Schoon to reproduce. The brother, no children; the sister, no children. Cousins, aunts, uncles—no kids. It looks like the end of the line for the Schoons."

"Does Elsa ever see her brother—or sister?"

"Never."

"Why?"

Fingertips smiled gently and sipped his wine: "They are a very conservative old Dutch family you know. I gather they find Elsa a bit gamey, a bit flashy."

116 ·

"Aaah," said Cassidy.

"That's why I like you, Cassidy, because you say Aaah like that. Nobody says Aaah any more. It's very nineteenth century. That Aaah."

"I'm a very nineteenth-century guy. How about your Rome man? Did he come up with anything?"

"Too much. It's all in the envelope. Very, very entertaining—if you're looking for entertainment. Also very unreliable."

Cassidy tossed down his Wild Turkey: "I've got another small assignment for the Rome man. Elsa di Castiglione is in Rome. I want to know who she's seeing there."

"And what they're talking about, I suppose."

"It would be nice to know that too, but I'll settle for just who." He handed Fingertips the little package from his breast pocket. "A little present," said Cassidy. "Don't sniff it all at once. It'll blow your head off."

·20·

"The Principessa would like to see you," said Lorenzo. He was polishing the great silver and gold meat tray, which was large enough for half a cow.

"She's back?" said Cassidy. "Since when?"

"In the conservatory," said Lorenzo, ducking the question.

The Principessa was snipping dead leaves, standing as always very straight, slim as a pencil. She was in a pale pink blouse over which she wore a heavily textured vest of pure gold and around her slender bottom a dove gray skirt with huge pockets and lots of pleats. All of it tidy as a bowstring. Her pale gold hair had been cut in a new way, close to her skull, giving her a boyish look. It made her extraordinary eyes even bigger.

The first meeting since bed.

"Nice trip?" inquired Cassidy.

"Not very," said the Principessa. She looked at him through eyelashes too long to be quite real. "Haven't you another suit, Professor?"

"What's the matter with this one?"

"Everything. You're to take us to lunch at the Windletop Club. I was hoping we might clean you up a bit for public display.":

"Many have tried, Madame."

"You look like an abandoned warehouse, Professor." Snip. Snip. It was a stunning arrangement of colors—her pale gold hair, violet eyes, and the deep green of the foliage. "It doesn't matter. We can place you at the window against the light where no one can see you."

"Under the table might be even better," said Cassidy. "Might I ask, Madame, why I am to be given the great honor of accompanying the Contessa and the Principessa to lunch?"

"Must I have a reason for everything, Professor?"

"You always do, Madame?"

The Principessa smiled: "I had no idea my life was so structured, Professor. I've been called a butterfly."

"They don't know you as well as I do."

She rebuked him with her eyes for that one. "Some of them do, Professor," she said very distinctly. Snip. Snip. "Actually, there *is* a reason."

I thought so, said Cassidy. Not aloud.

"I thought you might—during lunch—in the intervals of what I devoutly hope...."

Snip. Snip.

"...will be exquisitely amusing conversation...study the restaurant for security reasons. I'm thinking about my party."

Cassidy put his hands behind his head, walked to the window and stared out, rocking on his heels. *The Lights Are Going Out All Over Europe, said the Foreign Minister:* Who was it who played that part? Not Paul Muni. He let her wait for it. She was snipping away.

"I think the party should be called off."

Snip. Snip. Long pause.

"Why?"

Cassidy wheeled on his heels and faced her solemnly: "Because it has attracted too much attention. Stories in the *Post* and the *Times.* Now they're all doing it. Fenella de Hartung has called it The Party of the Year in her column."

"Fenella de Hartung is a cretin." Snip. Snip. "The same mildewed people—all of us getting a little more so—doing the same things, and *saying* the same things, as at a hundred other parties. Only the clothes have been changed to protect the innocent—as if there were any."

Snip. Snip. She didn't look at him.

"This party would have been harmless if it had taken place like all your other parties, as a sort of fashionable get-together known only to the insiders on the chic scene—or even the outsiders. It's got way beyond that. The publicity has made you and your party a very inviting target—the very symbol of bourgeois decadence."

He couldn't have selected a worse combination of words: "Decadent, perhaps," snapped the Principessa. "Bourgeois *never!*"

A mistake, Cassidy swiftly saw, and one that could hardly be rectified by any more arguments along that line. There were much deeper arguments for abandoning the party. A power hungry Number 2 man who needed a boost in the hierarchy and was throwing a little bread on the waters to get it (and never mind who got hurt). He might have told her about Alison and about Jefferson Lee, and later—in *The Legend of the di Castigliones, Annotated*—Cassidy admitted he'd made a great mistake. It was the *only* argument that would have swayed her at this point, and he should have used it. He didn't because there were powerful reasons for not telling the amateurs what the professionals were doing. The professionals were a race apart, and many of their concerns and their activities were almost unexplainable to the amateurs. There were very great precedents for silence. In almost every case in which candor had been attempted, disaster had followed.

It wasn't discipline, Cassidy was to write later, that kept him silent. It was bad habit.

Snip. Snip. The Principessa's exasperation had vanished, and she was again radiant.

"Do wash your hands, Professor, like a good boy."

The Windletop Club was rarely crowded, which was part of its panache. Usually ten servitors were in evidence to every club member. Bartenders waited at the empty bar, waiters stood expectantly in a restaurant almost devoid of diners.

Lucia was wearing a red velvet dress with gold buttons, looking Victorian and demure, unlike her nursery appearance. Her face had been scrubbed pink, and she was very subdued.

"I feel threadbare," said Cassidy.

"I'm overjoyed to hear it," said the Principessa. "Hurry along. We don't want to display you any longer than necessary."

The rooftop restaurant was unusually full of beautifully dressed club members, engaging in the ritual of lunch in which food played the smallest role. The important thing was how you looked and how the people around you looked and who they were with and who *you* were with. And why? And did her husband know?

The tables were covered with heavy pink linen tablecloths, bright with flowers, and awash with silver, glasses, the club's own red and white bone china and, on one of those plates, butter in round serrated balls resting on ice. Busboys poured water and dreamed of being waiters—perhaps even authors.

"Not the usual table, Robert," said the Principessa. "*That* one by the window. We're trying to keep the Professor out of sight."

Robert placed Cassidy in front of the plate-glass window, his back to Manhattan, a good place to study the diners. They all looked rich and harmless, but then that was the new technique among terrorists—dress well and look intensely bourgeois.

The Principessa was studying the menu, an enormous one written in French and printed in huge block type. "Lucia, you must have the trout. You look low on iodine."

"I'd rather have the child's menu, Mama. You get crayons with the hamburger, don't you Robert?"

Crayons, Cassidy was thinking. Sometimes Lucia acted six. Sometimes sixty.

"Robert, might Lucia have crayons with the trout?"

"Certainly, Madame."

Lucia looked mutinous: "And Captain Marvel, too, Robert."

"Captain Marvel!" The Principessa's voice fluted with astonishment.

"You get to color Captain Marvel whatever you choose."

"Coloring Captain Marvel! At twelve!" Deep in the menu, the Principessa threw the line away.

"It's for Titi, Mama," Lucia was not going to let her mother get away with throwaway lines.

"Even less excuse for Titi. She's eighteen."

Titi coloring Captain Marvel, Cassidy was thinking, was a very droll idea. More likely to play Captain Marvel.

"No one knows how old Titi is," said Lucia.

"Eighteen," said the Principessa. "I can tell by her teeth. Professor, what is your thinking about lunch?"

Cassidy rubbed his nose plaintively: "If you're ordering for all of us, Madame, I'm deficient in magnesium, zinc, and most of the lesser metals—lithium, for example."

The Principessa's gaze shifted from the menu to Cassidy but her tone of detached irony didn't change a bit. "*Omlette aux fines herbes* for the Professor, Robert—and throw in any magnesium, zinc, and lesser metals that happen to be around the kitchen."

"Yes, Principessa."

"And for me, spinach—the usual way."

Robert picked up the menus and handed them to the floor waiter. He took the wine menu from the captain—the table teemed with servitors as befitted a princess—and handed it to the Principessa. Just here the Principessa became very feminine and old world and handed the wine card to Cassidy. Cassidy didn't even open it. He handed it straight back to Robert, barking: "Château Montrachet, Robert. Only wine in the world that goes with spinach."

Spinach. No wonder she looked like a pencil.

"Spinach abounds in metals, Professor," said the Principessa demurely. "It adds steel to one's determination."

As if you need any more of that, said Cassidy to himself. He couldn't say things like that aloud in front of Lucia.

Lucia had detached herself from the conversation. She was gazing over Cassidy's head out the window at the Empire State Building shimmering in the distance, mouth agape, deep in her secret child's glee where adults couldn't follow. She loved restaurants, Cassidy guessed, loved every minute outside the apartment.

Cassidy fell to counting the exits. The one nearest them led to the kitchen; another on the highest bank led to a small garden with flagstone paths, green plants, and a countrified air (fifty-five stories up) for those who wished to take the air (few did, though the little garden cost a bundle to maintain). Straight ahead of him was the small landing where Robert held forth—and that led to the elevator which brought the guests up from the street. There was a service elevator next to the kitchens that complicated Cassidy's problems unbearably.

"This place will be dangerous no matter what we do the night of your party," said Cassidy.

"I'll tell the guests," said the Principessa brightly. "It'll add a little spice to the affair which, God knows, needs something like that. It's gone on a little too long—the di Castiglione party."

"If that's the case, why not call it off?"

The Principessa turned the full candlepower of her violet eyes on him reproachfully as if he'd emitted a bad smell: "How can you even suggest such a thing, Professor? Call my friends and tell them not to come to my party! Why, they would inquire? And what should I say to that—that I am a coward? That I've gone senile? That I have succumbed to your irrational fears that something *might* happen when, quite clearly, it is far more likely it might *not*."

The violet eyes blazed with passion. Over a party! The gulf between them yawned like the Grand Canyon.

She was smiling mockingly at him now: "We decadent bourgeois cannot abandon a party simply because revolutionaries are underfoot. We are chained to behavior patterns as fixed and changeless as the mating habits of fish, Professor, and to *us* just as important."

Blowing her trumpet defiantly for this idiotic party, as if civilization itself were at stake, as indeed *her* civilization was. If you took away the parties, the gathering together of the international rich to celebrate their uniqueness, their glitter, their charm, then you didn't leave them very much. Cassidy doubted the Principessa had thought this through exactly in those terms. She was reacting instinctively, spreading her feathers in the only way nature would permit her. Cassidy felt a sinking in his spirits. If the revolutionaries studied Marighela— and they studied Marighela like scriptures—they would certainly zero in on this fixed incapacity of the international aristocracy of the rich to change its habits—and make its plans accordingly.

"My dear Professor," the Principessa was nibbling on her spinach delicately, imbibing iron for her soul, "my freinds are coming from London, Paris, Rome, Brazil. They've already ordered their *shoes* for my party."

"Their shoes!" said Cassidy hopelessly. "Their *shoes*!"

"You didn't think they were coming barefoot," said the Principessa.

Cassidy tucked into his *omelette aux fine herbes* and sipped the Montrachet. Lucia and the Principessa were chattering in Italian, Lucia's little hands waving gracefully in the air. Her personality changed altogether when she spoke Italian. She became European—deeper, older, more cultivated. In the American language she was a tomboy; In Italian she was all female. Also she was closer to her mother. He felt out of it.

"We're discussing Mr. Struthers," said the Principessa. "The reason we're talking Italian is because Lucia...."

"*Mama!*" wailed Lucia.

"...thinks you're sexually naive."

"Which one is Mr. Struthers?" asked Cassidy.

The Principessa leveled her eyelashes at a boney, hawk-faced, white-haired man who lunched alone three tables away at the window.

"Professor! You're *staring*!" said Lucia. "It's *rude*!"

Cassidy was remembering that it was on Struthers floor, the thirty-ninth, he'd encountered Hugo Dorn, the Good Nazi. Well! Well!

"You are *staring*," commented the Principessa. "Do you know Mr. Struthers?"

"A nodding acquaintanceship," said Cassidy. "Many years ago."

When his name wasn't Struthers.

As Fingertips had said, the Fabrizio material was gamey and there was an enormous amount of it. Cassidy read it all swiftly, picking, choosing, putting some bits aside, underlined for later study, making his own judgments. He was in his pajamas on the bed at midnight.

> Elsa has been pictured as a grasping scheming divorcee only interested in becoming a Principessa. Or as an adventuress madly in love with Nicki who was the most beautiful man in Rome. Or as a nymphomaniac who needed an indulgent husband to condone and conceal her lusts...she was none of these really. I knew her very well. She was almost a mother to Nicki, taking care of him—and God knows he needed taking care of—trying to keep him out of trouble and out of the headlines....

Fabrizzio had got that from an English lady of advanced years (and somehow credibility increased with age in gossip like this) who had known the di Castigliones very well.

Now why do I pick that bit out, thought Cassidy, examining

his motives. It clashes with almost every other bit of information about Elsa. Is it because I want to believe it? Or is it because it fits the facts better than other more lurid, more sexual, more accepted, gossip about Elsa. Because it was a difficult mosaic to fit together. Why had this Prince of depraved habits married a woman much older than himself and comparatively penniless?

His father Augusto was an even bigger swinger than Nicki, one of the great hell raisers of the early 1900s. It was said that Nicki was always trying to overtake his father's reputation for depravity and that he'd never manage it.

Fabrizio had crammed in every last bit of gossip. He'd got some out of the papers and much of it from friends who didn't know they were being interviewed, who thought the conversation was just private gossip mongering and who had therefore opened up with all they knew. Which didn't make it any more reliable.

Cassidy read on for an hour.

The whisper now all over Rome is that the Mafia infiltrated the kidnapping and made off with the money. This is so popular a theory that I wonder about it. Next year there will probably be another rumor. The new twist is that one man ran off with all the money, and now the Mafia is looking for him because he was their man....

Cassidy turned out the light. His head was beginning to split with the possibilities.

She slipped into his room that night just after 2 A.M. when she returned from whatever party she'd been to. This time Cassidy didn't reach for the gun. Even half awake in the blackness, he recognized the rustlings, the faint feminine exhalations.

"This is to become a regular thing then, Principessa?" A whisper so as not to wake Lucia—or anyone.

"Why not?" The voice light as a moth.

"*Droit de Principessa?*"

"You have a nasty tongue, Professor."

She was climbing into his bed as she said it, the voice husky with lust which she made no effort to conceal.

"Principessa,..." emitted Cassidy pushing at the naked body feebly. A token protest in the name of his integrity.

"Let's fuck, Professor. We can talk later."

Same line. Cassidy wondered if she used it on all her lovers.

This time it was very different from the first time. Then it had been subtle and delicate, full of touchings and nuances. This time—total abandon; panting and exertion and little choked cries. To his chagrin, Cassidy found himself this time participating more than he wished. Also wishing more than he wished to wish, desiring more than he desired to desire. The Principessa was a force of nature devoid of taboos.

Except one.

Afterward they lay in silence uncovered. Cassidy had an urge to see the Principessa's body naked and unadorned. He reached for the bedside table. Quck as a fox, she grasped his arm and pulled it away.

"Never!" Exploding like a champagne cork.

"Afraid, Madame? Of what?"

"The light, Professor."

She was out of bed now, putting on whatever she had taken off.

Swiftly.

"You're very expert at dressing in the dark." He was as affronted by her swift abandonment as by her uninvited assault. "How do you manage?"

"Practice," said the Principessa. "*Auf wiedersehen,* Horatio."

She was gone.

Horatio.

We're on a first name basis, thought Horatio P. Cassidy. Next thing you know we'll be exchanging recipes.

She came every night. Always after dining out or partying or whatever she did on her ceaseless social round. Each visitation Cassidy greeted with a fresh mockery, feeling that, if he didn't, her very identity would be permanently altered.

"Why don't you invite your escort in for a drink," he'd say as the silken rustlings of her discarded clothes pierced the darkness. "He could *listen.* That's the latest thing—listening."

"Let's fuck, Horatio. We can talk later."

Always the same line. But there was precious little talk later. After a brief exchange, all of it barbed, she left.

"I feel like the male spider," he said *sotto voce*, always mindful of Lucia. "Having fulfilled my function, I expect one day you'll eat me."

Her response was immediate. She bit him.

"Ouch!"

"You taste," all the time slipping out of bed and into her clothes, "like a lapsed Catholic. Bitter."

The mockery was brazen on both sides.

"You'll find a little something in an envelope on the mantelpiece," he said once.

"The other girls at the nunnery say you very stingy, Signor," she said, taking him up on it. "Good lay, lousy pay—they say."

Time and again he tried to turn on the light. For the pleasure of her panic. The only thing that panicked her. Each time she grabbed his arm in a surprisingly iron grip and stopped him.

"There are certain sights a woman of sensibility should be spared," she hissed at him once. "One of them—you."

He accused her of shameless class distinction. "It's all right to fuck the lower classes. To let them see you naked might give us ideas above our station."

"All your ideas are above your station, Horatio."

Always Horatio. In the dark.

·21·

In the daylight, their relationship and their speech was rigorously correct. She summoned him along with Lorenzo to the foot of her bed, as she breakfasted, to confer about The Party, as it was now capitalized not only in the newspapers but in their own minds. Everything now centered on The Party. All other considerations, including Lucia's education, were secondary.

The newspapers called every day and were turned over to Cassidy who said the Principessa was out and he knew nothing. Click. When inadvertently the Principessa found herself on the telephone with a reporter, she forgot all her English and lapsed into Italian. Fishwife Italian.

Over party policy they clashed sharply. Cassidy wanted to stay in the apartment with the Contessa during the festivities. The Principessa wanted him upstairs to keep an eye on things.

"The target," said Cassidy, "is the Contessa. I don't give a damn if they kidnap all the 225 guests."

"How about me?" inquired the Principessa.

"Your ransom potential is zero, you said yourself."

"You don't think Lucia will be safe behind all those steel doors you put in at such vast expense?"

"No."

Lucia settled this one by announcing flatly that she intended to go the The Party. "I'm twelve years old, and I've never been to one of your parties. I can sleep all next day."

"Did you put her up to this, Professor?"

"Lucia is quite capable of reaching these decisions by herself."

The Principessa assented to this, largely because it settled where Cassidy should be stationed—at the rooftop restaurant.

The locksmith came unexpectedly one morning when the Principessa was still asleep, ushered in by Lorenzo.

"He says you sent for him, Signor," said Lorenzo reproachfully. "I told him we have already changed the locks once."

"This locksmith is simply to check the work of the other locksmith—a routine precaution in high security, Lorenzo."

There was no such routine precaution in high security, but Cassidy hoped the old man wouldn't know about such things. Lorenzo looked doubtful and retreated to his pantry, muttering in Italian under his breath.

"Abadu," said the locksmith—the agreed word—if it was a word.

"Yeah," said Cassidy. He took him down the corridor, keeping an eye out for Titi. Or Lucia.

"If someone comes, just make for a lock—any lock."

"I know."

First, Cassidy showed him the Tintoretto in the library—Helen and the golden apple she'd won in fair fight. The art expert disguised as a locksmith took less than thirty seconds. He shook his head.

The portrait of Pope Constant in the corridor took a little longer—three minutes. The Fragonard took five minutes. The Titian a minute and a half. After each examination, the art expert whose name was Stamm shook his head.

"You're sure?" asked Cassidy.

"Absolutely. They're not even very good fakes. You can do much better than that. Good fakes need X rays. Not these."

Good enough to fool clucks like me, thought Cassidy. Or the Principessa?

Meanwhile, there was Lucia. She had developed suspicions. Or perhaps, thought Cassidy, it is I who suspect her of suspicions. My guilt about a relationship with her mother that is totally concealed. At least I *think* totally concealed. Who knows what a child knows. Always a dark brooding child, Lucia had become more open under his teaching, more American, less European. Recently she had reverted to her brooding, her Europeanness. Her dark eyes constantly searched Cassidy's these days for...what? Did she suspect? Or am I making it all up?

Guilt, thought Cassidy, who didn't believe in guilt.

That day he tried to slip out of the apartment because Alison had dispatched another letter to the tree drop. He found Lucia standing beside the steel gates in the no-longer fuchsia foyer.

"I'm going with you," she announced darkly. "You're neglecting my education."

Cassidy rang for the elevator: "I never thought I would live to hear a twelve-year-old girl complain about *that*."

She faced the elevator glumly: "One day I'm going to have to be an adult and have immense responsibility on my shoulders, and I must be trained to exercise them. Your very words."

Coming home to roost, thought Cassidy. A teacher is a time bomb. Who knows when his words will blow up in his face?

In the park, she guessed instantly. "We're going to that same tree. I'll race you."

"Jupiter Jehoshaphat," yelled Cassidy. "No!"

Because she was faster than he was. She was off already, swift as a deer, Cassidy puffing along behind. She beat him to the tree by ten feet and got the letter out of the hole. He rescued it before she could open it and thrust it into his inside jacket pocket, panting indignantly: "You shouldn't read other people's mail."

"Who's it from?"

"My girl friend."

"You're too old to have a girl friend. Your *woman* friend."

Anyone over eighteen was middle-aged to Lucia. The Professor was older than middle age, older than antiquity. She sat on the grass, knees pulled up to her chin, solemn as a catacomb.

"Why didn't you ever have any children, Professor?"

"I never had time." An inadequate explanation.

"I don't think you like children."

"You're groveling for sympathy."

She was not to be deterred. "I don't think *anyone* likes children very much. They just have them because they make love, and they can't avoid it."

"There are many ways to avoid it."

"Well then, they have children because they think they want them and when they arrive, they don't want them. Or anyway, they don't want the ones they get."

This was becoming a Freudian nightmare. "If you feel unwanted, Lucia, just come out and say so."

130 ·

Passionately. "All children feel unwanted."

"That's a little sweeping: Any sentence that starts—*all* children, *all* men, *all* women, is immature."

"I'm only twelve!" she blazed. "Do you expect maturity?"

"Yes," said Cassidy calmly, "I do."

For some reason, that remark pleased Lucia to her very bottom. She smiled a secret smile, as if she'd been fishing for just that remark and had got it. "How nice!" she said. "You really are the most marvelous man, Professor, because you don't treat me like a child. Not ever!"

"That's because I don't know how to treat a child," cried Cassidy. "Because, if you must know, you're the first child I ever had any dealings with. Come on, I've got things to do."

"Wait," she begged. "Just a *little* while." They sat awhile, listening to the birds.

"Have you got your gun, Professor. Let's fire it. Can I fire it? Please? You always said I should learn to defend myself."

She never forgot anything he said, and whenever she could she turned it against him. Lately he'd been teaching her a little basic Kung Fu. Weaponry? He was against it on principle. Certainly for a child. The trouble was this affair was beginning to shape up very badly. So many imponderables, and so many forces at work, all pulling in different directions. In the middle of it all—Lucia. If she wasn't rich, she wouldn't be in this predicament, wouldn't be a prisoner in her own apartment, wouldn't be sitting there with him. Victimized by her own money.

Cassidy peered about him. They were deep in the park, in the northernmost third of it which was the wildest bit, screened by heavy bushes and trees, an area shunned even by rapists. "It's very much against the law," said Cassidy. Nevertheless, he pulled out the silenced .22. It lay in the palm of his hand, ominous as evil. She stared at it, fascinated and a little scared.

"Very, very dangerous," said Cassidy. "You are never to use a gun except in the most dire emergency, Lucia."

"What is a dire emergency?"

"You'll know," said Cassidy gloomily, "when it comes."

He explained about the gun, the safety, the loading clip, the trigger.

"Roll over on your stomach. Now line up the rear sight and

the front sight on that big tree. Aim dead center."

"How can I miss a tree that big?" said Lucia squinting down the barrel.

"That's why I picked out a big one. So you don't miss. Otherwise you could kill a bystander on Central Park West. Now squeeze—slowly, slowly, slowly...."

She hit the tree dead center.

"Kill or be killed," said Cassidy savagely, almost to himself. "An idea whose time has come—if it ever went away. I hate it! But I don't know what to do about it." Arguing with himself. "I'm in a quandary. I don't know whether what I'm doing is right or wrong." Talking to himself. Lucia staring at him as if he were demented. He leaned over her and slipped on the safety catch. With the .22 in his hand he walked to the tree and with his knife marked it at head level, shoulder level, crotch level—using his own dimensions as a model. In the upper third where the heart would be he slashed an X.

"When danger looms," said Cassidy, playing *Hamlet* now. Even with Lucia there, it was still a soliloquy.

"What danger?"

"You'll know—when it comes. And when it does, hit the ground! Don't wait for anyone to tell you to hit the ground! Hit it! Go flat as you are now! Aim where I put that X."

"The *heart*!" said Lucia gleefully.

"Yeah." Handing her the gun. "Hold it in both hands—that's right, just like Kojak. Aim! Steady! Squeeze! Slowly! Slowly!"

She hit the X first try.

"Now roll—arms outstretched—with gun in them. Roll."

"I'll get my fall coat filthy. Titi will be furious."

"Never mind Titi. Roll! Now fire!"

Under Cassidy's tutelage she squeezed off nine shots, rolling after each one, and achieving a quite respectable score.

Her accuracy should have pleased him; instead it filled him with foreboding. Cassidy didn't believe in God, but no Irishman has ever successfully extricated himself altogether from demonology. The fates had a terrible way of reversing a man's precautions so that in place of protecting you, they hit you in the face, he thought.

·22·

"Golly," said Lucia.

The apartment was as he'd left it—books helter-skelter on the floor, mattress ripped open, screaming disorder. "I like the place to look lived in," said Cassidy.

"Oogh!" Lucia had discovered the moving stepladder that ran around the bookshelves. She pushed it the length of the room standing on the bottom rung, using it like a scooter, after which she ran up it like a monkey. On the top rung she sat down and picked up a book.

"*This Plundered Planet,*" she called down to Cassidy who was heading into the bathroom where he could read Alison's letter in peace.

"Very good book," said Cassidy. "Read it."

He locked the bathroom door and dug out the code book from the little floor safe underneath the bathtub. Decoded, Alison's message was brief: Fourteen man combat team RAF RW RA trained Iraq mockup patterned windletop in Amsterdam believed emplaning next week usa where from knows nobody apple.

RAF meant red army faction from Germany. Very bad news because they were very efficient. RW was the Red Wind from Italy who were so good they were believed not to be Italian at all. RA was the Red Army from Japan, also very hot commandos at terror operation. As for the *where from knows nobody*, Cassidy took the liberty of doubting it. If they had that much information, they probably had the rest of it, too. So why didn't they stop the operation in its tracks? Because they didn't want to stop it in its tracks is why. An ambitious man at Langley needed a little shootout to increase his prestige, enlarge the office staff, and perhaps jump up a step on the slippery ladder of Langley.

On the other hand—if he wanted it to happen, why was he warning Cassidy at all? Because Alsion didn't dare not do *something*, that's why. If there were a later investigation, he needed a little communication on file—and God knows this was little enough. Enough to scare you half to death and not enough to go on. No names, no guesses as to method. Nothing.

Cassidy deposited Lucia on a bar stool at the Spumi, Henry wailing: "You know it's against regulations, Cassidy. She ain't eighteen."

"Actually she's twenty-six," said Cassidy reaching for the bar phone. "She looks that way because she's a Contessa. This is Henry, Lucia, a Teuton knight who has been unhorsed." Dialing all the while.

Alison answered with a simple: "Yes."

"I'm very unhappy with this message, Apple."

"Gung ho," said Alison—and rang off.

Cassidy was left with a dead telephone in his hand at which he scowled as if it was its fault. Gung ho meant action stations which was very serious indeed. Or it meant he had somebody there and couldn't talk. Or it meant only that Alison didn't want to be bothered and was throwing sand in his eyes.

"Your woman hung up on you," guessed Lucia. "Oho!"

"His woman don't hang up on him." said Henry. "He hangs up on her. Sophy was in last week. She's broke. Some fellow ran off with her purse on 42nd Street."

"What was she doing on 42nd Street?"

"Seeing *Deep Throat*. She says it reminds her of you. Sophy says she's the only one who goes to *Deep Throat* and cries."

"She read it somewhere," said Cassidy exasperated. "Give her some money, Henry."

"I already gave her some money."

"Put it on the bill."

"I already did."

"You're a good friend, Henry—with a keen sense of double entry bookkeeping."

"Can I have a Coke?" asked Lucia.

"By all means," said Cassidy rubbing his hands over his face. "Give her a Coke, please, Henry."

The Red Army faction were the only ones with skyscraper

experience. They could take the Windletop if they wanted it. Why did they want to? Because it was there. That was such a comfortable theory that Cassidy doubted it very much. There were other darker forces at work here. Somebody wanted him to think—or everyone to think—that this was an ordinary terror operation. But it wasn't all that simple. In fact, it was so complicated it was beginning to give Cassidy a severe headache.

It was Marlborough who was first to sidestep the fortresses (which the French had made close to impregnable) and take the cities. You don't have to assault the fortresses, said Marlborough very sensibly. Capture the cities and let the fortresses rot. Fortresses hadn't amounted to much since Marlborough's day, including the Maginot Line. Now people were thinking in fortress terms again. Lunacy. There was no ideological sense in assaulting a fortress when all you wanted was headlines. Or cash—both available elsewhere. There was no point in assaulting the Windletop unless that wasn't the point at all, unless there was something else they wanted, and the ideology was just a smoke screen.

He led Lucia out of the Spumi and into a taxicab and gave the address of the Windletop.

"Back to prison," snarled Lucia.

"We all have our prisons," said Cassidy. "Your's is no worse than most."

"Oh, yes it is," cried Lucia. "You don't know!"

No, thought Cassidy. He didn't, but he was trying, against a very great pressure of time, to find out. He deposited Lucia in the hands of her fencing teacher, each exceedingly reluctant to share the other's company—and slipped out.

The Gypper had been waiting at the Ariadne for a very long time and the ruddiness of his face showed it. "How many have you had?" growled Cassidy.

"Aah, here comes Mary Poppins now," said the Gypper in his teddibly British accent. "We're conducting a temperance crusade, are we? The nursery has had a deplorable effect on your tolerance, dear boy."

"Stuff it, you bloody Limey," said Cassidy feeling, as always in the Gypper's presence, a glow of fellowship that warmed his bitter heart. His relationship with the Gypper, which stretched over thirty years, was one of those obsolete friendships of the old-fashioned sort, not relevant to modern life—at least not in Manhattan. ("We waste each other's time," the Gypper used to say cheerfully, "neither of us furthering the other's career by so much as a hairsbreadth.")

"Give this nurseryman a slosh of Wild Turkey," said the Gypper to the bartender. "Tell me about life among the twelve-year-old set. What are you teaching the poor child?"

"Decency, honor, loyalty, integrity," said Cassidy, studying the bourbon in his glass.

"God save the mark," murmured the Gypper. "You'll ruin the child for all practical purposes."

"What luck did you have?" asked Cassidy.

"Not much. She lost me so professionally that I'm very curious to know who taught her that trick. One minute we were going together—me fifty steps behind—but well in view, down the inside pathway to the Park. The next minute she'd vanished from the face of the earth. A very good trick. I would like to know it."

Cassidy was neither surprised nor displeased. "Tell me exactly where?" A map of the park he'd squirreled out of the Park Department was spread out on the bar. "This is Fifth Avenue and here is the Seventy-second Street entrance. Now just where?"

The Gypper pointed to the spot and Cassidy drew an X there. "You sure you had the right girl?"

"I took a few pictures for your collection." He handed them over. Titi all right—without her scarf and with big glasses, unmistakably her—striding along under the falling brown leaves of Central Park.

"That's her," said Cassidy. "How about the prints I gave you?"

"Zilch," said the Gypper. "Whatever transgressions she's committed—and I'm willing to bet she's committed a few—she's kept out of sight of the FBI and the police. She's got no record at all. Why don't you get the Principessa to fire her?"

"Because I haven't a thing on her except my suspicions. I was hoping you might come up with something I could lay on her."

"Sorry, old boy. Perhaps next time...."

"We've run out of time. The party is three days away. Titi won't have another day off before then."

"Then I most earnestly advise you to keep a sharp eye on the lady," said the Gypper.

Back in his room, Cassidy read for an hour from the book he'd got out of the library that very day, *The World Beneath The City*, "where you will find sewers, stores and subways, men, mains and even alligators." One of the first things he encountered in the book was the dismaying news (he'd rather suspected) that there was nothing resembling a master map of underground New York. There were thousands of specialist maps showing where the telephone wires, the TV cables, the subways, the water mains, and the steam pipes were, but he didn't have time to peruse that many maps even if he could find them.

Fascinating stuff, but it didn't solve his problem and it was twenty years out of date. The Subterranean New York changed every year, sometimes drastically, and always for the worse. Cassidy turned out the light.

He was awakened in the darkness by the familiar rustlings of silk mixed with the faint whisper of her breath.

Mockery and lust, mockery and lust
Go together like ashes and dust.
This time, no.

She was in bed with him naked as a Botticelli, but her opening line—Let's-fuck-We-can-talk-later—was missing. In its place, a kiss. *Tendresse*, reluctant on both sides, crept into the embrace, perhaps because of the darkness and the lateness of the hour. Their bodies assumed the usual postures with the sweetness and—yes, softness—of familiarity. The embrace contained a certain *tristesse*, in place of the usual expertise. The Principessa was not altogether in control of that supple body as always before she had been.

When it was all over, she sighed, as if dying. Not her style at all.

No words passed.

Emotionally devastating, Cassidy found it. He lay back on the pillow, uncertain how to procede under this new circumstance.

He raised his arm toward the lamp anticipating her iron grip, her fierce resistance. There was none. No response at all. He hesitated because he was going into new territory here. The rules had changed with this new . . . situation. In the end he had to force himself—and it took some doing—to turn on the light because it was the next move in their unceasing chess game and it had to come some time. Therefore. . . .

The Principessa was asleep, an unprecedented surrender.

It was a face he'd never seen before. She lay in the pool of yellow light wrinkled, vulnerable, as old as the earth. She's as old as I am, thought Cassidy, older; he found that touching. The steel in her had been washed away by slumber. In sleep she looked forlorn and lost, a little girl grown old, now even—and this he found shocking—beautiful.

He gazed four seconds too long.

The Principessa awoke. A shattering experience.

The violet eyes flew open, luminous with outrage, as if he, Cassidy, had perpetrated a deed so base as to be mentioned only in whispers till the end of time.

"*You* . . . bastard!" she said, spinning the *You* into a long throbbing curse.

This was followed by a most extraordinary sight. The Principessa reassembled her features into youth—well, absence of age, at any rate—and beauty. By sheer force of character, wrinkles and weariness were banished. By titanic will power, the Principessa *assumed* beauty, adorning herself with it, as if it were her prerogative, donning it like raiment. All in a magical moment.

Then—aaah, then—the face contorted with hatred, beautiful but malignant. Now she was the Witch of Endor.

She opened her mouth to utter the scream that would bring the household running—Lucia included. Cassidy closed the furious mouth with both strong hands while holding the flailing body in a scissorlock, and whispering into a most unwilling ear. "You cannot afford that scream. You are in the most awful peril of your useless life, Principessa!"

He couldn't tell her the whole story—even if he knew it—not with her struggling like that with her strong muscles, her white teeth, and her furious will.

With infinite reluctance, Cassidy played his top card: "She isn't your child, Elsa, and if you force the issue I'll have to tell her."

First time he'd ever called her Elsa.

The Principessa went limp as a dead fish. The furious face turned to stone, eyes forlorn and distant as stars.

Cassidy turned out the light.

A terrible minute went by.

The Principessa slipped out of his bed, into her clothes, and out of the room.

BOOK TWO
The Party

They came by Concorde, by private jet, in their own yachts, silent as snowfall—the Big Rich and the ordinary Not-Big-But-Old-Rich and some not at all rich but deeply established internationally, all of them as at home in Paris and New York and London as in Buenos Aires or Madrid or Athens. These were the people who always get out just before war. Or revolution. The money safely in Switzerland. Their homes, alas, temporarily occupied by the Nazis. Before that, Genghis Khan. Before that, the Visigoths.

Always. In the nick of time. These are the monied who remain monied, no matter what, temporarily inconvenienced by massacres and other social upheavals but not quite losing their heads. Somebody else's head rolls, perhaps even a cousin's, but not theirs, and they survive—slim, beautifully dressed, all knowing one another intimately....

"Darling Elsa...."

"Bibi, how very, very...."

"Have you seen Sacha? So awful *about Sacha!..."*

And so forth.

They were coming for Elsa's party which all of them had gone to for years. Once Nicki and Elsa's party. But then that terrible thing happened, never mind, it was all so long ago....

They came from Rome, Lisbon, Hong Kong, London, and They opened the New York flats which remained closed and empty eleven months of the year (but dusted and ready in case Paul came over for les affaires*). The moment they arrived they were on the phone to darling Gigi whom They haven't seen since Deauville August or to Bibi whom They haven't seen since Venice.*

"So much to tell you, darling! And how is Gerald? Not really! How perfectly ghastly!"

And so on.

The Party was three days away.

·23·

Cassidy was inspecting the doors of the rooftop restaurant starting with the big plexiglass one leading from the elevators to the entrance landing where the guests assembled to face Robert, the maitre d' with his lists and his scornful smile, standing behind the velvet cord which kept the unwashed in their proper place.

All except Cassidy who had the run of the place by order of Alfred the Great. Robert didn't like it, but there was absolutely nothing he could do about it.

"Let's go through the drill," said Cassidy gently. "Let's say someone pulls a gun...."

"We lock the door." As if explained to a child.

"With your foot," said Cassidy. Robert had hated to part with that information. That was his little secret—or had been his little secret—that foot-operated lock.

"Let's see you do it, Robert, just for the thrill of the thing "

Robert demonstrated. The inch-thick bolts shot into the four inch thick plexiglass door, bullet resistant, as they said now because few things were bulletproof 'Very impressive," said Cassidy. "What happens if someone gets off that elevator, all dressed up in his dinner jacket, well-shaven, and all that—and then pulls a gun and shoots you right through that scornful smile, Robert? What happens then? You fall down, all bloody and very dead, that's what. *Before* you get your foot on that thing."

That was the trouble with this drill. It would work fine against bank robbers or rapists or ordinary murderers but not against Carlos or Greta or any of the other more modern terrorists who simply blew away the man at the gate in what was once called cold blood. Even professional hit men were not quite so indifferent about mowing down the innocent and, in fact, the men with contracts on them were not at all innocent usually. There was a reason for killing them. For the terrorists it was reason enough if you got in the way. Blooie....

Cassidy went from the plexiglass door to another door to the left of the elevator—this one of steel and locked against all fire regulations.

"In case of fire, we unlock," said Robert frostily.

"Who's we—you and God?" asked Cassidy. "I want a key to this door, Robert, of my very own until after the night of the party. Then you and God can have sole access again. Let's look at the backstairs."

Same story there. The backstairs, which also served the Windletop, were next to the service elevator which brought up food and waiters from the outside world. The door was of steel and kept locked. "I want a key to this one, too."

"What do you want these keys for, Professor Cassidy," said Robert haughtily. "To let people in? Or out?"

"Maybe both," said Cassidy. "Would you mind opening the door?"

Robert minded very much, but he did as he was told. Cassidy gave him a wolfish smile and started down the steps, Robert watching with his fishy gaze. "Those doors are locked all the way to street level, Professor. Fifty-five stories down. A long walk."

Cassidy disappeared around the stairwell. After a moment he heard the clang of the steel door as it closed, locking automatically. Then there were only his footfalls echoing down the dismal gray stairwell, Cassidy thinking sad thoughts.

There had been no more nightly visits from the Principessa. He had never thought he would miss them, certainly not so badly as he did. Still, there it was. He missed his nightly carnality very very much, and what was one to make of that, eh?

Clomp. Clomp.

He felt guilty, himself a man who didn't believe in guilt. Especially over so trivial a matter. What did I do? I turned on the light. It was she who invaded my sanctum, raped me, seduced me, so why do I feel guilty? But he did. He'd blundered in where he had no business.

146 ·

The TV cameras were probably watching him, as he went down. But then the cameras were no threat to him any longer, so compliant was Hugo now that Cassidy had used the muscle. Clever Hugo. Giving out just enough information to stop the agony. But by no means all. Hugo, Cassidy was sure, had hoarded a bit for rainy days, for other perhaps more profitable betrayals.

At the thirty-ninth floor, Cassidy paused for a very long time, listening at the steel door. According to Hugo, none of Struthers pretty boys was in residence. If one trusted Hugo. Cassidy didn't.

He pulled out the set of gretchels, fifty of them which made an unsightly lump in his pocket. He selected one, A-25, and tried it on the lock. Too thick. He tried another; this time the steel stairwell door opened inward. Now he was on Struthers's private landing on the backstairs. The rear service elevator was to his right, Struthers's backdoor straight ahead. Cassidy strained his ears. Nothing. But then his ears weren't what they'd once been. Nothing was. Ears, legs, cock. Desuetude settling in all down the line.

Struthers's rear door lock was a very tough proposition. An Odheim from Germany, one of the best locks around. Cassidy selected the thinnest of gretchels and tried it. Too thin, too wide. He picked another. It was wrong too. Still another. Also wrong. It was ten minutes—it seemed hours—before the Odheim yielded. Cassidy stepped into Struthers's kitchen, pumping adrenalin. Perhaps he'd have to take this up for a living. The corridors of government were closed to him, the halls of academe almost shut. The Principessa could queer him forevermore as tutor to the well born. Cassidy grinned. The situation contained a certain desolate humor, no two ways about it.

All the while, listening, poised, ready to scuttle if there'd been a sound.

No sound. Struthers had no servants, except that bodyguard who was queer as a treeful of owls. Struthers trusted few people. In fact, no one. The bodyguard would be with Struthers. Wherever that was. Struthers went out very little and then with an excess of caution that made the rest of the folk at the Windletop seem positively reckless. And for good reason. His name wasn't Struthers.

Cassidy moved swiftly out of the kitchen. Now he was in a

long wide corridor—the layout wasn't all that much different from the Principessa's apartment—and he traversed it rapidly on tiptoe, catching glimpses through apertures of a sitting room heavy with walnut furniture, much of it carved into excruciatingly medieval corkscrew legs, claw feet, demons' faces on the knobs of chairs, all looking like the sort of furniture Henry VIII might have had. The apartment was bathed in a peculiar unhealthy light stemming from stained glass windows in improbable places—in interior doors, as well as exterior windows. Cassidy couldn't escape the feeling he was 100 feet underground rather than on the thirty-ninth floor.

The master bedroom was at the end of the corridor—a corner room like the Principessa's. This one had stained glass outside windows as well as inside windows, throwing splashes of purple, red, pink, and blue light all over the Bokkhara carpets. All very expensive and in what Cassidy thought perfectly awful taste—but that meant only it wasn't *his* taste. There was no such thing as good or bad taste, just different fashions at different times. This place would have been the last word in Milwaukee in 1905. Put into a super-efficient skyscraper apartment in Manhattan in the late 1970s it was very odd.

Also German. Not modern German, God knows. They went for the most contemporary art and architecture of all, a deliberate turning of the back on the past. No, this was old pre-World War II German, perhaps even earlier.

In the center of the room was a vast circular bed. In the ceiling of course, a mirror exactly as round as the bed. Also in the ceiling, heavy-duty hooks, strong enough to support a body or two. The whips would be around the place somewhere. All very interesting. Was this where Struthers entertained those beautiful young Swedish boys?

It was all out of key. Struthers hadn't looked capable of that sort of exercise. Anyway, it wasn't his thing. Cassidy was sure of that.

No time for speculation. Work to be done. Cassidy cased the whole room for possibilities and then started on the vast, heavily carved, locked, oak door. His sense of room layout told him that behind it must lie a closet. Who locked closets? Unless there was something to protect. Booze?

Again an Odheim; and very tough, even tougher than the

one on the back door. It was as complicated as a chess problem and, in any other circumstances, fulfilling. But Cassidy was in a hurry. Inside was a walk-in closet hung with clothes, some heavy tweedy stuff, some very formal pin-striped business clothes. Struthers was a very formal fellow.

Cassidy felt behind the clothes carefully, inch by inch. This would be the place for it. He hoped.

Aah!

Cassidy pushed the heavy formal suits out of the way, exposing the thing. Jupiter Jehoshaphat! Another Odheim. The man must have stock in the place. A triple knob job. Cassidy had never even seen one except in color photographs. He didn't know whether the Stemmler could handle it.

He pulled it out of his side pocket. A bit of loot from the CIA. The scope went into his ears with some reluctance because it meant he couldn't hear what was going on—or *not* going on in the rest of the apartment. No time to worry. He adjusted the oscilloscope, and pressed the starter. The needle fluctuated wildly, then steadied at ten millitres. Cassidy rubbed his fingers on his trousers hard, then turned the lead knob ever so delicately to the right. The lead should be right turn, second lead left turn, third lead right again. If not, he was in trouble. With each twist the needle gave a leap, then settled back to 15. In his ears, a steady hum. Slowly, slowly, Cassidy turned the knob 20, 30, 40. At 45 the needle leaped to 85 and the hum in his ears turned to a high squeal.

Cassidy turned to the second lead knob. Before dialing, he took the scope out of his ear and had a good listen for sounds in the apartment. Struthers was a very dangerous fellow, and here he was with his hands full of Stemmler. If the queer bodyguard showed up at the closet door, Cassidy would be half a minute dropping the Stemmler and getting his gun out.

The second knob was a poser. Cassidy went around twice, very slowly, before deciding that he was going the wrong direction and reversed the twist. That did it. The high squeal and the dial coincided within minutes.

On the third knob he mistook direction again, wasting minutes, before he discovered it was a right turn like the second lead.

The handle to the safe turned easily and Cassidy reached his arm into it. He brought out a packet of letters. In Italian. How nice! The names meant nothing. He fished again. This time he got a thick manila envelope full of photographs.

Aaaah!

The photographs were solid pornography. All the homosexual positions, including a few postures Cassidy had never suspected. But then Lucia was right. He was a prude in these matters. He didn't suspect the right things. A few heterosexual attitudes thrown in for good measure. Or bad measure.

Cassidy studied them all very carefully because he wasn't interested in the bodies but the faces. Some very interesting faces—beautiful, cruel, despairing. Ultimately this sort of thrill was an exercise in despair. Or was that Cassidy The Prude talking?

When he found it, it wasn't what he was looking for at all. So surprising, so unexpected was it that it shocked him to the core. For a full minute, he stared at the photograph, the implications in his brain fluctuating as wildly as the needle on the Stemmler. He couldn't believe it, didn't want to believe it! The evidence of his own eyes.

When he came around to belief, it unloosed something even more painful. If the photograph told the truth—and how could you argue with a photograph?—what in hell did it mean?

Every theory Cassidy possessed went out the window.

From far away in the apartment came the sound, a soft implosion. Cassidy felt it on his skin rather than heard it. A barely perceptible shudder, the kind of shock wave a heavy front door makes when it closes.

Cassidy thrust the photograph into his inner breast pocket, closed the safe and spun the three knobs. He closed the heavily carved oak door and locked it with the gretchel. It was a full thirty seconds before he succeeded in getting out of the bedroom and into the corridor. There were two exits to the apartment—the front door and the kitchen—and from where he stood he was blocked from both.

He had to make up his mind in a great hurry. Already the murmur of voices was drawing closer. Next to the bedroom stood a doorway. Cassidy stepped into it for lack of anywhere else to go, and flattened himself against the wall. There was no door, only an aperture.

In the corridor, the voices approached, speaking...Italian!

That made everything even more confusing because Cassidy expected the language to be German. All his theories were undergoing intensive revision, even as he flattened himself against the bookshelves. It was a kind of library he was in. Bookshelves stretched from floor to ceiling, but it was a very small room, especially in light of the size of all the other rooms there. It had only a single window of stained glass which made the light mercifully dim. If someone walked in, Cassidy had no protection at all. His gun was in his waistband and he dared not risk the noise of pulling it.

The voices were passing him now, two or three feet away. The silky smooth catarrhs of Hugo Dorn, the Good Nazi, talking excellent... well, unhesitating and very confident Italian. Cassidy's Italian wasn't good enough to tell whether it was excellent Italian or not or even to understand what they were talking about. He caught only one word.

Paura was the Italian word for fear. One of Hugo Dorn's favorite words, *fear*, in all languages. *Wealth and fear are the two common denominators here*, Hugo had said. Cassidy began to revise his estimates of Hugo Dorn. Fear, he thought, was perhaps less a common denominators of the Windletop than of Hugo Dorn himself. It was a constant preoccupation of the Good Nazi, his constant companion and what did that mean except that Hugo lived it every second of his life? He was an expert on fear was our Hugo.

Just as they passed the aperture, Struthers's gravelly voice spoke up. Cassidy comprehended only a name which floated out through the gravelly Italian. *Gianini Gennaro.*

Gianini Gennaro? Where had he heard that name? Or read that name?

Where was that queer bodyguard? With them in the bedroom? The murmuring voices had passed and entered the bedroom. Cassidy heard the bedroom door close.

What were they going to do in there—look at dirty pictures? Or make some?

Cassidy pulled out the silenced .22 and stepped into the corridor, chancing the presence of the bodyguard because he had no choice.

The corridor was empty. Cassidy walked swiftly down the corridor and turned into the kitchen—gun at the ready. Just in case.

There was no one there.

He slipped out the back door and leaned against it, uttering a long, noiseless, sigh of relief.

I'd thank God—if I believed in the fellow. I don't even really believe in Jupiter whom I invoke all the time, but I like that particular deity because he's so human—which so few humans are.

·24·

Alvin Feinberg's hands were behind his head and he was leaning far back in the old-fashioned swivel chair, eyes on the ceiling, his best posture for reminiscence.

· "Vittorio Pietroangeli," he was saying, "was way out of the usual run of Mafiosi. An intellectual, of all things. He'd actually *read* Karl Marx. Hated the man and his teachings, but at least he knew what he was hating. A very interesting and unusual old crook. I met him once—in Milan."

"So did I," said Cassidy.

Feinberg straightened up with a great squeaking of his ancient chair, and leveled the intelligent eyes behind the gold-rimmed glasses on Cassidy with a penetration that Cassidy found very discomforting: "Oh, did you now, Cassidy? And how did you happen to know so eminent a Mafiosi as Vittorio Pietroangeli?"

"We used him in the OSS—him and Luciano and some others during the war." Cassidy was sure Feinberg knew all this. It was difficult to find anything Feinberg didn't know.

"Why are you bringing him up now?" asked Feinberg softly.

The old fire horse smells smoke, thought Cassidy. Damn!

"I wondered what had become of him."

"He's been dead for twelve years, didn't you know?"

"No," said Cassidy. "I didn't. Tell me about it."

"I gather he was holding out on the boys. He was always exceedingly greedy. He went his own way—which is a dangerous thing to do in the Mafia—and they gunned him down in Milan."

"If it made the papers, I must have missed it."

Feinberg was still bending that inquisitive stare at him.

"Horatio," he said softly, "you didn't come all the way to Forty-third Street to discuss a dead man, now did you?"

"No," said Cassidy, "I didn't. I want to know the name of your informant about the death of Prince di Castiglione. The life of a twelve-year-old child might depend on it."

"Balls!" said Feinberg emphatically. He rose, a small, tubby, figure of a man, and took short mincing steps around his little glassed-in cubicle as if to shake his thoughts loose. "What are you playing at, Cassidy? You're hired as a bodyguard, not an investigator."

"The two things go together!" cried Cassidy. "I'm trying to get her to call off this damned party. It's an invitation to homicide."

"Why don't you go to the police?" asked Feinberg.

"The police are not interested in calling off the party. They promise *protection!*" Incredulity in his voice.

"And you don't think they can provide it? Are you serious, Cassidy? Yes, by God, you are!"

Jupiter, Cassidy was thinking. I want him to be concerned but not *that* concerned.

"I'll make a deal!"

Confirming Cassidy's worst fears.

"Deals!" barked Cassidy as rigid as George M. Cohan would have played the scene, focussing attention squarely on the *evenement*. "A child's life is at stake and you talk...*deals!*"

"Yeah," said Feinberg, tough as bootleather. "I'll be Jane Atchison's escort at that damned party."

"That's not possible," said Cassidy. "I can't steal another invitation."

"Then no deal." Feinberg wore a cherubic smile on his little round face. He hadn't been the greatest newsman in the Far East without learning a few trading tricks, one of which was to know when you're ahead. He leaned back in his revolving chair and contemplated the ceiling. "I'll tell you something else you're not going to like. I'm going right along with you when you see her because I want to hear the questions you're asking."

"Oh, it's a her!" said Cassidy.

"You're opening all sorts of doors that should remain decently locked." Everything she said contradicted what she really meant, thought Cassidy. She'd dying to open doors. "The 1960s in Rome! Oh, my dear! Such marvelous fun and laughter! It'll never be like that again. Well, you were there Alvin! You know."

"We were younger then, weren't we, Marietta?" Feinberg leading her on, opening her up like a can of sardines.

Marietta looked used up. "How beautiful Nicki was in those days! Like one of the statues on the Via Attica. Hands on his hips, that scornful smile on his face." She placed her hands on her hips mimicking. "A beautiful boy!"

"Much good it did you girls," said Alvin.

He was giving her the needle and she responded like one of Pavlov's dogs. "Alvin, that's not so! Nicki was as interested in girls as he was in boys." A wave of her hand. "I speak with authority."

"I'll bet you do," said Feinberg.

Cassidy had stayed well out of it, letting Feinberg run with it, but he couldn't stay out much longer.

"I might have married Nicki—but for those damn Trustees."

Cassidy jumped in right there. "Who *are* the Trustees, exactly?"

Marietta bent her gaze on Cassidy, coldly, as if wondering what he was doing there. "Clothilde," she said distinctly, "his sister, was the chief Trustee."

"She was older than Nicki, wasn't she?"

"Oh, my God, she was old the day she was born. She *hated* everything about Nicki—the fact *he* was getting the money, the life he led. She spent most of *her* life on her knees—like her mother. She disapproved of everything."

All very good stuff. Cassidy had never before heard anything about the mother.

"Mama was the bride of Christ," said Marietta dripping female venon, "which didn't leave much for Nicki."

"Aaah," said Cassidy. That explained a lot of things.

"Trustees?" said Feinberg, getting her back on course.

"They ran the fortune, you know. It was Nicki's, but Nicki had about as much control over his own money as I did. Or you. The Trustees told him what paintings to buy—and what to sell. They passed on his house, his horses. They could turn off the money like that." Snapping her fingers like Edward G.

Robinson. "Several times they did. I tell you Nicki was so hard up once, he borrowed money—actually—from *me*! They ran him absolutely!"

Feinberg zeroed in, journalist that he was. "You mean they found Elsa for him."

"Oh no no no no no no no no." Marietta spewing out No's like the chorus in *No, No Nanette*. "Elsa was *around*, you know. She'd left that cowboy she married. She was *available* in Rome and," here the soubrettish face darkened, "beautiful if you like that sort of thing. I find it cold."

It was late in the afternoon, and the sun was long gone from the east-facing windows of the old Broadway apartment building which, on the outside, was turretted, recessed, crenelated and adorned with spiky towers and corniced windows.

"Oh, the Trustees didn't find Elsa. Elsa found Nicki, if you know what I mean. The Trustees were only interested in finding a Principessa. There had to be a Principessa, don't you know?"

Marietta laughed viciously in the fading afternoon light.

"You know why there had to be a Principessa? The Trustees needed an heir. Nicki couldn't have cared less. He would have gone on indefinitely screwing the girls—and the boys—having his little parties. But the *Trustees* needed an heir because if he died without one the estate would have gone to some cousin in Turin and they'd be out on their fat behinds. That's why. *They* wanted marriage. He didn't. *Marriage*, said Nicki to me. Just like that! Scornful! *Marriage!* he said. A *wife*, he said. An *heir*, he said. What a *bore*, he said."

She fell back in the over-stuffed armchair, exhausted with the exertion of playing Nicki. The whole apartment was overstuffed, looking a little like a barbershop of 1922—potted palms, great leather armchairs studded with brass nails, mother of pearl magazine racks. The place looked like a waiting room for men to make themselves comfortable while waiting their turn.

"What was he like as a lover?" Feinberg's question stunned Cassidy because it was a question he wanted to ask and didn't dare. But why was Feinberg thinking along those lines?

"Oh, Alvin! You are a naughty boy to ask questions like

156 ·

that!" Clearly no one had asked her such a thing in years. "Well, what they all said—and all the girls said it—was absolutely true. You had to do everything for Nicki—if you know what I mean, and I think that you do. The girl had to do all the work. Not that we minded because he was so beautiful. But there's no denying, Alvin, that Nicki was the prince of narcissists—in love with himself, as they all are."

Cassidy leaped in with the question he'd long wondered about. "Why did so beautiful a man have so plain a daughter?"

"I've never laid eyes on Lucia, but I have heard that she looks just like him—and in spite of it is not beautiful at all. Well, sometimes that happens. A little bit off here." Tapping her nose. "A little bit off here." Tapping the mouth. "And beauty becomes," an expressive wave, "plainness, don't you know."

Brushing crumbs from the cake she'd served Cassidy and Feinberg into the palm of her hand, her eyes absent. She rose, putting a stop to the interview, picking up teacups, busying herself with the tea tray. They were being dismissed, as if they'd gone too far, and the memories of the 1960s were too precious for the likes of them. The face was sad and remote now, as if she'd opened cupboards she wished she hadn't.

Now they were standing in the big old-fashioned hall next to the immense front door, Cassidy still peppering her with questions she was increasingly reluctant to answer. "Who was the last girl before Elsa? Was it you?"

An impertinence to shock some sort of answer out of her. He knew it wasn't Marietta.

"No no no no no no, we'd parted long before." Not *he left me.* But *we parted.* "The last girl ... so many, you know ... was ... yes, little Jennie Feathers, an English girl. She died the summer Nicki and Elsa were married, and some said she committed suicide but I don't believe it. Not Jenny. She was so smart she'd have found another man in a month. I'm sure she died of something else."

Childbirth, said Cassidy. To himself.

They shared a cab, Feinberg insisting on dropping Cassidy at the Windletop which was miles out of his way.

This scenario is trapped in the past, Cassidy was thinking.

What has been has been like something out of Ibsen, forming the present and shaping the future, but it doesn't matter a tinker's damn what I do or don't do. It's going to happen anyway.

Cassidy became aware that Feinberg was speaking.

"...not a single known link with any American extremist organization. Not the Weather People, not the Black Panthers, not any of them." Feinberg's round intelligent eyes twinkled behind the gold-rimmed glasses. "All I'm trying to tell you is that it's got to be all foreign talent—if there's a shootout at the Principessa's party. Not local talent at all! How is so much firepower to get into the country without being detected?"

"Perhaps it's been detected," said Cassidy. "Even encouraged. There are depths to this perfidy undreamt of in your philosophy, me boyo," Cassidy swung out of the taxicab at the Windletop's front door. "Journalists around to the rear, me lad, with the serving classes." Feinberg was staring with frank journalistic curiosity at the Front's huge top hat. "That's where the party enters, back there. Mind you come properly dressed, you ink-stained wretch."

"Black tie and shoulder holsters," said Feinberg.

Jupiter, thought Cassidy. The day *The New York Times* starts packing guns, on that day civilization begins to glimmer in the West. He stood on the sidewalk, ignoring the bullet-proof door held open by the Front, and looked at the sun-drenched towers of Manhattan on the Central Park skyline, seeing them in his mind's eye in ruins. Not new ruins, centuries old ruins, grass growing in the foyers, and trees bursting their buds through the lower windows.

Rome in the Middle Ages had fallen to a population of twenty-five thousand. New York would do the same one day. Cassidy was sure of it.

·25·

"Count Otto is a talker in German and French. Not very much English," said the Principessa. "He must be put next to a listener in one of those languages. Have we one? So many talkers in the world. So few listeners."

The Principessa was arranging the tables with the help of the plump Englishwoman who acted as her social secretary when she needed one. A round-faced, smiling, English lady down on her luck, name of Phoebe Cass, who had once been invited to parties like these—until the money ran out. Now a social secretary. Still smiling, though, thought Cassidy. He was on the scene as advisor on security—and not smiling. Two hundred twenty-five guests. He wanted to know who they all were and where they would be sitting.

They were in the immense sitting room, the Principessa and Mrs. Cass seated at her red and gold desk, Cassidy leaning against the painted woodwork. The Principessa would select a white place card on which a name was written in Phoebe Cass's beautiful eighteenth-century calligraphy and expatiate on the guest—wickedly, telling Cassidy all the things he didn't want to know and little of what he did.

"Chantal de Niailles," she was proclaiming now. Princesse de Niailles, Cassidy noted from the guest list in his hand. "Poor Chantal has lost Hubert Casals to Jennifer Honeycutt and has not found another lover, poor sweet. She turned forty last week— the witching point at which she must learn pursuit and capture—she who was *always* pursued...."

"And always captured," said Phoebe Cass drily.

"It's not easy for one so beautiful to learn to do her own hunting. Let's put her next to John Spaulding."

"A bore!" complained Phoebe Cass

"A clay pigeon for her to practice on," commented the Principessa.

Was this aimed at Cassidy, all this pursuit and capture talk?

"Jeremy Wild," proclaimed the Principessa, squinting at the white card. "They'll all want him."

Jeremy Wild was a famous novelist, playwright, and conversationalist, queer as a hatrack, who lived all over the place—Hollywood, Rome, New York, Tangier—and who went to all the parties and threw some pretty good ones. Much prized as a dinner table companion.

"I think we'd better award him to Jessica de Angelis."

Jessica de Angelis, witty and rich, was known as the Flying Duchess because she barnstormed around the world from Biarritz to Hong Kong partly to escape boredom, partly to escape her Duke, a drunken sot. She threw smashing parties.

"At her last party," murmured the Principessa, "she put me next to Hector Lamb, having discarded him herself that very morning. Hector needed consolation and I'm not bad at consolation."

"Jeremy Wild is no good at consolation, only conversation," commented Phoebe Cass.

As each name was settled, the white card was slipped into a small rectangular block of wood, designating a table, each one numbered. Partygoers were seated loosely according to intellect—the stupid with other stupids, bright with bright. Sexual leanings were generally ignored in favor of conversational aptitude. In general the homosexuals of both sexes were the wittiest and most ruthless talkers and therefore had to be seated next to passives who were expected to listen and nod in the right places.

Some of the guests were asexual (as far as anyone knew) and these were wild cards, much prized by hostesses, because they fitted in anywhere. Many of these were professional partytrotters, full of the right kind of conversation which is to say reasonably literate gossip about people, plays, books, places, sex, and money—and expert at avoiding polemics on politics, sociology, and all religions, including Marxism.

The Principessa discoursed freely on the nuances of parties, trying, Cassidy suspected, to give this one some reason for

160 ·

existence important enough to override reasons of safety. Putting him in his proper place. At one point, she lifted her golden head and talked to him directly, smiling her thin smile.

"And what is it all about, you are saying to yourself, aren't you, Professor? What is the *point* of these expensive gatherings—all these rich people flying around the world to see people they've seen many times before, saying the same things they've said before, growing older every year? What's it all about? That's what you're asking yourself now, isn't it?"

"Oh, is that what I'm asking myself," said Cassidy, very stage Irish (because she wasn't far wrong).

The Principessa bent over her white cards again, continuing in her thrilling voice throbbing with sex appeal. (Had he noticed before how full of sex appeal her voice was? No, he hadn't.) "Many of us are quite fond of each other, unlikely as that seems to the non-*invités*. We are anxious to hear about one another's children, husbands, and even health and money problems—just like the poor folk. The poor have their *fiestas*, the rich their parties, and why not? It's a refreshment, Professor, and what is that lovely word—rededication."

Mocking him now. Rededication!

"One remembers a great party all one's long life. It becomes part of the tapestry of one's existence—and an important part. I have known parties, Professor, where the conversation was so brilliant, the people so beautiful, the music so divine, the whole experience so ravishing that they have modified my life, changed my character, and shaped my personality, would you believe it, Professor?"

"No," said Cassidy.

"That's only because you've never been to a really great party. Anyone who has would know exactly what I'm talking about because they've had the same experience. An hour or two of beauty and bliss and self-fulfillment, that's what a party is for. You mustn't underestimate parties, Professor. I have never known such happiness as I have experienced at some parties—or such despair. Because, of course, there *are* parties that plunge you into the abyss—and even they must be respected for the depth of feeling they arouse. The one thing I forbid my parties to be is trivial. They can be heaven or hell—or both—but trivial never!"

She looked at him challengingly: "We are the last survivors, Professor, expiring in a shower of expensive sparks. After us, the deluge."

"After Louis Quatorze, it wasn't the deluge," said Cassidy, the historian. "It was *toujours la même chose.*"

The golden head bent over the cards again sorting and arranging, calling out names. "Bibi Pilenski. Oh dear! Oh dear!" the Principessa was deep in revery. "She's *married* so many of them. Someone should tell Bibi there are other ways of getting rid of a man. Six marriages! There should be a bag limit. Heterosexual men are a dwindling species, perhaps even an endangered one. What do you think of putting her next to George Luvacs, that garrulous Hungarian?"

"They're *both* garrulous," complained Phoebe Cass.

"Neither one listens. They can chatter simultaneously in their separate languages, deliciously at cross purposes."

"George Luvacs," interposed Cassidy sharply.

"You know him?" murmured the Principessa.

"I know *a* George Luvacs."

"There can't be two George Luvacs. Hungarian? Handsome in a seedy Balkan way?"

That was George all right. Sold himself to the highest bidder after the family estate was made a collective.

Cassidy said: "I don't remember a George Luvacs on the list, Madame."

"He called three days ago—deeply wounded that he wasn't included. So I included."

"Didn't that call strike you, Madame, as propitious."

"Professor, you must learn to curb your paranoia."

"George Luvacs is a KGB agent, Madame, and a very high-ranking one—seedy or not."

"I can't believe George Luvacs is KGB," said the Principessa. "He's a Magyar Prince. His family goes back to 1262. Possibly even 1261. He might have dabbled in KGB once...."

"There is no such thing as ex-KGB—except dead ones."

"If you are suggesting that I disinvite George Luvacs, an old friend...."

And lover, thought Cassidy grimly. He was taking the temperature of the Principessa's tantrum, studying it for its sexual implications like an astronomer studying the red shift in a star.

162 ·

"...it's out of the question."

They had a flaming row, which centered on paranoia (his) and feather-headed recklessness (hers), neither of which (as both were intensely aware) was the real issue. While raging at one another's brains—or lack of them—each was more concerned about the state of the other's loins and, having discovered through the sheer heat of the blaze, that the other one was equally bereft, the row flamed out quite suddenly.

Both won—in a manner of speaking. George Luvacs remained an *invité*. Cassidy won out on reinforcements to help him police the party, something the Principessa had resisted savagely. Armpits with bulges under them, she called them. "You'll have to find your own armpits," snarled the Principessa, "I have no idea where to go to find armpits."

"They're already hired," said Cassidy. "Four of them."

She glared at him exasperated: "Sometimes you go too far, Cassidy. In fact, always."

"We *must* get on," said Phoebe Cass, bewildered by this charade. "We haven't even discussed the shape of the *pâté*."

"A swan," said the Principessa triumphantly. She picked up a colored sketch at her elbow—a crayon drawying of a swan with its tail feathers fully spread. "I've sent for Angeli and he's flying in from Venice. Very expensive but well worth it. He carves *pâtés*, Professor, into any shape you ask. This one will be a swan two feet high and three feet long, every feather carved out of a different kind of *pâté*. Isn't it amusing, Professor?"

Showing him the drawing and laughing openly in his face because she knew he'd hate it.

"Sometimes, Madame," said Cassidy, "I think I'm on the wrong side of this business."

"Oh, you are! Professor, you are! You're definitely on the wrong side of the tracks."

·26·

Lucia waylaid him in the corridor as he hurried to the elevator.
"I wallow in ignorance! Aren't you ashamed?"

"Mortally," said Cassidy, "It's this damned party...."

"I hate the party!"

"We all do. What are you going to wear?"

Lucia underwent a lightning change of mood: "Oh, it's
beautiful, my dress! Come see!"

"Later. When I get back."

"You're never here any more. How can you protect me when
you're not *here*?"

"I'm not even leaving the building." Cassidy did an
unexpected thing then. He put his arms around the thin
Contessa and held her close for a moment, very tight. He left her
there stunned by his embrace and rang for the elevator.

In Hugo Dorn's office, Cassidy plopped himself uninvited
into a chair. Hugo was on the telephone, his eyes acknowledging
Cassidy's presence with a somber gleam in which there was no
hostility. Relations between the two men had gotten extraordinarily intimate since Cassidy had applied the muscle, about the
only thing he'd got out of that encounter. Little that Hugo had
divulged could be trusted. He hadn't learned anything about the
building and its defenses he didn't already know (though Hugo,
he was convinced, knew a lot he wasn't telling even under
torture).

What had emerged from the torment was not so much
information as this extraordinary intimacy. Hugo and Cassidy
now knew each other very well, had as it were, explored one
another's nature in the camaraderie of the thumbscrew. At least

on the surface, Cassidy had his will of Hugo—but only on the surface. If Cassidy ever let down his guard, retribution would be swift and terrible. That was the rule of thumb. Cassidy bore it in mind always when dealing with Hugo. Hugo treated him with an outward deference, customary between torturee and torturer, but inside the man lurked something besides deference. What *was* it like inside Hugo's suave, dyed, mummified, ageless facade? What went on inside a man who was unhampered by any fixed goals except survival; who hedged, trimmed, changed direction, allies, principles, plans, everything at a moment's notice, depending on who held the knife to his throat at that moment? On the outside, Hugo appeared hypercivilized, but actually he was as basic as a field mouse. Survival was the first law of nature. Winning was staying alive at all costs—including pain, humiliation, degradation. Cassidy was at sea about Hugo's hopes, plans, wishes, aims. The only sure thing was that Hugo was unquestionably alive against all the odds, and that was not only remarkable but ominous.

Hugo was doing a great deal of listening. Cassidy strained his ears to catch some of it, but he had no idea of the sex of the person on the other end of the phone conversation.

"I regret, Madame," said Hugo finally, "that you find our security apparatus oppressive, but I'm afraid there is no possibility of modifying it. However, if Madame wishes to discuss the termination of her lease, the management would be happy to listen.... Thank you, Madame."

He hung up.

Malarkey, thought Cassidy. A signal to tell the caller to get off because other ears were listening.

Hugo was silent, watching him with his velvety questioning eyes. "You wished something, Professor?"

"About tomorrow night, Alfred...." Always Alfred in the office.... "I'll have four of my own men in the building. I want there to be no confusion about that."

"The Principessa has agreed?"

"Of course."

"I'll tell Robert—and alert Security. They'll need identification."

"I'll get you photographs. What I expect from you, Alfred, is security at the bottom—in the foyer at street level and around the entrance. You're in full charge down there, including any bit of sidewalk the police don't cover, and it would help if your foot soldiers had walkie-talkies. I'll take over the dance floor and all of the rooftop." Cassidy didn't want Hugo's men anywhere near the restaurant.

"Who is going to check these people in?" inquired Hugo mildly. "The Principessa is adamant against having anything so aggressive as a check list. An insult to her guests, she says."

"Phoebe Cass will be in the lobby to greet the guests—all of whom she knows by sight. Also, I believe, by smell."

"Smell?"

"The rich smell different from you and me. Haven't you noticed?" He rose. "I'll be in the lobby during the arrival period if you don't mind." He had to get Jane Atchison and Alvin Feinberg past Phoebe Cass.

"I'll want a music box, too, Alfred." Music box was Cassidy's name for the gadget that opened the door to the super secret subcellar. Hugo was most reluctant to part with a music box. Nevertheless he went to his office safe, got one and handed it to Cassidy. Like a genie doing his master's bidding. It was a little eerie, this compliance.

"You wouldn't have changed the tune on this thing, Alfred? You wouldn't do a thing like that?"

Hugo smiled wearily: "If you'd like a test...."

"No." It wouldn't do any good. Hugo could change the tune five minutes after the test. Cassidy would have to go with it.

"I hope the Principessa has a lovely party," murmured Hugo, his eyes fathomless. "I rather doubt it."

"Oh, do you now?"

"My feeling is there has been too much publicity, too much fanfare, even too much security. All this fuss.... Hugo smiled directly at Cassidy... "adds *weight* to a party, and that is the one thing a party should not have. A party should be light as a *mousse*, effervescent as champagne. This affair is heavy as lead—already."

"I had no idea you were so full of opinion about something so trivial as parties, Alfred."

"There's nothing trivial about this party," said Hugo quietly.

166 ·

He could hear the laughter when he stepped off the elevator, rippling down the corridor from the nursery. A mixture of innocence, malice, and complicity. They were chattering in Italian.

He found them in front of the big nursery mirror, Lucia in her party dress which was royal blue with white lace collar and cuffs, full skirted with a flounce of petticoats that made it billow out at the bottom. It fell all the way to her heels.

"Titi says I look like something out of *Heidi*. She thinks I should bring a goat." Lucia pealed with laughter, not joined in by Titi who always went *farouche* when Cassidy stepped in the room.

Cassidy did one of his Alfred Lunt bows: "May I have this dance, Contessa?"

"Oh, yes, please. Titi put on a record. No, not that one. The Mozart."

"They won't be playing Mozart at your mother's party."

They did a minuet, Lucia leading him through it carefully, as if through a minefield.

"You're not very good," she said.

"The minuet is not one of my things. I'm surprised it's one of yours."

"Lorenzo taught me. Lorenzo said every Contessa should know the minuet—even if she never does it," all the while leading him through the slow stately dance, "because it would lend her grace in other things. No, the *left* foot, Professor. Now the right. Really, you're as graceful as an ostrich."

"How very true. Shall we have our lesson?"

Last lesson? Cassidy doubted there'd ever be another.

She sat in the window seat, overlooking Manhattan, Cassidy pacing like a caged lion, hands clasped behind him. "In the twelfth century, the vassals sold their fiefs as if they owned them which, of course, they didn't. In theory, the vassal held his bit of territory only in the name of his lord, but having occupied the land for hundreds of years, the vassal simply took possession. This practice was forbidden by decree of the Holy Roman Emperor Barbarossa—much good it did. When law clashes with the facts of life, the law ceases to be observed—then as now.

"Even more piquant—in the light of our contemporary experience—was the clash of loyalties in the late Middle Ages. So tangled were a man's loyalties after hundreds of years of vassalage that sometimes when two knights were at war, the vassal might owe fealty to them both. He would send thirty men to one side, perhaps a hundred to the other—sons killing their own fathers. In the long cool light of history, loyalty, when followed slavishly rather than intelligently, is seen as an aberration, a form of insanity. Civilizations founder on obedience to the law, rather than the other way around."

"What am I to deduce from all this, Professor?" asked Lucia, puzzled.

"You must review your loyalties from time to time, Contessa, in the light of changed circumstances."

The last lesson had to be pertinent.

Titi, in her corner, glowered.

Cassidy heard the Principessa come home that night. Two A.M. Fine time to be coming home the night before her own party. Laughter light as silver bells. The murmur of voices in the sitting room. Then silence. The implications of silence rode roughshod over Cassidy, alarming him. Am I *jealous*? A weakness in the young, an absurdity at his age.

Worse, it was keeping him awake when he should be getting his sleep the night before The Party.

An hour of silence was too much.

Cassidy clipped on his ancient robe and opened the door. Silence gripped the apartment. Cassidy tiptoed stealthily down the corridor to the sitting room which was black and still. If there were lovers there, they were asleep or dead. He switched on the crystal chandelier. The room was empty.

He walked the corridor now without stealth and entered the Principessa's room. Her light breathing pierced the stillness like an accusation. She was asleep. She was alone. Cassidy felt relief and shame. I've wronged her.

Hand on the knob.

He had difficulty leaving. The Principessa beckoned—even in sleep. No, certainly not! It would amount to rape. Or, at very least, blackmail. But then, after all, hadn't she? Repeatedly? He had been raped, then blackmailed, finally seduced by the Madame. All the time protesting.

Now, here he was, hand on knob, in the stillness of the night quite free to go back to bed unraped, unblackmailed, unseduced. Except that he had been robbed of his free will by her continuous and repeated possession of himself—and this had corroded his resolve, his fierce sexual integrity (Irish sexual integrity was most peculiar), and his loyalty to Lucia.

Hell and damnation! (Not only strong words for Cassidy but altogether ridiculous since he believed in neither.)

He took off his robe.

I am only human, he said. I have been weakened in my resolve by circumstances beyond my control, Your Honor (not believing in God he had to set the scene in a sort of mythical higher court in Upper Ruritania). I plead guilty with extenuation.

He took off his pajamas, first top, then the bottom, continuing his defense to the Magistrate. *It is the last night, and there is much to discuss. Much misunderstanding to be cleared up, Your Honor.*

In short, it wasn't sex exactly. Or anyway, not primarily. It was to be a meeting of minds, not bodies. If bodies got mixed into this encounter it was only parenthetically, *ex parte nolte, summa extenuensis,* if you see what I mean, Your Honor.

Stark naked, he slipped into bed with her.

She awoke slowly, painfully, bringing herself out of the depths of sleep like returning from the nether world of the dead—an interminable process during which Cassidy was impaled on the knowledge of his own perfidy.

"Professor," she said, the voice unsurprised, languorous with sleep.

"How would you know," asked Cassidy, surprised and pleased, "among all the naked bodies of your experience that *this* one was mine?"

The bed shook with her laughter, soft as feathers: "Yours has an odor of Irish sanctity about it, Professor, quite unmistakable. As a lover, you're an anachronism, Cassidy, altogether in the wrong century." With a touch of sadness. "And the wrong time. You should have come into my life long ago."

"How many of your lovers have you used that line on, Madame?"

"I think only six," she said. "Shall we fuck, Professor?"

"Let's talk. We can do that other thing later."

She was slipping out of her silk nightgown: "The greater urgencies come first in an ordered world, Professor."

Afterward, she fell instantly asleep, precluding talk.

Cassidy lay awake, caressing her nakedness absently! "I wanted to talk about your loyalties and motivations in this affair, Elsa, which remain shrouded in mystery. Your father died leaving you the legacy of aristocracy and no money. Therefore the marriage to a drunken moneybags of good family was fairly comprehensible Even the marriage to a cowboy movie star who had a few dollars and great sex appeal makes sense. But why Nicki? Everyone thought you married for the title, but I think it was some other more basic urge."

These musings in the stillness of the night were interrupted by a soft click followed by a sssshing noise—like velvet on velvet. Cassidy snapped on the bedside light just quickly enough to catch the sight of the bit of ceiling directly over the Principessa's bed, which was rimmed with ornamental plaster in the shape of flowers and leaves, sliding back into place. Just for a moment, he looked directly into the blackness of a hole and saw the lens of a camera. Then the bit of ceiling settled into place and all was still.

Cassidy slithered out of the bed, as if stung by a rattlesnake. He groped his way into his pajamas, eyes thunderous. Cameras, he was thinking, can operate in almost total darkness now and it was not totally dark in the room. Manhattan's never-ending street lights cast a faint glow over everything. Plenty of light for hypersensitive cameras, both moving and still.

Cassidy snapped out the bedside lamp and made his way back to his room, his mind in a torrent.

·27·

The crowd stretched clear around the block from Fifth to Madison down both side streets. Thousands of the curious stood antlike under the floodlights put there at the insistence of the police over the loud objections both of Cassidy and the Principessa.

"Nothing like a little light to scare away the hoods," said Inspector Kilpatrick heartily, six foot four inches of Irish cop. (Every inch brainless, said Cassidy.)

The police had penned the crowd against barriers across the streets from the Windletop, pushing the Fifth Avenue onlookers almost into Central Park. They stood in the cold air, rows of silent eyeballs, drinking it all in.

"It's not like it was movie stars," said Inspector Kilpatrick jovially. "Not even one of them rock stars. Just a bunch of furriners. What the devil are they staring at?"

"Floodlights," said Cassidy. "Turn out the lights, and they'll all go home. And you could go home, too, Inspector." The two men stood in the center of an empty Fifth Avenue just to the left of the canopy under which the guests got out of their cars.

"You can't combat terrorists if you can't see 'em," said the Inspector, chuckling at his own cleverness.

"Have you any backup, Inspector?" asked Cassidy.

"Forty of the finest," said the Inspector. "Enough firepower here to quell the Middle East."

A comedian, thought Cassidy. Another limousine was pulling up to the canopy. Out stepped Feinberg, and then Jane Atchison, dressed to the nines in red velvet and ermine.

"Don't shoot any innocent bystanders, Inspector," said Cassidy, "unless you're quite sure they're white Anglo-Saxon

Protestants." He stepped quickly to the sidewalk and slipped his arm in Feinberg's. "This way."

Next to the elevator stood Phoebe Cass, her welcoming smile thin and strained. At sight of Feinberg and Atchison, neither of whom she expected, the smile sagged.

"Security," muttered Cassidy into Phoebe Cass's ear. Aloud he sang out: "You look like a new rose in the mornin' light, my dear." Phoebe Cass blushed scarlet.

The elevator door closed behind them, and they started up, Cassidy shaking his head at Feinberg and Atchison to keep them buttoned up in the presence of the elevator operator.

Conversationally, he said: "Not many here yet. There's dinner parties all over Manhattan. They'll be converging here in about half an hour. The Principessa is still presiding over her own dinner party in her own apartment."

The three of them stepped out on the landing of the Windletop Club. Robert stood there with his list and his frozen smile.

"Security," barked Cassidy.

Robert was not so easily intimidated as Phoebe Cass. "I have not been told about two more...."

Cassidy cut him off sharply: "Robert, the world is full of things you have not been told about. You'd better get cracking if you're ever to catch up with the rest of us." He pushed Feinberg and Atchison ahead of him into the gloom of the restaurant.

"Oh!" gasped Jane Atchison. "It's beautiful!" She was a thin bony blonde, not very intelligent but pushy and ambitious, which counted for more than brains in society journalism.

"No expense has been spared," said Cassidy.

The rooftop restaurant was candlelit like the eighteenth century, every inch of it. Three great chandeliers from the di Castiglione collection had been hung from the ceiling in place of the usual electricity. The tables—all but one empty—were set in pink damask with oceans of silver bearing the di Castiglione crest in gold. Each table carried a crystal vase with fresh flowers and blazed with candlelight from silver candelabra all carved by Fironi in the seventeenth century expressly for the di Castigliones.

Set against the walls farthest from the entrance lobby was a vast refectory table made for a mountaintop monastery in Tuscany in the twelfth century, lit by enormous, many-armed,

Meissen candelabra and bearing the lobsters, the caviar, the truffled eggs in glaciers of cracked ice—presided over by the immense swan carved out of *pâté de fois gras* by Angeli.

"Christ," said Feinberg, eyes glittering. "I'd forgotten all about the swan. Nicki and Elsa had that swan at all their parties."

"The ship is sinking with all guns firing," said Cassidy.

On the dance floor, a single couple was doing the Gargle—badly. "John Spaulding," announced Jane Atchison. "He always arrives first."

"A bore," said Cassidy. "I speak from hearsay."

"Not in bed," said Jane Atchison. "I speak also from hearsay."

Well back from the dance floor, at the only occupied table, sat an ancient couple, skins like parchment in the candlelight, their bodies bolt upright, their ancient lineaments stiff with disapproval—not only of this scene but of everything in the modern world—disapproval that looked as if it had been imprinted on their faces and passed on down the centuries like hemophilia.

"Prince and Princess di Rapallo," said Jane Atchison, delighted with her recognition.

"They flew all the way from Venice for this party," said Cassidy, "and they're hating it."

"All the old Venetian aristocracy look that way," said Jane Atchison. "They've hated everything that's happened since 1524."

The scene was immensely ominous, Cassidy was thinking. The single couple dancing frantically and badly, a modern dance they didn't understand, a lone couple watching and hating. All around them a sea of empty tables, candles flickering and smoking. Over the stereo system the Renegades screeched. The Principessa might have hired the Renegades to shriek the song out in person, but this year it was more chic to play the records. Next year, who knows? Maybe there wouldn't be a next year.

"Fellini would love the scene," murmured Feinberg, eyes glittering behind the gold-rimmed spectacles. "Especially the faces on that Venetian couple. He'd zero in on that *pâté* swan with his camera while that awful music played."

"What's so awful about that music?" complained Jane

Atchison. "I think the Renegades are absolutely delightful."

"The difference in our generations, my dear," said Feinberg.

Cassidy propelled them through the gloom to the security table, which was pushed against the wall next to the entrance from the kitchen, well back in the darkness. Fingertips sat there drinking a glass of water, his brown eyes mournful. "Fingertips," introduced Cassidy. "Atchison and Feinberg." Apologetically, he added. "*The New York Times* deserves better, Alvin, but all those tables out there bear place cards at every seat, and your name is not among them. You can watch the action from here without being seen—at least I hope so."

"If we are seen....?"

"Blame it all on Cassidy. I'll leave you now."

Dinner was over, and the dinner guests were scattered across the vast sitting room—first time Cassidy had ever seen the room decently used. He stood in the hall behind the ebony screen of carved acanthus leaves which had taken a Cambodian monk twenty years to complete—the spaces between the leaves providing excellent eyeholes to count the house.

The Principessa was standing, slim and straight, in the center of the room, listening to Jeremy Wild, who wore a satyr's smile while holding forth on Crispin's latest movie: "It's quite clear he thinks he's Chekhov. It's also quite clear he isn't."

The Principessa laughed her easy enchanting hostess laugh, eyes never leaving those of the celebrated writer. She was a marvelous listener, absorbing the words with her whole body, appreciating the wit, the thought, the syntax, as if savoring a meal. She was dressed in a simple sheath of sapphire blue velvet with a white lace collar that covered the neck (very important, covering the neck at her age) and long bouffant sleeves which muted the aging arms, the gown displaying to fullest advantage the slender body and radiant face.

Under the radiance the face looked a little tired.

Lounging like a question mark on the onyx loveseat with its sphinx-faced ends was the Earl of Canossa, who was twenty-six and enjoyed—so they said—both sexes. He was deep in talk with Jessica de Angelis, the Flying Duchess, who was slim and restless as a racehorse, eyes darting about the room as if worrying she was missing something somewhere, not listening at all. With Gogo Canossa it hardly mattered. He was listening to himself talk, admiring the flow of his own discourse with great self-appreciation, a form of masturbation for which he was famous.

Standing next to the window was a fleshy, white-haired man with eyes that had seen everything and condoned everything, a Middle European face, exquisitely accommodating. George Luvacs, once Prince Luvacs, had adjusted with Middle European agility to his change of circumstances. He'd aged since their last meeting, thought Cassidy, but then perpetual accommodation must be a tough life. He was listening to Bibi Pilenski with his air of tired languor. She was talking about the old days in Poland with intense regret. "I miss the shooting. So simple, so natural! Shooting in the old forests. Now they *raise* the bird for slaughter! So positively indecent!"

"Youth is what you're missing, Bibi," said George Luvacs.

"So painful my youth, so boring my middle age. Life is a disappointment, George."

"You must lower your expectations, Bibi. That's the latest American craze—lowered expectations. They play it like parchesi."

Cassidy walked to the Principessa, a long walk, her cool glance on him all the way. "Ten thirty, Principessa," he said.

"Oh...yes," she said with an abstracted smile. She plucked at Cassidy's sleeve and led him a little way from Jeremy Wild, the face not changing expression by so much as a hair. *Sotto voce,* she said: "Trouble! Titi's disappeared! Lucia's in hysterics!" Cassidy was struck foremost not by the bleak facts but by the total control of the Principessa in giving them to him.

"Do something!" commanded the Principessa quietly.

"Immediately, Madame," said Cassidy—and made his exit, thinking: *It's started.* Behind him he could hear her rounding up the others in her hostess voice, charming them with her beauty and brains, grace under pressure they knew nothing about.

"I hate you!"

It was worse than he imagined because it was unexpected.

Lucia was in her blue ankle-length Heidi-like ballgown that ballooned around her like a picture out of a Hans Christian Anderson fairy story, her face contorted in the same expression Cassidy had seen there once before—when she'd beaten at her mother's face with little fists.

"I hate you! I hate you! I hate you!"

There was something very peculiar about this rage. As if it were an old rage that had lost some of its steam through repetition, a rehearsed rage that didn't quite come off.

"Where's Titi?" asked Cassidy.

Lucia dissolved into tears, her face crumpling, and this emotion, Cassidy felt, was genuine. "She's *gone*!" A long woebegone wail, as if this was something beyond her understanding. Lucia knelt on the floor and buried her face in the Heidi-like blue dress, sobbing. Cassidy couldn't resist. He leaned over the girl and caressed her arched back. She reacted like a scalded cat.

"Don't touch me, Lover Boy!"

Lover Boy! Cassidy saw again in his mind's eye the camera disappearing behind the moving ceiling.

He straightened up, trying to think straight. You should never get emotionally involved. It fries the brains.

Calmly, he asked: "When did you last see Titi? It's important."

"*Hours* and *hours* ago!"

A child's hours could mean anything.

"When *exactly*, Lucia?"

"I don't know....Maybe...eight o'clock. I've been here alone for *hours*."

Cassidy looked at his watch. 10:35. Two hours and a half. The operation had begun at about the time he'd expected, but not in the way he'd expected. Certainly, not Titi's disappearance. That was really throwing it right into his face, jeering....

"How did she disappear exactly?"

Lucia's voice was tear-drenched: "She went to the laundry room to do her stockings. She *never* came back. She's *never* coming back! Not *ever*!"

"Well," said Cassidy, "I think you've outgrown your pet mouse. Get off the floor, Lucia. It's time to go to the party."

"I don't *want* to go to the party!"

Cassidy knew her better than that. She *did* want to go to the party. She wanted very badly to go to the party. She wanted to be urged. That was what she wanted. Then she would say no and be stubborn. Cassidy didn't have time for these games. Not with the operation already underway.

"All right," said Cassidy. "We won't go to the party. I'll stay with you."

A gamble.

"I don't want to stay here alone with you, Lover Boy," snarled Lucia.

"It's either that or go to the party. I can't leave you here alone."

That settled it. Lucia got off the floor and removed herself to the bathroom to repair her face.

Where in hell was Titi? She couldn't have left the building. Or could she? Cassidy pulled the Radox from his inner breast pocket and pushed the Number 3 button. The Gypper came on immediately. "Yeah, man," said the Gypper which was as close to radio discipline as you could get the Gypper. Cassidy had positioned him in the lower lobby just inside the entrance. "Gypper has Titi left the building?"

"No boss. None of our group has gone out this door."

"Okay, Gypper, listen, it's started. Come up to the restaurant in five minutes. Repeat, back over."

"Restaurant in five minutes. Got it."

Cassidy slipped the gadget back into his breast pocket, beating Lucia's reappearance by an eyelash. He'd have to check with Rooftop at the rear entrance later. Titi knew all the entrances and too many of the procedures. The possibilities were endless and dreadful.

Lucia stood before him, tearstains wiped off, the plain face sullen but not mutinous. "I'm ready," she said.

Cassidy marched her out of the nursery but not, as she expected, to the elevator. Instead they went to his room where he pushed her on to the bed.

"I'm under age, Lover Boy," yelped Lucia.

"You're under-witted, too," snapped Cassidy. He was reaching under the mattress drawing out the little .22, unscrewing the silencer from the muzzle. That made it into quite a small handgun. "It could save your life, Contessa," he said.

Roughly he pushed up her skirt with its bouffant petticoats and taped the little gun to the outside of her right thigh where the petticoats would conceal it.

"How can I dance with that thing stuck to my leg?" wailed Lucia.

"You won't even know it's there in a minute," said Cassidy sternly. "You're not to tell anyone it's there, and remember you're not to use it except in *dire* emergency."

Pulling her by the hand toward the elevator they both faced the steel gates, avoiding each other's eyes in a highly uncomfortable silence.

"If it comes, don't forget to squeeze slowly. Don't let yourself be hurried, and *don't* waste shots. You have only nine," said Cassidy.

·28·

The noise was earsplitting.

In the half hour since Cassidy had left, the party had begun to take hold, the dance floor alive with dancers, the tables—filling with the gowned, the jeweled, the dinner-jacketted—all looking a little misty and unreal in the candlelit gloom.

Lucia was bewitched. "I've never been to a grownup party before," she whispered. "There's Gogo. Hello, Gogo."

The Earl of Canossa was lounging languidly at the side of the dance floor, swaying slightly to his own interior rhythms. When he caught sight of Lucia, his face lit up with his famous smile. "Shall we have a whirl, Contessa?" he said. To Cassidy. "Will you forgive us, sir."

He had marvelous manners, no question of it. Cassidy watched a little sadly as Gogo Canossa bore Lucia away to the dance floor where they plunged precipitately into the Fregesi, Canossa moving languorously, voluptuously. Lucia coltishly, her mousy hair flying, eyes bright as harvest moons. Whatever emotional problems she had had were pushed aside by the physical urgencies of the Fregesi.

Cassidy circled the dance floor, keeping an eye on Lucia, looking around to see what he could see. Chantal de Niailles was dancing with John Spaulding. Gigi Cadwallader was doing his extraordinarily dignified version of the Fregesi with Bibi Pilenski.

At the security table, Jane Atchison was taking notes in her lap, keeping pencil and paper out of sight, while keeping up a running commentary to Feinberg.

"That little blonde with George Luvacs is Tessa de Ouvranche from Brazil. Only eighteen and supposed to be the hottest fuck in the western hemisphere. Poor child, she's out of fashion. Nymphomania was *last* year. This year chastity is very hot."

"Hot chastity," said Feinberg. "I like that."

The Principessa, Cassidy noted, was going from table to table, greeting her guests, radiant in the candlelight which she had probably planned just for that purpose.

Cassidy drew Fingertips away from the table.

'What's up?" asked Fingertips, sensing the trouble.

"Everything," said Cassidy. "Keep an eye on Lucia, will you? Don't let her out of your sight."

"Right."

Cassidy picked up the phone on the security table and asked for Alfred the Great. Through the gloom he could see the di Rapallos, their faces etched with disapproval which had deepened in the half hour he'd been gone to an expression approaching horror. Had the Principessa just invited them for contrast with the smiles, the laughter, the blaring music? She was quite mischievous enough to do something like that.

"Well, where the hell is he?" barked Cassidy. Alfred was neither at the restaurant lobby, the front lobby, or in his office.

"I don't know, sir!" said the operator, a fierce old spinster who ran the switchboard from 10 P.M. till 6 A.M. at the Windletop because she needed the money. "He always leaves word. Always!"

"What does the Front say?" The Front had been bribed into working until dawn for the Principessa's party.

"He doesn't know either."

"Try his room!"

"I've tried it."

"Try it again."

Cassidy watched Lucia whirling in Gogo Canossa's arms, as he hung on the phone. She was having a very good time, her plain face lustrous. Girlhood's last gasp, Cassidy thought. Soon, she'd be eighteen like Tessa de Ouvranche and would she too be the hottest? . . . no, not Lucia. Cassidy was glad chastity was back in fashion again.

"What's the matter?" asked Feinberg, sensing the urgency.

"Nothing! Everything!" said Cassidy, trying to throw Feinberg off. He didn't want *The New York Times* around his neck when there was so much to be done. "Remember those old

Joan Crawford movies when somebody said 'What's the matter?' she'd say 'Nothing. Everything!' and laugh, Ha ha ha.''

"She never did," said Feinberg wisely. "And Charles Boyer never said 'Come wiz me to ze Casbah' to Hedy Lamarr either. Those are just myths. Something *is* the matter."

Miss Jasper came back on: "No answer in his room."

"Ask Rooftop if he's seen him. 502."

"Yes, sir," said Miss Jasper. Cassidy heard her ring 502—a long ring. Cassidy looked at his watch—11:15.

Cassidy watched the Principessa making her rounds of the tables, joy pinned on her features like an orchid on a dress. At each table, there were embraces and kisses and bursts of greeting like shooting stars. She'd sit for a while before moving on, to hear the latest gossip from Peru—or wherever. At that moment, she was at a banquette by the window overlooking Manhattan, straight and slim as always, the golden hair shining through the candlelight. Even at that distance he lusted after her savagely and, in that moment of unbridled lust, he knew as well as he knew his own name he'd never have her again. Not ever.

Miss Jasper was back on the phone: "No answer!"

"Try 506, he might be on the elevator."

Miss Jasper rang 506.

The dance floor had got very crowded, and the tumult was deafening. The Principessa had hired Joald Frantic, the world renowned disco expert, a wizard at controlling the pace, tempo, and volume at parties so as to produce the maximum orgasmic effect on the dancers. At that second he was lashing on the dancers with *Anyone But You*, which was Number 1 on the charts:

> I'll love
> Anyone but you

The Antichrist were singing it in their falsetto voices that contrasted so strangely with their virile appearance on the dust jacket of the albums.

> I'll fly with
> I'll lie with
> I'll die with
> Anyone but you.

Lovely song.

Miss Jasper was back on the phone: "No answer there, sir."

The worst news of all. He'd told Rooftop not to leave his post under any circumstances and if, for some unforeseen reason, he had to take the elevator, to stay in it—not to leave it. If he wasn't available on 502, he should be on 506. If reachable on neither....

"Mr. Cassidy, I have another call. I can't hang on any longer."

"Go ahead, Miss Jasper," said Cassidy politely. "I've got to think." He hung up, head spinning. He didn't want to leave the dance floor but he had to find out. That had always been the weak spot in the defense, that back door—and with Titi missing....

The Antichrist were caroling:

I'll do anything
And everything
With anyone
But you, baby."

The Gypper stood at his elbow.

"Sorry, I took so long. The lady at the elevator took a bit of talking to. Didn't know about me."

"Come on," said Cassidy. He rose and started toward the rear exit. Then he stopped.

Where was Lucia? Cassidy had caught sight of Gogo Canossa who had been Lucia's partner, now dancing with Bibi Pilenski. Or rather *not* dancing with Bibi Pilenski.

There was Lucia—dancing with George Luvacs. Why? She didn't look as if she were liking it either. Where before she had looked as if she were in heaven, she now looked pained, dancing dutifully with the Hungarian who was himself a very suave dancer.

Cassidy turned back to the security table and bent over Alvin Feinberg. "Alvin, go cut in on Lucia. She's out there dancing with George Luvacs and hating it."

"I thought I was supposed to stay out of sight."

"This is an emergency. Go ahead."

"I don't know any of these dances," protested Feinberg, rising to his feet reluctantly. "I never got beyond the fox trot."

"Lucia does an elegant minuet and if you don't know how, she'll teach you," said Cassidy propelling him in the general direction of the dance floor. "Whatever you do, don't let her out of your sight until I'm back."

He watched a moment as the little butterball of a newspaperman in the gold-rimmed spectacles made his way to the floor and cut in on a startled Lucia.

It was this sudden interference in the natural order of things, Cassidy was later to write in *The Legend of the di Castigliones, Annotated*, that saved Feinberg's life. Otherwise, he'd have been cut down by the same burst of automatic fire that killed Jane Atchison, next to whom he'd been sitting. The odd thing, Cassidy wrote, was that in retrospect he couldn't understand *why* he'd done it. It was very foolish and reckless of him to expose Feinberg (who was his own secret) to the gaze of the Principessa at that time. It was as if he'd been forewarned.

Cassidy was almost at the rear exit heading for the back elevator, when his eye was caught again. Lorenzo was at the refectory table carving a bit of the beautiful three-foot swan for a lone guest whose back was to Cassidy. This was very odd because it was much too early for any guest to be eating supper since all of them had been at dinner parties. Also, he thought he recognized that back.

"Wait!" commanded Cassidy to the Gypper. He threaded his way back through the tables to the refectory table. Hugh Alison was holding his plate out for the slice of *pâté* which Lorenzo put on his plate, solemn as if he was performing High Mass.

"Try the truffled eggs," suggested Cassidy into Alison's ear. "The KGB flew them in especially for you."

"Always the needle," complained Alison. He took his plate and made his way along the edge of the dance floor to an empty table. Alison selected a seat and sat down. Cassidy sat next to him.

"Who let you in?"

"Hugo's our pigeon," said Alison, tucking into the food.

"Hugo's everyone's pigeon," said Cassidy. "What are you trying to do—provoke a massacre?"

"Prevent one." Alison smiled his party smile and accepted a glass of wine from a waiter. Cassidy shook his head fiercely at the

· 183

waiter who tried to offer him wine, his eyes never leaving Alison's bland face. "We had to come, Horatio. The Principessa is in this thing deeper than you think."

"Oh, you've finally got wise to the Principessa?" said Cassidy.

Alison was eating and sipping wine coolly: "You were a little late in wising up to the Principessa yourself, weren't you, Horatio?" Alison's eyes were roving the room, his face fixed in a half smile. "Lovely party."

"It's going to be even lovelier in a minute," snarled Cassidy. "I think they're in the building already. I'm going down to find out. Where are the rest of your troops?"

"That waiter is one of them. Others in the kitchen."

Cassidy rose from the table. "Hold everything until I get back."

"We might not have the choice," said Alsion, munching quietly.

Cassidy bounded through the restaurant, picking up Gypper under the exit sign. The two men passed under it and walked rapidly down the bare corridor leading to the elevator. Freddie was in position back against the cement wall keeping an eye on the service elevator and the door leading to the rear stairwell.

"Not even a mouse stirring," he called out cheerfully, both his hands in his side pocket resting, Cassidy knew, on the guns in those pockets.

"Red alert," said Cassidy. "I think it's underway. Has anyone used the elevator?"

"Very active," said Freddie cheerfully. "Nobody's got off at this floor but it's been going up and down, up and down."

"Jupiter," said Cassidy pushing the button. "You should have reported it." Nobody should have been using the back elevator at this hour. "Do you remember where it stopped?"

The rear elevator had a big old-fashioned dial which showed where it was.

"Thirty-nine," said Freddie. "Three times."

"Juno!" said Cassidy, a very large cuss word. He invoked Jupiter's wife only on special occasions.

The two men stepped into the elevator, and Cassidy pushed Main. Too late, he was thinking, too late.

He was right. Rooftop was sitting back against his glass

cubicle, mouth open as if greeting someone, legs akimbo in a comical position like a Raggedy Ann doll, eyes open. A little trickle of spit had coursed down the side of the open mouth.

"Icepick job." said the Gypper professionally. "Very old-fashioned. Who do you know who owns an icepick? They're not so easy to find any more."

"Come on," said Cassidy morosely. He'd been fond of Rooftop. Everyone was. Sweet-tempered little man. That's what got you into trouble. It wasn't the right time for sweet temper. The two men got back into the elevator and Cassidy pushed thirty-nine.

"He looked at peace with the world," said the Gypper. "As if he was good friends with the guy who slipped it to him."

"Or the girl," said Cassidy. "From here on in, its *silenzia*, Gypper. Thirty-nine is where the operation's being run from."

Gypper put his hand to his mouth, signifying he'd got his orders.

It was 11:35. They'd been gone from the dance floor eleven minutes.

·29·

I wished I trusted someone, anyone, Cassidy was thinking, as the elevator shot up toward thirty-nine. Gypper and I are not enough firepower—if they're in thirty-nine. And if they're *not* in thirty-nine.... Cassidy didn't like to think about that.

Cassidy gave the silence signal again as the elevator stopped, the little button glowing thirty-nine. He opened the door soundlessly and listened. Far up the stairwell he heard a slippered sound, but it was very faint and he brushed it aside for more immediate concerns. (A mistake, he was to admit much later in *The Legend of the di Castigliones, Annotated.*)

Cassidy and the Gypper stepped out of the elevator soundlessly. At Struthers's rear door. Cassidy strained his ears. Cassidy slipped the gretchel into the lock and opened it easily. Too easily? It had been double-locked before. This time, it was only on catch as if someone didn't give a damn.

Cassidy gritted his teeth, angry at himself. I'm running behind on this operation, and the terrible thing was I don't know how *far* behind. Thirty minutes? The two men stepped into Struthers's kitchen and closed the door. The lights were on. Very peculiar, and very ominous. Cassidy strained his ears again but could hear no sound.

The two men stepped out of the kitchen and into the corridor. Lights on again. Here Cassidy thrust caution aside. Speed was more essential at this point. On tiptoe but swiftly he traversed the long corridor toward Struthers's bedroom. At the door he paused only long enough to pull his .38 out of his shoulder holster before stepping into the room which, like the others, was brightly lit.

Struthers lay on his unopened bed, eyes on the ceiling. He was in a dressing gown and pajamas.

"Another icepick job," said the Gypper, looking it over. "Very neat. Couldn't do it better myself."

Cassidy felt the man's forehead, then tried to bend the arm which was stiff as cement. "Been dead for at least an hour," he said.

"Do we know this character?" asked the Gypper.

"He went under the name of Struthers," said Cassidy. "His real name is Vittorio Pietroangeli. The Mob has been looking for him for a very long time."

"And they found him."

"No," said Cassidy. "Somebody else found him."

The closet door stood open. Cassidy marched in, knowing in advance there was no point. He was right. The safe was open and empty.

Damnation. It was beginning to come together, all of it. I've been outwitted at every bloody turn, Cassidy was thinking. The only consolation was that Vittorio Pietroangeli had been outwitted in the end—and Vittorio Pietroangeli was both bright and tough. It would take a deal of outwitting to slip an icepick into him, if that was any comfort. And it wasn't much.

"Come on," said Cassidy. "They're ahead of us."

As they left the bedroom, Cassidy glanced into the doorway of the little library-type room where he'd hid out last time he'd been in the apartment. Unlike all the other rooms, it was dark. Something very funny about that.

Cassidy leaned against the corridor wall, keeping his body well back, and snapped the overhead light with the switch on the library wall. He took a quick look.

The face that stared at him was only barely recognizable as Hugo's. Eyes starting out of their sockets, mouth wide open as if caught in midscream—a scream that had been going on for some time. The body was tied with nylon cord—a great deal of it—to the big chair behind the desk. On Hugo the silent scream was a horrifying sight. Screaming wasn't Hugo's style and someone had made him scream—something Cassidy hadn't managed even with the Vivaldi.

"Someone worked him over real good," said the Gypper. "Icepick in the kidney. That's very unkind."

"Poor Hugo was always getting it in the kidneys."

"Is this guy a friend?" asked Gypper.

"Oh, Hugo was everyone's friend," said Cassidy absently. "That was his big problem." He was going through Hugo's dinner jacket pocket by pocket.

"You were close to this stiff?"

"Oh, very close." After you'd tortured a man, Cassidy was thinking, you were his uncle—until death do you part. Death had them parted but Hugo might have a little malevolence left in him which was what he was searching for. "Hugo was a very great expert at survival, Gypper."

"If that's survival, I don't want any," said Gypper.

"He ran out his string," said Cassidy gently. "It'll happen to you and me some day."

"Not with icepicks. I'm pretty good against icepicks."

He found it in a special pocket sewed into Hugo's trousers on the inside seam near the bottom of the right leg. It was a music box, the little gadget that opened doors.

"Now, we shall see what we shall see," said Cassidy. He pulled out the music box Hugo had given him and pushed the button. It emitted three clear notes. He tried it with Hugo's box. It emitted three quite different notes.

"Aah," said Cassidy. "He vindicated my total lack of trust. Betrayal to the bloody end, Gypper. Hugo had an unbroken record of duplicity."

Very careless of them to leave the music box on Hugo. Clearly they'd frisked him because the body contained nothing else—no wallet or keys. They just hadn't quite finished the job.

Their first mistake. Perhaps their only one.

The lights went out.

All the light—the light in the little library, the corridor, the whole apartment—was extinguished at once, as if someone had thrown the switch.

In the blackness, Cassidy thought, with paralyzing certainty, they've switched off the whole building. There was only one place they could do that—the control room Hugo Dorn had shown him.

"The one thing I didn't think of, Gypper, was a flashlight," said Cassidy apologetically in the darkness.

The Gypper's torch cut through the blackness at that moment, cheerful as a ray of sunshine, playing on the dead man's black eyes. "Never travel without one, Boss. Not since Korea. Bloody dark in Korea!"

Gypper's last words

Or almost. That last word of all was a half screech...
"Cass...." He never quite finished that word, Cassidy. It ended
in an exclamation point of silence but that half screech sent
Cassidy to the floor, rolling to get away from the spot he'd been
in. In the nick of time.

In the light of Gypper's torch, now doing a parabola which
ended on the floor where it went out abruptly, Cassidy caught a
surreal impression in black and white, like one of those old
German silent films, of an icepick clutched in a female hand.
Even at the speed the icepick was traveling through the air, and
it was going very fast indeed, Cassidy clearly distinguished the
hand that clutched it as a female hand. By the width of a straw,
the icepick missed Cassidy's skull, his rolling shoulder, his
revolving body; it went into the wooden floor with such force
that the hand could not pull it loose.

The Gypper's torch had gone out at that instant but Cassidy
still rolling—a roll which ended painfully with a crash into the
wall of the library—heard a hiss of rage at the impervious
icepick, a hiss that sound like "Gltl."

Cassidy put his head down and threw a body block where the
arm was last seen, but she was darting quick. His legs cutting
through the air struck her legbone, but not nearly hard enough.
In the pitch blackness, he heard rather than felt her go on hands
and knees, then her fingers whistled past his ear. Even in total
darkness, he knew a dike shot, and he riposted with a short
openhand chop at where he thought the head should be. He
caught only the shoulder bone—but hard—and heard an
exclamation of pain.

She must be on hands and knees now, couldn't be anywhere
else considering where his chop had hit, and Cassidy did a bull
rush, arms outstretched. Again she was fast, and he crashed
against bookshelves. He heard a quick scuttling sound and knew
she'd got out of the library. She was scuttling down the corridor
on all fours from the sound of it. It was the first chance Cassidy
had to pull his gun.

The shot from the .38 lit up the blackness of the corridor for
an instant like a lightning flash and in that flash Cassidy caught
a glimpse of his antagonist.

Two bits of information registered—one after another:
1. It was Titi.

2. She had a gun and it was pointed at him.

The last bit of information was easily the most urgent. Cassidy rolled to his left, and her shot missed him by a considerable margin. Her second shot was closer, and this time Cassidy bounded right through the bedroom door to get out of range.

In the blackness, he heard her taking to her heels down the corridor, running through the blackness as surefootedly as a cat. He would have taken after her, but his Radox came alive at that moment, uttering its high shrill command.

Cassidy pulled it out of his breast pocket and pushed the INCOM button.

"May Day," screeched Fingertips in tones that sounded both anguished and hopeless. "May Day! May Day!"

Behind it Cassidy heard the crackle of automatic fire—a lot of fire from more than one gun.

"May Day! May Day!" The voice was weakening. Clearly some of that fire had got to Fingertips. Presently the voice stopped and there was only the sound of the guns on a crowded dance floor where 225 people were screaming. The screams of the super-rich and super-sophisticated, Cassidy noted at the time, were no more well-bred than anyone else's screams. If anything, a little louder, because the rich were better fed and had better lungs.

Cassidy crawled through the blackness, feeling his way into the little library, his fingertips groping for Gypper's flashlight. A door slammed at the kitchen end of the apartment. Titi had left the apartment.

His fingers closed on the flashlight. Cassidy jiggled it and it came on, the ribbon of white light cutting across Gypper's dead and open eyes. With the tip of his index finger Cassidy closed the two eyes, then permitted himself a single caress of the tough cheek. "Not with icepicks. I'm pretty good with icepicks," Gypper had said. But it *was* with an icepick, and that was just that, after twenty years—Korea, Bulgaria, and a lot of other places.

Cassidy permitted himself the luxury of a moment's grief— and, in retrospect, he thought this may have saved his life because it slowed him down, it gave him a moment's reflection, and he needed that very badly. If Gypper had been alive, the pair of them would have hurtled after Titi, up the stairs, into the maelstrom at the rooftop restaurant. And probably been killed.

Lying on the floor in the blackness next to his dead comrade, the Radox spitting out screams and rifle fire, Cassidy thought things over.

If you were assaulting a fortification—and what was the Windletop but a fortification—take command first of the cellar where the underpinnings of the castle are. Then command the stairwells. Who said that? I said that, said Cassidy, to Lucia— Titi listening in, crouching in her corner like an animal. They're in control of the controls. No elevators so the cops can't get up, and they got the stairwells. I taught her all that.

So what do I do now....

·30·

Excerpted from *The Legend of the di Castigliones, Annotated*

Of all the great massacres of the twentieth century, that of the Windletop is believed to be the only one by candlelight.[1] Candlelight was, in fact, a very great strategic problem to the planners of this massacre. Their original plan had been to douse the lights before the shooting began and control of the light switch was always essential to the plan. Only the combat team was to have had flashlights. However, this twentieth century tactic ran headlong into the eighteenth-century esthetics of the Principessa who personally determined the disposition of all the 7,265 candles which lit the party.

There is no known way of shooting out 7,265 candles or putting them out in a hurry,[2] and therefore the plan had to be changed slightly which meant we are aware of details of the raid that would not have been known if the restaurant had been

1 The most famous massacre over dinner is, of course, that by the Campbell clan of the McGregors after having served them dinner at Inverary, an inconceivable breach of good manners which took place in the seventeenth century and has not been forgotten or forgiven to this very day. It took place by torchlight. Of massacres by candlelight probably the best known is that of the Stirglesi family—father, mother, eight children including a babe in arms—extinguished in Venice in 1365 in the great hall of the Stirglesi *palazzo* on the Grand Canal by the light of six superb Venetian chandeliers, each bearing over 100 candles designed and made by Faschetti in 1126. The Stirglesi is still considered the most elegantly lit atrocity of its or any other day.

2 *Warfare by Candlelight*, by British Major General R.L.S. Padgett (Ret.), the definitive work on this subject, estimates it would take ten men working at top speed at least five minutes to extinguish 1,000 candles and therefore half an hour or more to put out 7,000 candles. Only the British can do such military research with a straight face.

plunged, as originally planned, into total darkness. The combat team—all of it—came up the stairs eschewing the elevator for reasons, we presume, of surprise. In superb condition after intensive mountain training in Iraq, the twenty-two man combat team ran up the thirteen flights of stairs in roughly seven and a half minutes.[3]

The team poured first into the kitchen, where two men held the kitchen crew at gunpoint[4] while their teammates poured out the door next to the strategic table where sat the *Times* society reporter Jane Atchison and Fingertips. The gunmen fanned out along the upper rim of the restaurant, holding their fire for twenty-six seconds. This gave them time to go clear to the end of the restaurant before firing or even attracting very much attention, carrying their automatic weapons inconspicuously straight down parallel with the seams of their trousers.

One of the few to notice was Fingertips, who dove under the table seconds after he saw the gunmen. Apparently Jane Atchison stayed in her chair, notebook poised in her lap like a good reporter, trying to understand what was happening, when she was cut down by one of the first bursts of fire, still in her chair.[5]

Fire was not altogether at random. Of my four men, all armed, three, Fingertips, Freddie, and Jacoby, were all killed early on, apparently by design. Of the CIA's known four men, two were cut down, and it is thought another waiter was killed because he was thought to be CIA. Alison escaped by diving under a table so thickly surrounded by dancers that the bullets aimed at him found instead the merrymakers on the dance floor. Summing up, this meant that of the nine men, myself and Alison included, at the party for security reasons, the Red Wind combat team cut down five and missed four; which is a fairly normal rate of success for an operation this size. For reasons they could not

3 My report here deviates sharply from the FBI's. The FBI is, as usual, full of prune juice.

4 The Red Wind combat team was careful to avoid martyring any true members of the proletariat, confining bloodshed to the rich and the security men, except for one Puerto Rican waiter killed by accident who left seven children in quite authentic proletarian misery.

5 The last of Jane Atchison's notes, deciphered by FBI cryptologists and found still clutched in her dead hand, reported that the Duchess de Angelis' hairdo was coming unstruck from the severity of her dancing the Pendulum.

have foreseen, Gypper and I were not on the floor, Alison was preserved by accident, one waiter was shot by mistaken identity. From all this we deduce that it had been planned to eliminate all of us. This shows not only the thoroughness of their preparation but the brilliance of their intelligence, which penetrated the CIA.

Even after the fire became general, the gunmen firing into the mass of dancers and diners, it was fairly selective. Analysis of the dead and wounded clearly shows that the prime targets were the most dissolute, featherbrained, and useless of the very rich—Gogo Canossa, the Duchess de Angelis, the Princesse de Bruxelles, and others whose names were bywords in the gossip columns for insensate triviality—whose slaughter would excite headlines without censure (and perhaps even with approval) from the masses and derision from the intellectuals.

As a public relations coup this careful selection of victims was superbly planned but not always that well executed. Robert, the headwaiter, was gunned down, possibly because he got in the way, or perhaps because of some ideological confusion as to which category—bourgeois or proletarian—one properly puts a headwaiter in. Or maybe some gunman didn't like the scornful smile, which was found fixed on Robert's face even in death.

We come now to the Principals in the case—Lucia and the Principessa. The Principessa was continuing her round of the tables, greeting her guests, and there are four different sworn statements in the FBI files, claiming that at the moment the storm of bullets started, she was at this particular table, all of them different ones.

A waiter swore to the FBI that the Principessa remained standing throughout the entire massacre while everyone else threw themselves to the floor. According to three other witnesses, she was almost the most conspicuous person in the entire room for one reason or another.[6] The fact that she didn't get killed or wounded in spite of this is significant, of course. There was intense speculation as to what she was doing during the sixty-seven seconds[7] of the massacre, some saying she just stood there,

6 "Elsa was a beacon of courage in a sea of craven cowardice," Chantel de Niailles was quoted as saying in *The New York Daily News*.

7 The FBI is slightly demented in the matter of numbers, relishing idiot statistics like fine caviar. It may well have been sixty-eight seconds or even sixty-nine.

others that she continued to dance as a gesture of defiance, one that she was weeping, another that she was laughing. Actually, she told me afterward, she was searching the dance floor for her daughter.

Fortunately, Lucia was dancing with the most combat-wise man in the whole room, Alvin Feinberg, a veteran of eleven wars, and within an instant of the first shot, Feinberg pulled Lucia to the floor and sprawled on top of her to protect her. There was, however, tremendous competition for floor space from the other dancers who pushed and shoved in an effort to get as flat as possible. Somewhere in this maelstrom, Lucia slipped out from under the protecting body of Alvin Feinberg and disappeared. Feinberg himself thinks she wriggled away, and he's not at all sure she wasn't helped by someone whom he couldn't identify because of the crush of bodies on him at the time.

There were enormous discrepancies in the accounts of how long the operation took, ranging from half an hour to two minutes. From all accounts, added up and known times of blackout, it appears the elapsed time from the moment when the gunmen first entered from the kitchen to the moment when they left the same way they came, was about five and a half minutes.

During all that time, both elevators were shut off from the main control room in the sub-subbasement which meant police were cut off from the rooftop by fifty-three flights of stairs.

·31·

In his stocking feet Cassidy descended the pitch dark stairwell by memory, the flashlight in his left hand, the .38 in his right. (And the Gypper's .44 in his waistband.) The flashlight would have made things easier but Cassidy now was consumed by caution. Bravado was for other times, other people. He'd lost the Gypper and Fingertips. He didn't yet know he'd also lost Jacoby and Freddie, but he suspected it, and anyway they were nowhere near.

There was just himself. He had to be careful, and being careful meant he was slow. The blackness did things to his wits—sharpened them. Or over-sharpened them until he saw Titi in that brief terrible instant way out of scale, big as the Minotaur and as menacing.

Meanwhile, counting each landing.

Thirty-eight, thirty-seven, thirty-six, thirty-five....

He stopped and listened hard for sounds of pursuit, sounds of anything....Nothing.

Thirty-four, thirty-three....

Had they left a guard on the stairwell? They had to get out of the building and it would tell a lot about their plans if they had left a guard. If they had. Would he be disciplined enough to remain in total darkness, silent and still. Or she? (Terror was completely bisexual, conceivably the first occupation to have equal pay, equal rights, equal opportunity for both sexes.)

Twenty-one, twenty, nineteen....

Then came the noise which, in the terrible silence of the stairwell, sounded like the crack of doom. A tremendous clang and then a shhhhrrrrrr sound, sustained and approaching.

They'd put the elevator back in commission, but not the lights. Very clever.

The elevator passed Cassidy as he was between sixteen and fifteen. He could hear it descend and stop far below him. How far below? He didn't know.

After a ten-second interval, during which he could hear them decanting from the elevator (but on which landing? Rooftop's?) the elevator door clanged shut again with its ear-splitting bang and started up again.

Bringing them down in relays?

Cassidy picked up the pace. He had a long way to go in the pitch blackness. He abandoned caution. Or perhaps "abandon" is too sweeping a word. No one past fifty, thought Cassidy, feeling his way down the blackness, *abandons* caution. Past a certain age a man plays a little fast and loose with it. That's the best he can do.

Still on stockinged tiptoe, keeping very quiet, just picking up the pace a little, Cassidy rounded down twelve, eleven, ten. . . .

The shot came as he rounded the midpoint between the landings on nine and eight and came from the eighth landing. The noise on the enclosed stairwell was headsplitting. The shot missed, largely (he decided much later) because he was crouched sideways to make the turn.

The muzzle flash lit up the shooter perfectly and Cassidy shot him in the heart from a crouch, with a noise like a thousand thunderclaps.

Cassidy changed position. fast, scooting to the landing and crouching to reduce his targetability, in case there were two of them. Even if there weren't, he was thinking, the terrible noise would bring a platoon of Red Wind.

Or perhaps not.

The Red Wind was notorious for leaving their fallen where they lay and proceeding according to the blueprints.

The elevator was coming down from the rooftop restaurant. It passed in darkness and silence and proceeded down. Far down. Cassidy listened to the stop—as if life depended on it. Lower than street level. Much lower.

He used his flash for the first time, confident there was no one else on that stairwell within shooting distance.

A very ordinary man, almost a boy, wearing almost too

ordinary street clothes. Collar and tie, even. What a way to come a-murdering. All dressed up for church. But that was the fashion in terror. Merge with the crowd (like a fish in the sea, according to Mao) and if you were urban, you must look like what you most despised—bourgeois—because that's what the masses looked like these days. The most romantic new occupation, that of terrorist, dressed like a file clerk.

Cassidy snapped off the flash and started down again in his stockinged feet, this time really tearing along. He doubted there'd be another one.

The blackness conjuring up little pictures in his brain. Out of the past! His one and only wife accusing him with her level stare of loving another. But you're dead, cried Cassidy in the noiselessness of his mind. It's not adultery, it's . . . anyway, I was raped. Imagine you caring, after fourteen years dead. I thought there was a statute of limitations. Jupiter, what am I doing maundering around in the past when I am mired so viciously and dangerously in the right now of it. . . .

They say that in the darkness you lose all sense of time. Maybe it's three days later. Certainly my spatial is out of whack. I've been on these stairs for forty miles at least.

Five, four. . . .

The obstruction was on the third floor landing—a triple-plated steel door that had no ordinary look. Cassidy felt his way down in the blackness, step by step, encountering nothing. The triple-plated steel door was open. Why? Had they expected him? More probably it was left that way as the escape hatch for that terrorist dressed like a file clerk.

The elevator had not gone back up again.

That meant . . . what? They were all down there. How many? Must be at least twenty. Otherwise, they'd all have gone in one load. Me, against twenty. Who said a man does not abandon caution after age fifty? I said it. I'm now about to make a liar of me.

He counted the flights, one, two, three. Stiflingly hot, which meant that he was in the basement with its array of steam pipes and those ancient red pumps. Twice he risked a momentary beam from the flashlight in order to pick his way through the antique machinery.

He ran into the steel wall at the end of the room with his nose.

Mankind's great glory is his unpredictability. Sainthood is only one step away from foolishness. From deviltry, only an inch. His head ringing like a great bell.

Feeling his nose and listening for sound behind the steel wall.

Cassidy tucked the .38 in his waistband of his trousers at the front. (The Gypper's .44 was in his waistband at the back.) He stuffed the flashlight in his side pocket and drew out the music box. He had two now—the one the late Hugo Dorn had given him and the one he'd taken from the seam of Hugo's trousers.

He tried the first one. Just in case.

Three musical notes: pong, ping, pang.

Nothing at all happened.

He put the box carefully on the floor at his feet, took out the second one.

Put his ear again to the steel door just in case he'd not listened hard enough the first time. Or perhaps just stalling. If the door opened, life was going to be very perilous indeed for the next little while.

Cassidy sighed. A luxury in the blackness.

Here goes one unemployed medievalist locked in a twentieth-century fairy castle about to enter the dragon's lair to rescue the fairy princess.

Three musical notes—the steel door sank into the concrete floor.

Cassidy went down on his belly fast, head up.

Ahead of him the circular stone steps, lit by two faint light bulbs, stretched, curving down and out of sight.

A murmur of voices drifted up the stairs, insubstantial as air. He couldn't even make out the language.

They couldn't get a little girl in a Heidi-like blue dress out of the building without attracting attention. On the other hand, they couldn't stay even in so secret a hideout as this indefinitely.

Whatever it was they had figured it out long in advance, and I've got thirty seconds to make up my weak wits.

Thirteen steps to the curve of the wall which concealed him from them. From there until the steps ended in the brick room with all its dials and computers and switches would be another ten steps in which he would be fully visible.

To procede cautiously, poking his head round that treacherous corner, trying to size up the situation, perhaps pick off a few on his belly while himself making only a smidgin of a target....

Or to rush guns blazing into a situation he knew nothing about. Not even how many there were there or whether Lucia or the Principessa was with them....

The first was just a cautious man's way of getting killed by inches and at snail's pace and what was the virtue of that?

The second was the speedy way of getting himself killed and perhaps Lucia, too.

To a man of his age and sagacity both courses were recipes for disaster. Not worth consideration, much less.... Yet he had no others.

Meanwhile, assembling the hardware. The .38 in his right hand, .44 in his left. No accuracy at all, two-fisted firepower, that was all. He deplored it. But, after all, the rush tactic had succeeded at Entebbe and at how many other spots where nothing else had?

The murmurings in the control room were split in half by a shrill cry in unmistakable tones of twelve-year-old fear and fury, the two so evenly blended he couldn't tell which emotion was uppermost.

In his stocking feet Cassidy ran down the twelve stairs around the curve of the wall and into full view of the control room and at that very instant he let loose a roar of sound from his lungs (a noise bomb would have been better if he had had one, but he didn't). "Eeeee-iiiii-o-o-o-eeee-aahhh-tii"—a Saracen cry that had terrorized the Christians when the walls of Acre tumbled down around their ears and the Saracens came charging in with their curved scimitars, a magnificent cry to curdle the blood of the infidel....

BOOK THREE
Lucia

In all the speculations, indignations, denunciations, and explanations that exploded in the press, pulpit, and street theater everyone agreed on only One Thing: even the Super-Rich shouldn't be massacred with Russian *weapons. Wielded by Germans and Italians. What was the matter with good old American weapons? To say nothing of good old American assassins? We'd always been pretty good at massacre. Had we grown so soft we had to import it?*

What on earth had gone wrong?

Cassidy missed most of this uproar because he was in a police station not answering questions. The police asked many questions about the dead and the living and Cassidy, who knew his rights as well as any lawyer, answered as few as he could.

The police gave him a very bad time. No one gave him a good time.

·32·

Excerpted from *The Legend of the di Castigliones, Annotated*

This is written in retrospect—as what isn't—and it's not what happened (as what is?) because time has blurred the fine edges. Reason has tried to sort out an essentially unreasonable—one is tempted to use the word insane—action. And made a mess of things, as reason usually does when it messes with the irrational.

The first part was by the book.

I hurtled down into the Control Room shrieking a Saracen war cry to freeze the blood of the New Infidels (not bad, the New Infidels, because that's what they are), and as I hit the light, I went down and to the right which meant to their left. As the Good Book says, always go to the left because it's harder to track a moving target left than right.

The scene, even after three months, four days, some hours, remains vivid and *pointilliste* in memory. I've tried not to add anything that wasn't there, and it's not easy, so creative are we with our most painful and precious recollections, to avoid adding a few touches that should have been there but were not.

Let us freeze the action for a moment and sketch the scene in full color. A scene from grand opera. Second act curtain with the full cast and chorus on stage, all singing at the top of their lungs.

In her Heidi-like dress Lucia dominated the center of the stage, struggling in the arms of a Titi who seemed to have grown in stature and certainly in viciousness.

Nearby stood three Red Wind, weapons at their sides. The Principessa stood near them under no restraint—at least no physical restraint. She stood there in her sapphire blue velvet sheath, as always erect, but for the first and only time since I had known her, in despair. Defeat was writ large all over that beautiful graven image of a face, a defeat she'd held at bay for twelve years.

Titi was trying to force Lucia through a hole blown in the rear facing wall. This was the exit I'd been looking for from the moment I saw that room, and had questioned Hugo closely about under the Vivaldi. Hugo had resisted the blandishments of the Vivaldi (no relation to the composer) simply because he didn't know. (Or perhaps he did. There are some things about Hugo we shall never know. So finely grained was his duplicity, he kept secrets from himself.)

I digress.

My Saracen war cry achieved one unexpected bonus. Designed to freeze (if only for the tiniest moment) all the participants (and it did that to some degree), it had the opposite effect on Lucia, who had been struggling against the bigger Titi. The war cry—eeeee-iiiii-o-o-o-eeee-aahhh-tii—gave Lucia just that extra bit of strength she needed to toss Titi over her shoulder in the back Motherwell I'd taught her.

I changed my shriek from Saracen to plain English. "Dire emergency! Dire! Dire!" Directed to Lucia. Meanwhile I shot from a crouch the three Red Wind warriors in their file clerk suits, moving all the time as the Good Book directs.

Lucia drew the .22 strapped to her thigh in the nick of time because Titi came out of her tumble with a gun in her hand, pointed at myself in what you might say was the final manifestation of a disapproval that had marked our relationship from the very beginning.

Her's was a pretty good shot, missing only because I was moving left and downward. Mine would have taken her out clean but the .44 jammed (they always do, invariably at the worst moment) and it was Lucia who shot Titi, directly in the face, rolling as I'd taught her to the left.

Still firing.

As I'd instructed her.

Perhaps too well instructed her.

"No! No!" shrieked the Principessa. "He's *your father.*"

For Lucia was still rolling, still firing at someone to my right

206 ·

outside my vision. The Principessa had thrown herself directly into the line of fire, whether deliberately or not—things being as they were—we'll never know.

I saw Lorenzo now, for the first time. He'd been at the console that controlled everything in that building, turning the lights back on in the Windletop (a clever ruse designed to keep the police from looking for the control room by obviating the need) when I had come hurtling in.

Lorenzo had caught Lucia's bullet directly in the heart—as if I'd marked an X there as I had marked those X's on the trees in Central Park—and he crumpled neatly into a small compact heap like a circus clown, playing it for laughs.

"Your Papa! Your Papa!" said the Principessa carefully, trying to undo mortality.

"Papa!" screamed Lucia and flung herself on the body as if she'd been looking for him all her life—as indeed she had.

The Principessa sat down slowly, the sapphire blue dress stained now with a shade of red she'd never have worn with that dress.

"I killed my Papa! I killed my Papa!"

The rage directed at me because, of course, I'd taught her. These things never work out quite as you plan.

Pointing the gun at me, directly at the heart.

Again, exactly as I'd instructed.

Click.

"I told you to count your shots," I said to her. "You had only nine."

·33·

Cassidy and Feinberg were lunching in the back room of the Spumi, each giving away as little as possible.

"Intelligence," said Cassidy at his most mellifluous, "is filling the function once so ably performed by journalism. You journalists have grown rich, respectable, and even famous, and with it has come sloth, greed, and layers of avoirdupois, whereas we in the intelligence profession...."

"You're no longer in that profession," commented Feinberg.

"...are poor starvelings, despised and misunderstood by the populace..."

"For very good reason."

"...our wits sharpened by deprivation, our bodies driven by hunger..."

"Balls!"

"...to uncover the sordid corruptions you journalists so persistently ignore—or worse—don't see at all, your myopia ripening into ignorance and eventually superstition which you inflict as news on your sycophantic readers who rival you in stupidity, greed, and impotence."

"Cassidy," said Feinberg with his cherubic smile, "you are a driveling idiot who has swallowed a dictionary. You mistake words for intelligence."

"I'm Irish," said Cassidy. "Words are the national pastime and idiocy our congenital weakness. How is the *canneloni?*"

"Adequate," said Feinberg.

"You sound like a drama critic," said Cassidy, "which is not a profession but an epithet."

Jabbing away to prevent Feinberg, a very good journalist, from asking all the questions Cassidy didn't want to answer.

Like trying to keep a hog from rooting.

"Why," said Feinberg, returning to a question Cassidy had twice sidestepped, "should Nicki expose himself in that restaurant in full view of people who had known him very well—people he'd been hiding from for years?"

"Freudians," said Cassidy, "would call it a cry for help." Followed by a three-minute disquisition on the lunacy of Freud, Freudians, and most modern literature. Feinberg bore it all with his implacable good nature (which had reduced many world statesmen to a bonhomie they later regretted when they read his dispatches), boring in finally with:

"I knew Nicki very well, and I looked at Lorenzo several times. It never occurred to me that was Nicki even though he looked like Nicki—an older ravaged Nicki. Now why was that, do you suppose?"

"You didn't expect to find a Prince of ancient lineage working as a butler. Function changes personality. *She Stoops to Conquer* in modern dress. Also you thought he was dead."

"Lorenzo looked older than Nicki would be, older than God really. How did he do that—makeup?"

"Acting," said Cassidy. "Nicki *believed* himself into old age so passionately you believed it, too. Zero Mostel didn't transform himself into a rhinoceros with makeup. He bulged out his eyes and pawed the ground. Inside himself he was a rhinoceros—so outside he was, too."

A stunning bit of acting, thought Cassidy, himself the connoisseur of acting that he was. He had himself seen many photographs of Nicki and never suspected it was Lorenzo. Then there was the other photo he'd taken from Pietroangeli's safe—a naked Titi whipping a naked Nicki. Cassidy had not recognized the whippee until after it was all over and done with as either Nicki or Lorenzo. Truly, Nicki was a man of many faces who changed personality—also character—at will. Dr. Jekyll and Mr. Hyde, as it were.

Feinberg was boring in again with a question Cassidy had no intention of answering: "How did Nicki get into livery in the first place?"

"Aaaah," said Cassidy with his expansive Irish smile.

"That's hardly an answer," complained Feinberg silkily.

The cards were by no means all in Cassidy's hands. Feinberg

had the entire newsgathering machinery of *The New York Times* at his elbow. He had a lot of information Cassidy badly wanted and he was not about to give it up for nothing. Also, Feinberg had been to Italy for the funeral. Cassidy couldn't afford to be too flippant. He needed Feinberg as badly as Feinberg needed him.

Feinberg picked at his canneloni patiently: "You were alone with the dying Principessa for the last hour of her life. The only one she would speak to, Horatio. Now why was that, do you suppose?"

"I would love to hear your speculations about that, Alvin," said Cassidy. "Your skill at putting words into other people's mouths is world renowned."

Feinberg smiled his cherubic smile: "Well then, hear this. Remember I knew Elsa before you did and just as well...."

Cassidy felt a stab of jealousy to his very toes. Ridiculous. Being jealous of the Principessa was liking being jealous of the sun for shining on everyone.

Feinberg was continuing with great calm: "Elsa would not like the legend of the di Castigliones to die untold or misunderstood. At the same time she would not like the story told *now* when so many of the living could be hurt. Therefore she would not tell me, a journalist, and she would not tell anyone so unreliable as the police. That left you."

"Oh, did it now?" retorted Cassidy. "The Principessa's friends were numbered in the thousands, few of them journalists or police."

Actually Cassidy knew very well why he'd been summoned to the bare room in New York Hospital into which the Principessa had been thrust too fast for Alison or his crew to mike.

"Sit down, Horatio, and shut up." In a thin whisper of a voice which was all she had left. She looked every minute of her age—and what was her age, fifty?—and she wanted no one but Cassidy who'd already seen her in her nakedness to see that ravaged face.

"*Cherchez la mere. Pas la femme, la mere,*" she whispered in that spidery voice. "Nicki's mother was on her knees in all of Rome's 2,000 churches. I gave him what he wanted—a mother—

what he'd never had. I was too indulgent a mother, too loving by miles, but then I'd never had a child before, you know. He was my only child—and spoiled."

Even in the extremity of circumstances, Cassidy couldn't forbear the raging question: "Why didn't Lucia recognize Lorenzo as her father?"

"Lucia had never seen her father. He wouldn't allow her in the room. He was horrified by paternity. A little boy who won't grow up can hardly have a daughter, can he now?"

She told him only carefully selected things he had to know, some of which he'd already guessed (but guessing wasn't knowing) and many of which he hadn't guessed at all and which astonished him.

Even if she had time, and she hadn't much, she wouldn't have told him everything. She was too subtle, too intelligent, and too feminine to tell all. She left selected holes in the air which had to be filled by other voices. But Feinberg was dead wrong in thinking she gave a damn about the di Castiglione legend. She had no interest in posterity. Only in Lucia. There was a good reason for every crumb of information she gave him. Those facts that didn't need divulging were not divulged. Cassidy was still digging them up elsewhere.

There were very good reasons for keeping the legend quiet now. There was Lucia, who had not spoken a word to him since that terrible night.

Cassidy turned on the Irish charm to get at what he so desperately needed to know. "Tell me about the funeral."

"Now why should I do that," said Feinberg, "when you have been so unforthcoming about everything else?"

"Because the whole story has already appeared on the front page of *The New York Times*."

"I must confess I enjoyed writing about the di Castiglione tomb."

The tomb in which reposed four hundred years of di Castiglione bones was one of Bernini's masterpieces, an immense edifice of marble and bronze that loomed over the Tuscany hills like a benison. That's what Feinberg had written.

"It was a beautiful day for a funeral," said Feinberg, telling Cassidy all the things he didn't want to know which is what

Cassidy had been doing to him for the whole luncheon, "sunny and warm. There were enough high Catholic clergy to elect a new Pope but not many di Castigliones."

"There are not many left," said Cassidy. "How did Lucia look?"

"Solemn—but then she was always a solemn child."

She wasn't. Thought Cassidy.

"She was with her Aunt Clothilde—a wizened crow...."

Poor Lucia.

"Dressed in black."

Lucia hated black.

"Where is Lucia now? You didn't say in your article," said Cassidy sweetly. His letter had been returned. Recipient unknown.

"No, I didn't," said Feinberg. "Did I?"

"Where is she, Feinberg?"

Alvin Feinberg buttered a piece of bread and then chewed on it reflectively, letting Cassidy wait. He sipped his wine. He wiped his mouth meticulously with his napkin.

"It was, of course, the second identical burial in the same bronze casket. There had been a body in that casket for years. Whose body? The police say they have no idea. The police are lying. This time, they took fingerprints. They know very well who that is but they're not saying for reasons I can only guess at, all of them discreditable. Now who was it, Cassidy, who lay in Nicki's tomb all those years?"

"Gianini Gennaro," said Cassidy negligently. You had to give a little to get a little.

Feinberg slammed his napkin down on the table. "That's who I thought, too, but I didn't *know*. Gennaro! The guy the Mob thought ran off with all the ransom money. They've been looking for him ever since. The Principessa knew the whole bit all along and she told you...."

"Listen, you bastard, if you mention my name in connection with any of this, I'll cut your balls off and eat them in front of your very eyes. I'm not even an unnamed source. These are your own sleazy speculations."

Feinberg's eyes glittered in triumph behind the gold-rimmed glasses. He'd found out what he'd come for. He'd have liked a little more, as what journalist wouldn't, but this was enough. He felt generous.

"I owe you a little something, Cassidy," said Feinberg, "and no one has ever said I'm not generous in victory. I've been talking to the lawyers—this is for your ears only, Cassidy, until my book is published—and they told me...."

"There's not a lira left of the di Castiglione fortune," said Cassidy wickedly. "What hasn't been already stolen the lawyers will steal, so in effect it's all gone."

It took the wind out of Feinberg's sails. He sighed: "Cassidy, you never fail to amaze me."

"Don't forget, my friend, I have been on this case longer than you and it has been my sole preoccupation while you and the other *Times* editors have had the rest of the world on your shoulders."

They both ate in silence, each pursuing his own quite different ruminations.

"Where is she, Feinberg?" Cassidy asked.

"I was told not to tell you."

"By Aunt Clothilde—or Lucia?"

"Both."

Feinberg's eyes were deeply sympathetic. It was brutal, that word *both*, but Cassidy deserved the truth. He's bleeding inside, thought Feinberg.

Cassidy grimaced in pain: "I've got to know, Alvin. It was the Principessa's dying wish. You can't hold out against that."

Feinberg thought it over. "She's in the Convent of the Holy Sepulchre above Siena."

"I feared as much," whispered Cassidy. "Thank you."

"It won't do you any good, Horatio. I had a few words with Lucia. She's bitter."

The waiter was standing there with the check in his hand. Cassidy plucked it from him and handed it to Feinberg. He smiled his Irish blarney smile: "It's not only the di Castigliones who haven't a dime to their names. It's the Cassidys, too. The Principessa died owing me two month's salary."

Excerpted from *The Legend of the di Castigliones, Annotated*

I should have thought of that 1920s railroad station that lay under the Windletop long before I did, if only because it was so exquisitely attuned to the rest of the story—a relic of the past—surfacing in the 1970s in a way never intended and causing havoc to a generation unborn when it was built.

The wall had long since been bricked up and the railroad station abandoned, actually with a private railroad car still sitting on a siding. It was an ornate little railroad station, with a great vaulted ceiling of ornamental brick interlaced with multicolored tiles, the whole confection looking a little like a Romanesque Church of the late Crusades.

Long abandoned. But not by everyone. Bums knew it was there and slept on its resplendent stone steps. They got there from the Grand Central tracks under Park Avenue. New York teems with abandoned underground stations (most of them old subway stops) and the underground hobo population knows them all. That's how the Red Wind got into the Windletop—by blowing a hole in the wall at the precise spot Titi told them to.

They got into the tunnel (as so many do) through the many manholes on Park Avenue and most of them left that way and got clean away.

·34·

Under the beneficent foliage of Georgetown's trees, Cassidy lurked for a full hour, choosing the nearest parking space to Alison's house. Alison would have trouble finding a parking place for the little Julietta, his latest extravagance. Georgetown was very short of parking and when other motorists zeroed in, Cassidy had to leap out from the shelter of his oak and wave them away peremptorily.

The parking space was a good two hundred yards from Alison's front door, which would give him time to present his case. Alison arrived, cruising slowly in the Julietta (whose roof was only four feet from the ground, a very sexy car that went 175 miles an hour and was at the moment going three). Cassidy stayed well out of sight behind his tree until Alison locked up the little sports car and started walking.

Cassidy fell in step beside him: "You've not returned my calls, Hugh. That's very short-sighted," said Cassidy.

"Go away," said Alison not looking at him. "You're an embarrassment Cassidy."

About to become even more so, thought Cassidy. Aloud he said: "I want to talk about Lucia, a small child whose life you've wrecked."

"She's all right. She's in a convent."

"She hates it. I've had a letter."

A lie.

"We can do nothing. She's in the custody of her aunt."

"Her aunt has disowned her. She's imprisoned in a convent. Once one of the richest heiresses in the world, penniless. Have you no heart, Alison?"

"Go away," said Alison picking up the pace.

They were two blocks away from Alison's Georgian residence which, he liked to tell friends, he'd bought for $30,000 (with his wife's money) and was now worth in the neighborhood of $500,000.

"A very simple request. An airline ticket delivered to her personally and in private because they open her mail. And a passport *not* in the name of di Castiglione which would set the hounds of hell on her trail both in Rome and here."

"You're out of your mind!"

Alison was almost running now, but he couldn't afford a full run because his neighbors had eyes and they talked. So Cassidy had a little time to lay it all out.

"She'll get out of that convent by herself. She's a very resourceful child. If she has some place to run to...."

Alison stopped dead and faced Cassidy. "Cassidy, it's finished! You know that! Why are you talking this gibberish?"

"A mother's dying wish, Alison."

"Eh!" said Alison—and resumed his walk, faster than ever. "She'd never get out of Italy. She's twelve years old, for God's sake!"

"Thirteen now. I've got friends in Pan Am who owe me some favors. They'll take care of her, get her on the plane—*if* she gets to Rome. They want no part of that convent. That's where you come in, Alison. You've got to come up with the bread for the ticket because I haven't got any. And a passport in some name besides di Castiglione."

"No!" said Alison, "I'm in enough hot water as it is!"

Almost running now.

"You'd be saving the child from a living death!"

"No!" Alison was heel-and-toeing it now as if he were in the Olympics, Cassidy dog-trotting beside him. They were close to the house now and once there Alison would slam the door in his face—and that would be that. Cassidy threw his rabbit punch.

"Alison, it was you personally who let twenty-two terrorists slip into this country deliberately so that the Terror Section would get a lot more money and more importance. You did it to beef up your own job over there at Langley...."

Alison had again stopped and faced Cassidy, his face wild. "Cassidy, I truly think you've gone over the edge this time. Who do you think would listen to these ravings?"

216 ·

"Alvin Feinberg is writing a book," said Cassidy sweetly. "The untold story behind the Windletop massacre. He's on my ass every twenty minutes to give him a few more juicy tidbits for a book that is already Book-of-the-Month though not yet finished. I lunched with him just yesterday and told him nothing much, but I could change that. Feinberg is a most respected journalist, and he knows his way around the laws of libel as well as any scribbler in the business. He could blacken you from head to toe without leaving an inch for the lawyers."

"You don't know my lawyer." Alison resumed walking, face working furiously. He'd been hurt, but not put out. "My lawyer would tie up Feinberg so that book wouldn't see publication until he's dead."

That left only one card to play and Cassidy played it.

"Now, about that black bag job you admitted committing over your own clear signature, Hugh."

That stopped Alison in his tracks. Cassidy had pulled out his Xerox copy of Alison's letter, and thrust it under his nose. *The black bag job was a pretext, as you know. We all did them in the old days and, when I authorized yours, I couldn't foresee Watergate, could I?*

"It would never hold up in court."

"It would hold up to MacGregor."

A long silence.

"All I'm asking, Hugh, is a plane ticket from your contingency fund and a little American passport from the printing department."

"What name do you want on the passport?" said Alison dully.

"Cassidy is a very nice name," said Cassidy.

·35·

The weeks stretched into months with no word, no anything. Alison had done the business—or said he had. Nothing at all happened.

Cassidy was teaching part time now at the New School for Social Research, a short walk from his house. The rest of his time was passed writing *The Legend of The di Castigliones, Annotated.* When he wasn't writing it, he was researching it.

It filled the days but not the nights.

Excerpted from *The Legend of the di Castigliones, Annotated*

I dwell on the boyhood because Nicki is impossible to explain without reference to those early years when he roamed the vast palazzo with its 223 rooms looking for his adored mother and father who were rarely there[1] and avoiding his detested Nanny who rarely caught him. (Only Nicki knew where all the secret passages were.)

"Nicki! You come out of there or you'll be sorry," was the battlecry of the detested Mrs. Storch, an English Nanny who considered both boyhood and Italy obscene.

Nicki would climb the narrow circular staircases behind the walls to one of the many huge empty baroque rooms in the upper stories whose ceilings and walls were alive with cherubim

---

1 His father was invariably in the arms of one of his twenty-six mistresses, his mother in the embrace of Christ, a form of lechery far more devastating to a child than the other kind.

and seraphim and painted plaster satyrs and goats and maidens—and Nicki would play with these painted and sculptured characters by the hour, never quite losing sight of himself in the many mirrors. In all his life, Nicki never saw anything so beautiful as that boy.[2]

Nicki's imagination peopled the rooms with imaginary characters, fairies, nymphs, satyrs, grotesques, and he never again found companionship quite so *interesting*. Sometimes Nicki would disappear for half a day, and only Clothilde, his elder and formidable sister, was clever enough to track him down.

"What are you doing, you naughty boy?" she would cry because she found Nicki in all respects inexcusable.

"Oh, Clothilde," he'd say. "You've interrupted the mysteries!"

"What mysteries?" she would say crossly, for she was always cross. "There's no one here."

"Not any more," he would say.

Nicki had no childhood friends until he went to secondary school in England[3] at the age of fifteen. At St. Edelbert's[4] he was introduced to homosexuality, whipping, cold baths, and the peculiarly Calvinist Catholicism of England where Papism is worn like a plume as evidence of aristocracy[5] (as opposed to the United States where Catholicism is regarded in upper class circles as a superstition largely harbored by waitressses).

From St. Edelbert's Nicki went to Oxford, which civilized him in other ways, many disastrous. His great friend the Marquis of Finisterre said of Nicki that he was "the most beautiful object outside the Bodleian Library," and this, in addition to his wealth and lineage, attracted women as well as

2 Nicki told all this to the Principessa who told me on her deathbed.

3 Constantine de Lesseps, a celebrated homosexual of Rome, who told me much about Nicki's Oxford years in a twenty-two-page letter of immense erudition and horrifying obscenity.

4 St. Edelbert's in Sussex, an aristocratic Catholic school, which boasted of producing more homosexual Catholic intellectuals than Eton, Harrow, and Westminster put together. Many of these aristocratic homosexuals later infested both Houses of Parliament where they were renowned for advocating such enlightening measures as the death penalty for abortion, restoration of hanging, and corporal punishment in kindergarten.

5 Evelyn Waugh became a Catholic, it is said, only to get into the better London clubs.

men. Although by now his sexual nature was fairly well established, he was besieged by beautiful women, and one of them bedded him successfully.[6] It was she who first noted that to Nicki sex was something better experienced passively. Better yet witnessed. He was not alone in this form of amusement at Oxford.

It must not be deduced from all this that sex was his only preoccupation. Actually it was one of his lesser activities. Nicki was a passionate fencer (said to be the narcissist's favorite exercise), wrestler, and body nut of all sorts (including jujitsu and other eastern fads just then coming into fashion), wit, bon vivant, and celebrated host. The parties in Nicki's rooms were sumptuous and remembered today for the erudition of his guests as well as the wit and charm of the host. Nicki himself was a scholar not of the first rank but well up in the second, "a man of immensely original mind but without tenacity of purpose or, in fact, any purpose," according to his tutor.[7]

He was also an actor, but he made little of this great talent which was a great pity. Oxford, then as now, abounded in drama groups, drama experiment, theater of all kinds in which student actors could try their wings. Nicki's great flaw—although many would not call it that—was that he wanted to be the whole show (actor, author, director, stage designer, everything) and he was accustomed to getting his own way. Theater is above all a collaborative enterprise, and Nicki wouldn't and couldn't collaborate. (As we will discover, he could submit—but that is something else again. Collaboration he didn't understand.)

When he returned to Rome from Oxford, Nicki was beautiful, rich, aristocratic—and twenty years old. As do so many who have had lonely childhoods, Nicki surrounded himself with too many people—snobs, intellectuals, revolution-

6 The celebrated English nymphomaniac Fiona Le Roy whose book *Passions and Perversions* has two chapters on Nicki.

7 His tutor was Simon Purefleet, an eccentric now eighty-nine, who was famous for his bad temper. He was said to be the second rudest man at Oxford, and his insults were treasured by the recipients as if he had bestowed knighthood on them. He was also the biggest snob at the University and in his last five years refused to tutor anyone below the rank of Viscount.

aries, amusing people in general, and also those who liked to be outrageous as a form of amusement. He was very restless and some of his parties were wicked indeed.[8]

8 Constantine de Lesseps tells of one in which a young girl of an impeccable Roman family had oral relations with a donkey. "The interesting thing was that we all watched the girl and the donkey, which Nicki watched us watching—a voyeur of voyeurs. He told me after the party he wished he were the donkey—because it was the only one at the party. Nicki always wanted to be alone in the crowd."

·36·

An eternity of silence came from Rome. Cassidy had no way of knowing what was going through Lucia's thirteen-year-old mind but no way of stopping the speculations that were going through his.

He had battered that little skull with anathema against the Church. "Never trust a man who says his is the True Church. He's telling you an untruth." And so forth and so on. He had heaped contempt, derision, and withering sarcasm on the Church and especially on its Holy Orders but how much of it had penetrated?

He had prided himself that his teaching had become, as it were, too much gospel for her to embrace The Gospels without bursting into laughter. Or tears. Still, there it was: Lucia was still in the convent even after Cassidy had pried it open a crack.

In his mind's eye he saw Lucia on her knees in a chapel full of flickering candles and nonflickering nuns, praying for...what...deliverance? Or acceptance? Religion is the opiate of the people, especially powerful on little girls. But she wasn't such a little girl any more. Thirteen? The age of reason? Or the age of hysteria?

Meanwhile, silence from Rome.

Excerpted from *The Legend of the di Castigliones, Annotated*

There were tremendous pressures on Nicki to get married from the other two trustees, his sister, Clothilde, and Monsignor

Carbonotti,[1] one of the Vatican's most trusted financial pirates, but the last person in the world they wanted Nicki to marry was a divorcee who was apparently permanently childless. As Marietta had pointed out, these two trustees desperately needed an heir to keep the fortune from slipping into the hands of a Turin industrialist whose first act would have been to toss them out on their ears.

Clothilde had done everything possible to push Jenny Feathers into Nicki's bed and tried hard to push Nicki into matrimony with her. But, as we know, Nicki didn't want a wife, he wanted a mother, and he personally picked Elsa for her childlessness. Thus, he never would have a rival for her maternal affections.

He was horrified when Clothilde told him Jenny Feathers was pregnant by him. His sexual relations with Jenny had been nebulous. Jenny Feathers gave birth to Lucia, June 23, 1966, three months after Nicki and Elsa's marriage, and died in childbirth—an unlikely story since she was healthy as a peasant. At my suggestion Italian police exhumed her and performed an autopsy. She had been poisoned by cyanide.

We hastily pass over who would do such a dastardly deed to get at the fact that Clothilde—now that the mother was out of the way—bore the child triumphantly to Nicki and thrust an heiress down his reluctant throat. He refused to have anything to do with the child, who was banished to the upper reaches of the *palazzo* and literally *never* saw her father. Lucia's stories about a marvelous father who taught her to ride and to swim and sang her songs were the fantasies of a child who wished they were true. Thus the *palazzo* had a second lonely child wandering through its vastness.

Nicki might have ended his life as a rich dilettante, collecting jade or some other harmless idiocy, but for the kidnapping. Almost everything said or written about his kidnapping is wrong.

1 Marietta was mistaken about Nicki having no voice in his fortune. He was himself a trustee, but he was consistently out-voted by his sister Clothilde and by Monsignor Carbonotti, whose great interest was in keeping the immense di Castiglione fortune in the Vatican portfolio with the aim eventually of expropriating it altogether. Vatican larceny of this nature is apparently beyond the juridical reach of the legal systems of all countries.

·37·

When the call came, it wasn't what he expected. "She's on Flight 212 from Rome. It landed twenty minutes ago," said the Pan Am man, a stranger to Cassidy.

"Why didn't you let me know?" shouted Cassidy.

"Because she told us not to. She didn't want you meeting her." The Pan Am voice was neutral, not wanting to get into the rights and wrongs of this in any way. "The limousine will deliver her to Thirteenth Street in about an hour and a half. Customs is backed up to the rafters—so it might even be longer than that."

It was longer than that by half an hour. Cassidy stood well back in the shadows watching the sidewalk through his fourteen-foot windows. He'd been running through the possibilities. It was physically exhausting and emotionally debilitating.

"I don't know if I want her here, and she doesn't want me," he shouted at no one at all. "This whole situation is fraught with cataclysm for both of us." Wandering back and forth, his hands behind his back in his deposed Archduke bit, talking to himself like John Barrymore's Hamlet with much twitching of eyebrows.

The driver had opened the rear door for Lucia, but she was taking the devil's own time in getting out. Finally she stepped out on the sidewalk, her head drawn into her shoulders like a turtle. She was dressed in black. Black dress. Black shoes. Little round black straw hat with a round upturned rim. Very schoolgirlish, all of it, and very black, a color she detested.

She was clutching a suitcase, and it, too, was black.

We must do some shopping, thought Cassidy. What with?

Lucia was fumbling in her black purse for some money. The driver was shaking his head and saying something. His palm had already been crossed with silver. He had also been coached. He was under no circumstance to leave until she was well off the sidewalk and into the building.

So he waited.

Lucia stood motionless, suitcase clutched to her chest, staring at the brownstone steps as if they were the Himalayas. The driver standing there, car door open, not saying anything. He'd been told not to get into this (whatever this was).

Lucia looked this way and that. Up and down the street—and at her toes.

She has no place else to go, thought Cassidy savagely, and when you come right down to it, neither have I.

She'd grown perceptibly taller, and she had aged five years in one. It tore his heart to see it. Robbed of five years of precious childhood, he was thinking. And how do you get that back? You don't.

The plain brow was longer, more adult, and sadder, and the chin was firmer. (It had always been pretty firm.) A stubborn child, no doubt about it.

She was moving finally, dragging herself up the brownstone steps, stopping at each one. Interminably.

He heard the outer door open—and then she was inside the building, standing just outside his own front door. The Pan Am limousine drove away. Cassidy kept one eye on the outside steps to be sure she didn't bolt for it.

She didn't bolt. Nor did she come in. She did nothing at all for so long Cassidy couldn't stand it any longer. He threw open the door.

She was standing there, solemn as an owl.

"Am I such a fearsome object you'll stand on my stoop for all eternity without ringing the bell? Come in! Come in!" Irritation to cover his nervousness.

Lucia looked at him, her black eyes deep with reproach.

Or perhaps that was his imagining.

She came in slowly, dragging each foot, in a way peculiar to teenage girls. She sat on his huge bed because, in Cassidy's great room, there was nowhere else to sit. Every chair was loaded with students' papers that needed correcting or books on the middle ages or Cassidy's trousers that needed pressing.

Lucia said nothing, the black suitcase between her legs.

Cassidy scratched his nose. He walked to the window, hands behind his back, and looked out at the church across the street. Antichurch as he was, he always found comfort in the severe classic facade of that church with its Doric columns, which clashed with everything architectural on the street and, for that very reason, struck joy in Cassidy's perverse heart. As churches go, it was pretty good—having a little theater in its basement and a gymnasium with showers and locker rooms at its rear. God had been relegated to the front one third of the first floor because God didn't draw very well in Greenwich Village whereas basketball and theater did. Putting God in his place—behind the actors and the basketball players. . . .

This sort of rumination was getting him nowhere. He had best get on with his prepared speech which now sounded to him like the subtitle from a silent film: "It was your mother's dying wish that you be raised in America by Americans. Your mother didn't want you wasting your life on your knees."

Lucia said nothing.

Cassidy plunged on, getting it all out: "You didn't have to come at all. I made it clear in my note, the choice was yours."

He was walking back and forth now, passing her, silent on the bed.

"I must say you deliberated at great length. I assume you reached a decision. At any rate, you are here, and there must be an accommodation between us. We cannot live with hostility, we cannot dwell on the past, in one room."

Silence in the high-ceilinged room with its tier after tier of books. Outside on Thirteenth Street a huge furniture van was blocking the thoroughfare, causing a traffic jam clear to Seventh Avenue. Someone was always moving out or moving in on Thirteenth. It was a restless street full of students, sitar players, poets who sniffed cocaine, and revolutionaries who smoked cigarettes. Splendid neighborhood for a growing girl. They were more interested in ideas than rape on Thirteenth Street.

Cassidy filled the silence watching a bearded man in an ankle-length greatcoat going through Spumi's garbage, which contained delicacies not known in ordinary garbage pails.

Life would come as a shock wherever she lived. The *palazzo*, the Windletop, the convent. She'd scarcely been out of doors alone in her whole life.

226 ·

He faced her, sternly. She looked in agony.

"If you hate it here, you can always return to the convent. Few things in life are irrevocable."

"Where is the bathroom?" whispered Lucia in real distress.

Cassidy pointed. Lucia scuttled in and closed the door.

Cassidy sighed and collapsed on top of the bed, eyes on the ceiling. He was as winded as if he'd run a race. It wasn't much but it was a milestone of sorts.

Once they had gone to the bathroom, marked out the territory with the smell of their urine....

Excerpted from *The Legend of the di Castiglione's, Annotated*

As we know, Nicki's was a long incarceration, made so by Clothilde's haggling over each lira of ransom.[1] Clothilde didn't think her brother was worth $7,500,000, which she thought might more properly go to the Church as a down payment for life everlasting for herself.[2]

During six weeks of haggling Nicki was held captive in a shabby house on the outskirts of Rome where he was subjected to a daily going over at the hands of Pieta Lavalla, a beautiful, rabidly Maoist revolutionary we later knew as Titi.

Now comes the most wonderful part of all. What Titi (as we are accustomed to calling her) didn't know, what Nicki didn't even himself suspect, was that Nicki was an advanced masochist in search of an ideology. Far from being revolted by Maoism,[3] he was enchanted and radicalized by it. Within two weeks Titi and Nicki were coconspirators,[4] conspiring against the other kidnappers whom Titi seriously (and quite rightly) distrusted. They were also lovers, Titi whipping Nicki savagely with both

---

1 Inspector Francetti who was in charge of the case actually thinks Clothilde was *trying* to get her brother killed with all this haggling, which would leave her and the Monsignor in charge of the money.

2 The Church's claim to be able to sell you life everlasting is not subject to the blue sky laws which prohibit all other swindles of this nature.

3 Maoism is even more boring than Scriptures, but not quite so boring as Marxism.

4 Nicki could have been home in a week but for Clothilde's haggling.

her tongue and her whips simultaneously—an exercise both found deeply fulfilling.

Titi was no fool. She suspected that her fellow kidnapper Gianini Gennaro was more interested in the loot than in revolution, and she was quite right. Actually Gennaro was a Mafia hoodlum who had infiltrated the Red Wind at the order of his Mafia boss Vittorio Pietroangeli. The idea was to give the kidnapping an aura of revolution, get the money, and make off with it, probably killing Titi on the way.

Titi turned the tables on them. Titi and Gennaro were dispatched to pick up the money, and Titi maneuvered things so that they brought Nicki along. In chains, but nevertheless it was two against one. Somewhere along the line, Nicki was unloosed and, as we know, he was a jujitsu expert and in superb physical condition. He overpowered Gennaro, and Titi finished him off with her knife.

Titi and Nicki dressed Gennaro's corpse in Nicki's fancy clothes, after which Titi slashed Gennaro's face to ribbons so that neither Elsa nor anyone else would recognize it. When Elsa arrived with the cash—alone, as had been ordered—Titi took it from her at gun point and vanished. The police found Elsa in hysterics—conceivably the only time this self-possessed woman lost control—embracing the bloody body of what she thought was her husband.

Where was Nicki during all this? In the bushes, engaged in his favorite pastime: watching.

·38·

Cassidy entered her in St. Theresa's, which was in walking distance. He detested parochial schools, but after a long wrestle with his conscience, he decided St. Theresa's was safer than the public school. Whether it was better to be raped by street hoodlums than by Christ, ah, that was the question. Cassidy decided he could parry the clericalism by a strong dose of derision administered in the home. That is, of course, if a sensible dialogue ever began between them. So far it hadn't.

In the meantime, until decent conversation sprang up, Cassidy took her to St. Theresa's by six different routes, varying them each day, as if she were still the object of kidnapping. "There is no point in tempting a rapist six times a week," he said to her. "Once a week is enough."

He taught her the safe ways to travel alone on a street, keeping well toward the gutter, where a nimble girl can dart out between the cars, well away from the doorways where she could be trapped and pulled into hallways. To the Kung Fu he had already taught her, he added some chops he had learned in the CIA which were lethal—not least to himself.

"I'm a rapist leaping from behind," Cassidy would shout, and she would knee him in the balls and knuckle him in the kidneys with such diligence he couldn't speak above a whisper for half an hour.

It broke down barriers slowly. In a way.

There was no avoiding Sophy. She would drop unasked into a chair at the Spumi when Cassidy and Lucia were having their supper. Cassidy would grunt. Lucia would eat. Nobody would say anything. When the silence became unbearable, Sophy's earnest, stupid, deplorable face would blurt out some earnest, stupid, deplorable observation.

"You'd better get custody or there'll be trouble."

"There's never any custody trouble when no one wants the child," said Cassidy. "No one wants an heiress when the money's gone."

Lucia ate stonily. That night as she was undressing behind her screen—she had her own little niche with a camp bed behind that screen—Lucia blurted out: "You don't want me either. You're only doing it because Mama asked you to."

"You're not believing that, Mavourneen?" said Cassidy and softly aimed it at the black screen behind which was Lucia.

"I do indeed!" Very fierce whisper.

"You're all I have," said Cassidy.

He had no idea how that went down behind the black screen because Lucia said no more, and presently he could hear her soft breathing, which meant she was asleep. She fell asleep moments after her head hit the pillow. In that respect, she was still a child.

When she was safely deep in slumber, Cassidy pulled out his notebook and went to work on *The Legend* whose existence she didn't suspect. And whose eyes was the *Legend* for then? Only hers. When, Cassidy hadn't decided. At first he thought, maybe twenty-one. Then he pushed it up to twenty-five, and lately he had been thinking she should be at least thirty before she found out the whole terrible story....

Excerpted from *The Legend of the di Castigliones, Annotated*

Because of the power and prestige of the family, the corpse was laid away in the di Castiglione mausoleum in the hills of Tuscany without anything so demeaning as fingerprints being taken. Elsa was kept in ignorance throughout the funeral (easier to pass as grieving widow if one thought one was indeed one, Nicki had decided). Nicki, who had been hiding out in the 233 room *palazzo* with Titi, made his appearance at 3 A.M. in her bedroom.

"A milestone in the theater of the absurd," the Principessa had whispered on her deathbed.

Nicki was in black leather from head to toe, dressing up for the role of terrorist with the exquisite care he gave always to costume. "My dearest one," he said rapturously, kissing the Principessa. "You must forgive me." Smothering her all the time with kisses, for wasn't she, after all, his darling mama? "Look what I have brought home to you?"

Presenting Titi to her, as if she were a rare jewel for his Mama's delectation. "I have fallen in love at last! Isn't that remarkable? Aren't you pleased, my dearest?"

The Principessa only half awake in a tumult of joy and astonishment.

"I don't recall what she wore, but mostly she was garbed only in her own sullenness which she wrapped around her like an ideological contraceptive." A mistress of the barbed phrase even in her last extremity.

The beginning of despair, said the Principessa.

She was undisturbed by Nicki embracing Titi but appalled by his embracing Maoism, not because she was Right Wing (she had no politics at all and considered politics demeaning, a topic for the lower orders) but because she knew it was fatal for Nicki.

"For what is terror but theater," he would say with his shining eyes.

"It isn't, Nicki! It's not theater at all," she would cry. "What you are engaged in, Nicki, is murder."

"A murderer! Me! These people have never been alive, my dearest one. How can you murder someone who has never been alive?"

For four years, Nicki and Titi hid in the upper reaches of the Rome *palazzo* during which they carried out many of the bombings and kidnappings of the Red Wind from the last place the police would think of looking. Nicki was back in his childhood haunt, playing a grown-up version of the acting games he had played as a child.

Through it all, the Principessa raged in private and was silent in public, following the *coda* that leads all others in the upper reaches of aristocracy the world over. If you have a skeleton in the cupboard, keep it there, if possible, for centuries. There is nothing more cleansing than a couple of centuries.

·39·

Lucia had dreams, so terrible they woke her up in a fit of screaming, and left her shaken and sobbing.

"Mavourneen," said Cassidy on one of these occasions, and tried to comfort her, him in his worn red dressing gown.

She pushed him away with revulsion, as if it were all his doing, and he never tried again. He could put up with much from Lucia—and he did—but revulsion was more than he could bear. The truth of it is, said Cassidy to himself, is that she's overwhelmed by self-loathing for killing her mother and her father—and it's *not* her mother and probably not her father. So what do I do? Make her fatherless and motherless—rob her even of her parents?

It was almost enough to drive him to the priests—but not quite.

She had her own key and came and went as she pleased now, always alone. "There must be some nice girls at the school," Cassidy said to her. "Why don't you bring a friend home?"

"I had a friend; I killed her," said Lucia fiercely.

"She wasn't your friend," said Cassidy—after a moment because he didn't know how to deal with this.

"I know," said Lucia, the voice throbbing with passion. "She hated me! All that time, she must have hated me!"

It was too much for a thirteen-year-old to deal with, duplicity of that scale. She burst forth with a terrible question: "Why did Mama put up with it? Why?"

Excerpted from *The Legend of the di Castigliones, Annotated*

The Principessa had permitted Titi to be with Nicki as a sort of advanced toy that a child of his immensely overcivilized temperament demanded. In that sense she was an aristocrat to her fingertips: one dealt with the unspeakable by not speaking. The aristocracy has its own simplicities, some of them so painfully obvious as to be—to the rest of us—invisible.

She drew the line at Titi as nursemaid: "No, Nicki, it is out of the question. I have gone along with this masquerade beyond the call of love or reason—but Titi as nursemaid to Lucia is just not on."

"My dearest one," he had said—he was on his knees, pleading with his shining smile and Italian passion, "you are signing my death warrant."

.The Mafia, said Nicki—a flat lie—had wised up to the fact that Gennaro had not run off with the money.[1] They were looking for Pieta Lavalla and if they found her, they would also find him, Nicki, and they'd both be dead. Pieta needed a disguise and they also needed a change of scene. In short, New York.[2] Nicki would come along as butler, a role he played with more passionate attention to detail than any butler ever did.[3]

The Principessa eventually started hiring tutors to counter any radical poisons Titi might be pouring into her daughter's ears.

The Principessa's last words to me were: "Clothilde will bury her in a nunnery where she'll die of despair. Promise me you'll get her out of there, Cassidy." I promised.

1 Nicki and Titi had actually spent most of the $7,500,000 on their terror operations. Terror is an enormously extravagant form of amusement, requiring equipment and staff more expensive and far-reaching than polo or yachting added together, and has taken their place as the most conspicuous consumption of all.

2 Nicki and Titi probably decided they had worked over Rome to the limit of its capacity, having slaughtered an Italian Foreign Minister and two Ambassadors and staged some truly thrilling bank robberies, which brought satisfying headlines. The ultimate headline lay in New York. If you didn't make it on Broadway, you were still in the boondocks.

3 Nicki was fond of quoting Baudelaire on the subject of acting as total enchantment "veiling the terrors of the abyss," symbolism celebrating before the world "the mystery of life." As Lorenzo, curiously enough, he got very close to Lucia. As butler he felt great affection for a girl whom, as daughter, he found abhorrent.

·40·

Something enormous was going on behind Lucia's black eyes and Cassidy had no idea what it was. Communication between them slowed to a dead stop. Cassidy peppered her with questions about school, the cooking, the shopping, her clothes. In reply, she would say: "It's okay." "That's okay." Or simply: "Okay."

When clearly nothing was okay.

"It's not even a word—okay," he would say to the heavens in which he didn't believe.

Cassidy's job at the New School was exceedingly part-time. His specialty—medieval literature, as it pertained to modern life—was needed only when sufficient students asked for it, and that wasn't often. There were long intervals when money came in from nowhere. It took careful money management, and here Lucia stepped in uninvited.

"We cannot afford restaurants," she said flatly one day.

"There's no kitchen here worthy of the name," said Cassidy.

"I'll manage," she said stubbornly. And she did. The cooking was fairly awful, but her shopping was a miracle of resourcefulness.

It gave her something to do to eke out the silences which were becoming longer and awkwarder.

"Judas Priest!" His strongest imprecation. "What do I do now?"

To give himself surcease, he buried himself in *The Legend of the di Castigliones*, as if somewhere in that tangled tormented story he would find the answer to her pain, her awful silence.

234 ·

Excerpted from *The Legend of the di Castigliones, Annotated*

In this saga of unremitting perversity the role of Vittorio Pietroangeli is almost refreshing in its straightforward treachery. Pietroangeli was a former henchman of Lucky Luciano who cozied up to the OSS during World War II, much later to the CIA (which is where I met him). He was totally unreliable and would sell out to the highest bidder—the CIA, KGB, or his own Mafia bosses. He had a lucrative blackmail racket on the side (the source of all those filthy pictures in his safe) that he was supposed to share with his Mob colleagues. He didn't.

Pietroangeli was in such bad odor in the Mob that he was about to get the chop. However, no one has ever accused Pietroangeli of stupidity. He heard the news of his pending assassination almost the moment it was decided upon and was out of Rome within the hour. He took up residence in the Windletop under his assumed name Struthers. He spoke excellent English taught him by the OSS. He rarely ventured out of the building. On a trip to the laundry, he ran into Titi and recognized her as Pieta Lavalla.

The blackmail started immediately. The di Castiglione fortune was thus subject to two enormous drains: one from Titi and Nicki to finance their Red Wind, the other to slake the unslakeable greed of Pietroangeli (alias Struthers). That is when the art objects started disappearing from the apartment and showing up at auction rooms. Lorenzo spent many of his mysterious days off scouting artists to make imitations of the real paintings they sold.

Struthers's apartment was also used by Nicki and Titi to play their whipping games, of which they had been deprived in the Windletop for lack of space. Pietroangeli, of course, took pictures—one of which I found in his safe—but so consummate was Nicki's acting that I did not recognize him either as Lorenzo or as Nicki. He was playing one of his roles. The beautiful Swedish boys were also imported by Pietroangeli, not for himself, but for Nicki. At great expense.

The fact is that Nicki—while playing butler with skill and terrorist with dedication—had not shed all his princely vices.

One of these was witnessing his wife's infidelities by means of the camera in the ceiling over her bed. "Most of my love life was staged for Nicki's amusement," the Principessa confessed on her death bed. "You were a refreshment, Horatio, because there were no cameras in that room, and also because I was fonder of you than you ever imagined." Her only words on the subject.

·41·

Cassidy had come home earlier than usual, and he caught her in the very act—scuttling up the ladder heading, much too late, for the hiding place.

"Betrayer!" bellowed Cassidy and leaped up the skinny library ladder after her. It was too much for the little ladder which skidded off its brass rail and overturned, bringing down Lucia and Cassidy—the pages of *The Legend of the di Castigliones, Annotated,* filling the air like a cloud of white pigeons.

Lucia fell headlong onto the wood floor and hurt her elbow. "Ow!" she wailed.

Her first childlike sound in many a month.

Cassidy wrapped his long arms around her and exploded with apology: "I'm sorry! Sorry! Sorry! I was too precipitate!"

"Ow!" wailed Lucia. And burst into tears, which Cassidy found infinitely easier to deal with than her silence.

He kissed the elbow to make it feel better and made contrite noises and held her very tight.

The sobs abated and presently stopped.

Neither of them wanted to say anything for a long, long while as if words might shatter the peace.

But they didn't. When Cassidy finally spoke up, it was in a colloquial offhand style, as if asking about the weather.

"How much of it did you read?"

"I was just getting to the most exciting bit!"

"What bit was that?"

"Coming to New York because the Mafia was after them."

Cassidy rubbed his face with his free hand, the one that

wasn't around Lucia's thin shoulders: "The Mafia wasn't really after them. Nicki made that up."

"I know."

The barrier between them had vanished, as if it had never existed.

"She wasn't really my mother," said Lucia simply.

"No."

"And he probably wasn't really my father."

"No."

"You really have an orphan on your hands, Cassidy."

"It's the blessing of God," said Cassidy, very Irish.

"You don't believe in God."

"Perhaps I do. Under the circumstances."

"I don't want you believing in God, Cassidy, just for me."

"Okay. *Your* word. Okay. I was getting very tired of it."

Lucia stirred restively in his arms and screwed her face up right: "Were you in love with my moth . . . with the Principessa."

Cassidy exploded: "This is not a fit conversation for a thirteen-year-old."

Lucia giggled: "You're a prude, Cassidy. You always were."

It was as if a spring had been released inside her. After that Lucia was at ease with life, unburdened by a past which wasn't hers, and which she shed with scarcely a backward look.

Only now and then would it bob to the surface, and then there were always surprises.

One of them came almost two years after the Windletop massacre when Cassidy, in one of his fits of unemployment, sat on a bench in Washington Square watching Lucia skateboard in and around the guitar players and coke sniffers. She was doing triple carry-alls which scared the wits out of Cassidy. She was wearing a gray T-shirt with St. Theresa on its front and No. 26 on its rear.

After a very scarey run (a double wingover) she flopped next to Cassidy on the bench, panting hard and said—out of a clear blue sky:

"Do you know why I really came out of the convent and back to you, Cassidy?"

"Because you didn't want to spend the rest of your life in a nunnery."

"That wasn't it at all. I was going to kill you, Cassidy. I was going to avenge my mother and my father. That's why I came back."

Cassidy ruminated about this blatant announcement, rubbing his nose. "And what made you decide against it, Mavourneen?"

"Killing's wrong," she said bluntly.

Cassidy smiled, deeply gratified she'd got that far in her education. "It's a lousy amusement. Always was. I hope the human race will outgrow it, Contessa."

"I'm not a Contessa," said Lucia. "I'm a Miss. A Miss ...Cassidy."

For some reason that amused her no end. She uttered a whoop of laughter as if it were the funniest thing in the world.